AWAY FROM KEYBOARD COLLECTION

SECOND
SIGHT

PATRICIA D. EDDY

A NOTE FROM PATRICIA...

If you love sexy vampires and demons, I'd love to send you the prequel to the upcoming Immortal Protectors series. FOR FREE! Sign up for my Unstoppable Newsletter on my website and tell me where to send your free book!
http://patriciadeddy.com.

PROLOGUE

Six Years Ago

Dax

A DIM HALO seeps around the heavy canvas our captors tack over the cell doors. After so long here, I can almost see in the dark. Small variations in the rock walls. The flutter of air moving a corner of the shroud. My toes—if I wiggle them. Not that I've tried recently. The infection will take my leg soon. Or my life.

Let me fucking die already.

Ry's gone. Escaped. Hours ago. Killed at least four on his way out. We were supposed to go together. But I can't walk. He set my broken femur two weeks ago. One of the few times they let us stay in the same cell. But what should have been a minor burn festered, and now my whole leg is swollen and hot to the touch. At least they don't tie me up anymore.

Booted footsteps shuffle down the hall. I'm not as good as Ry. I can't always tell who's coming. The canvas is ripped away, and I blink rapidly, the dim lights of the hall searing my eyes after so long in the dark.

Rough hands close around my arms, someone throws a bag over my head, and I'm dragged from my cell. My leg screams in agony, the white-hot pain sending me barreling towards unconsciousness. Until they drop me.

Breathe. In and out. Focus.

"Get him up," Kahlid—the guy in charge—says, and I'm hauled onto a table. Before I can try to fight, they've tied my wrists together, then lashed me down with ropes around my torso, my hips, and my ankles.

Oh fuck. This is new.

"Sergeant Dash. How are you today?" As Kahlid pulls off the hood, I spit at him, but he's too far away.

"Fuck you."

The punch to my jaw isn't unexpected. Hell, that's how the fucker says hello. I taste blood, the metallic flavor turning my stomach.

His smile worries me. As does the glint in his eyes. "Would you like some water?"

This is some sort of trick. Say yes, and they'll waterboard me. I grind my teeth together, glaring at him, but in my current state, I doubt it's very effective. After Kahlid nods, one of his lackeys grabs my jaw and digs in, forcing me to open my mouth. A pill lands at the back of my throat, followed by half a bottle of water, and unprepared, I swallow before I can stop myself.

"Antibiotics only, Dash. Do not look so...frightened." Starting to pace with his fingers laced behind his back, he continues. "Your friend Ryker killed several of my men last night."

"Good for him." Another punch, more blood staining my lips. "You gonna keep that up? You want me to talk, it ain't gonna happen if you break my jaw."

"I do not want to hurt you, Dash. I only want to know where your friend Ryker was going. He will not get far. We shot him many times. I am worried for him. Tell me his escape route, and I promise you, he will not be harmed when we find him. We will treat his wounds and send him to hospital."

"Yeah. And I'm Santa Claus." I don't have the energy to keep this up. My leg throbs with every beat of my heart, my split lip is swelling rapidly, and I'm nauseous from the water they forced down my throat.

Kahlid leans over me, and shit. The bastard's a good actor. He actually manages to look...concerned. "What I have to do, Dash... you will not heal from this."

Is he finally going to kill me? Fear snakes its cold, bony fingers around my heart, but I'm so far gone, so weak, in so much pain death would be a welcome relief. "That's not...my...fucking... name. Whatever you're...gonna do...just get it...over with."

Behind Kahlid, two of his lackeys pull on thick, rubber gloves, and my stomach churns. Not the blowtorch. Or a belt. Or even a metal rod. This...has to be something different. Kahlid grabs a fistful of my hair—it's longer now. Hangs into my eyes. "Where is he? Tell me and I will not have to do this."

"Go...to...hell," I grunt. "You'll never...find him."

Kahlid slams my head down on the wooden table, and the edges of my vision darken. His crooked smile is the last thing I see as a harsh, caustic liquid splashes into my eyes, and I start to scream.

THE METAL TRAY lands on the stone floor with a crash, and I jerk awake, my heart racing. The cell door slams shut, and a weak glow of light dims as the canvas flops back down. I don't know how long it's been since they blinded me. Kahlid told me I screamed for half a day. Then he broke the last two fingers on my left hand when I still wouldn't talk. The one time they dragged me out of this cell since, my whole world was a muted sea of dull, washed out colors and agony every time I forced my swollen eyes open.

Crawling slowly, only able to use one arm and one leg without passing out from the pain, I feel along the filthy stone floor until I find the edge of the tray.

Fuck. I hope Ry made it.

I scoop up a bit of the rice slurry with my uninjured hand, then let it fall through my fingers. I can't. They've taken everything. Dax Holloway doesn't exist anymore. Hell killed him. I don't know when it happened. Every beating. Every scar. Every time they threw me in that goddamned hole. Left me there until I was out of my mind with hunger.

I can't walk. Can't make a fist with my dominant hand. Can't... see. Why keep fighting? Months ago, I was ready to give up. Starved myself for what I think was a week. Until they force fed me, then whipped Ry until his back was bloody. But he's gone. Safe. Or dead.

Forcing myself to sit up, I grab the tray and fling it against the bars. That'll earn me another beating. More broken bones. I don't give a shit. "You want me to talk? How's this? You're all a bunch of sadistic fucks. You can carve me into a thousand pieces, and I'll still never tell you what you want to know!"

I collapse, my head hitting the dirty floor. Shouts echo down the winding stone hall, and I try to scramble back, knowing they'll come for me. I don't care what they do, but I won't make it easy for them.

Despite all the months I've been here, I still can't understand much Pashto. But Kahlid's men sound panicked. Heavy footsteps race down the hall past my cell, and then...

Gunfire.

Not AKs. Not Taliban guns. Colt M4s. SEALs. Special Forces. Rangers.

"Go, go, go!" someone shouts, a hint of a Southern twang coloring their words.

"Four hostiles down," another voice responds. "Clear."

Wrapping my good hand around the bars, I try to pull myself up. "American," I call weakly. "Here."

"Get that goddamn door open. Now." Light flares, bright enough to penetrate my swollen lids, as the canvas is ripped away, and a dark shadow looms as someone breaks the lock. "Holloway?"

"Yes." I reach out a tentative hand and find a tactical vest as the man kneels next to me. "Who—?"

"West Sampson. SEAL Team Eight on a joint op with ODA. Can you—"

"Where is he?" Ryker roars from down the hall.

Oh God. He made it.

"Third cell," West calls. "I'm bringing him out."

Only a few feet away now, Ryker growls, "No one touches him but me. Dax?"

I jerk my head towards his voice, opening my eyes, desperate to see him. Except...I can't. Not after what those fuckers did to me. The pale reddish glow from the hall brightens as the heat of a flashlight paints my face.

"Fuck. Dax, what the hell...? Your eyes."

"Questions later," West says. "This place is coming down as soon as we're clear. Get him up and move."

"Where's Kahlid?" Ryker asks as he hauls me over his shoulders in a fireman's carry, his arm hooking under one knee as he grips my wrist tightly. Unable to see or tell up from down, I can't orient myself, and nausea crawls up from my stomach when he starts hustling down the hall.

Shouts, another three shots. "Blue Team Alpha approaching egress point. Need a location on Target Zulu," West says.

We start to climb. I'm...safe. I'm going home. The tears gathering in my burned and blistered eyes send shooting pain through my skull, but I don't care.

"Roger that. Kahlid's down. They've got him at the mouth of the cave. He'll be dead in five minutes."

"Then we've got time." Ryker's voice lowers, turns grave. "He's ours, Sampson. Give us sixty seconds alone with him, then we're gone."

West doesn't respond—at least not that I can hear. The first whiff of fresh, free air smells like heaven, and then West orders everyone to fall back. Somewhere below me, I hear raspy, rattling breathing.

"I told you I'd kill you," Ryker says as he bends and sets me on my feet. Keeping an arm around my waist so I don't collapse, he presses a pistol into my hand.

"I can't see, Ry," I whisper. "You have to—"

He shifts me. "Put your other arm around my shoulders and hang on. I'll aim for you. We fire together."

With a nod, I clutch the back of his tactical vest so I don't fall, and he supports my left arm with his. To my right, he cocks his pistol.

"Fifteen months, asshole. Every day, I pictured this moment. When your last sight would be the two men who took down Hell. Say your prayers, fucker." After a beat, Ryker snorts. "On second thought...don't."

We fire together, and as the gun falls from my shaking hand, Ryker says, "We're going home, brother."

Home. As Ryker half-carries me down the mountain and a series of explosions shakes the ground under our feet, I start to sob. We might be going home, but I'll never see Boston again.

1

Dax

"CALL FROM: RYKER. CALL FROM: RYKER," my phone's calm, female British voice announces. Well, shit. The jerk actually kept his promise.

So why can't I pick up the damn phone? Pushing to my feet, I stalk over to the window and press my hands to the glass. Sun warms my palms, brightens the perpetual thick haze surrounding me, and I try to remember what the Boston skyline looked like. But...with every passing day, my memories fade.

I can call up colors. The blue of the sky. Of denim. Of my mother's eyes. Of those stupid Slushies Mark, my childhood best friend, and I used to save up for once a month. Red's easier. Blood. Lots and lots of blood. Red is the last color I remember. But the skyline? For all I know, it doesn't look anything like it did the last time I saw it—more than eight years ago. Before my last tour. Before Hell. Before a Taliban asshole decided pouring drain cleaner into my eyes was fitting retribution for Ry killing four of his men.

The phone falls silent, and I blow out a relieved breath. Except...now *I'm* the asshole.

Ten days ago, Ryker McCabe walked into my office. After more than six years, I'd written him off. My best friend. The only other person in the world who knows what fifteen months in Hell will do to a person.

And now...he wants to reconnect. I don't know how to do this. After he rescued me, he abandoned me at the hospital. Blind, in constant agony, malnourished, with dysentery, broken bones, and a fever of over 103, I didn't know how to function.

I asked about him every day. Hell, probably four or five times a day. Called him when I could finally hold a phone—and get a number for him. Message after message went unanswered.

And I had to heal alone. Had to learn how to brush my hair without being able to see it. How to shave. How to fucking walk. Even harder...how to sleep in a bed. Not panic every time a door opened. Or someone touched me. How to be...human again.

And then he strides back in here six years later thinking one conversation can fix everything. If Wren hadn't needed help, if Ry hadn't been so fucking stubborn, if I'd just refused to talk to him that day, I wouldn't feel like shit now.

But he stepped up for Wren when I failed. One of my best employees. A brilliant hacker. A friend. And I refused to help when she needed it most. Ry protected her. Then the fucker went and fell in love with her. Almost died for her.

"Maybe..." *I take off my glasses and rub my eyes. Raising my head, I can almost make out the dark blur in front of me as a person. Almost.* "Maybe you could give me a call sometime. To...uh...catch up."

"I'll call. You're...family, Dax. And family keeps their promises."

Family. We were family. Brothers in every way that counted. Now...I don't know what we are. Or what I want us to be. When he and Wren almost died, when no one could reach them that last terrible night in Russia, a wound I thought I'd buried years ago started to bleed. And it hasn't stopped since.

Talking to him brought up all the shit I buried after Hell. The terror of waking up blind that first, terrible day. Spending weeks in the hospital in Germany unable to walk. The fights with Lucy. The distance. The rough scratch of the pen as I signed my name on the divorce papers.

But I survived. All of it. Learned how to navigate my apartment. Then my neighborhood. Found a boxing gym with a patient trainer who helped me learn how to use what little vision I have left to see my opponent's tells. Met Ford there not long after, and we started Second Sight.

In four years, we turned this two-man operation into a thriving private investigation and security firm that's saved or helped hundreds. Including, just a couple of weeks ago, a kidnapped teen whose father was about to sell her to a human trafficking ring. We do good work, and the seven men and women who've joined us are the best in the business.

But I haven't slept more than three hours a night since Ryker showed up, even less now that he and Wren are across the country in Seattle, and when I'm huddled on my floor, shaking from the nightmares, everything I've accomplished? Doesn't mean shit. I thought...I thought I'd beaten my demons. And one visit from Ry brought them all back again.

Three raps on my door draw me out of my memories. Every member of my team has their own signal. Wren used to knock twice. Trevor uses that stupid "Shave and a Haircut" pattern. Vasquez? Five times.

"You coming?" Ford asks. "The car's downstairs."

"Go without me." The words escape almost on a grunt. "You don't need me there."

"The hell I don't. You're the owner of the company, dipshit." He grabs my arm, spinning me around and shoving me against the glass. "You have the best instincts of anyone I've ever met, Dax. Better than me. Hell, better than Trevor, and he trained with the CIA."

"No one wants to hire a blind man to oversee their security, Ford. I only go because you drag me along."

My phone buzzes on the desk, and I shake him off. *"Voice message from Ryker."*

Ford turns and takes two steps towards the door. "I don't know what crawled up your ass after the shit with Wren and Ryker, but I'm getting sick of it. The car's leaving in five minutes. With or without you."

His clipped footsteps fade as he heads to the elevator, and I fumble for my desk chair. My team doesn't deserve a boss who can't get his shit together.

After I tuck my Bluetooth into my ear, I grab my jacket off the back of the door, unfold my cane, and head for the elevator. The client's expecting both of us, and my pity party could jeopardize the contract. But somehow, I have to get my head on straight.

Once I'm on the elevator, I tap my phone. "Play voice message."

"Dax. I should have called sooner. I'm around. Not taking on any jobs for at least another week or two. Sampson just got back from his honeymoon. I...I went to the wedding. Bet you thought you'd never see—shit. I'm sorry, man. Wren says hi. Uh...call me back. If you want."

The elevator doors slide open, and I take two steps forward, listening for the telltale rumble of an idling engine. "About damn time," Ford says from somewhere off to my left. As the car door *thunks*, I get my bearings and wave him off when his shadow moves close to my elbow.

"I got this."

"Sure you do. Like you've got everything else in your life," he mutters under his breath.

"Enough." I slide into the back seat, fold my cane, and shut the door, giving him time to round the car and join me. "One more word, and you're handling these on your own. You want a fight, I'll bench you and put Trevor on intake. I'm still the fucking boss, Ford. Don't forget it."

THE OFFICE QUIETS down after five, my team leaving one-by-one. Trevor's the only one with an after-hours gig this week, and he's holed up in the media room watching surveillance video of the thief who hit the Boston Museum of Art two weeks ago.

The three raps startle me as I down the last of my lukewarm coffee. "What is it, Ford?"

"I was about to head home. But," he sighs, "I'm a glutton for punishment. You want to tell me what's going on with you and Ryker?"

"No. Talk to you tomorrow." I don't raise my head, don't bother moving my hands from my keyboard. I have to wrap up a few outstanding email inquiries before I can take a couple of days away from the office—try to shove all those fucking memories back where they belong. Out of my head.

"Jesus, Dax. You ended up in a fist fight with the guy because he ghosted you, and now when he calls, you ignore him? Make up your damn mind."

I try to glare at Ford, but since he knows I can't see him, I doubt it's very effective. "I'll call him back. Later."

"You mourned the loss of that friendship for six fucking years. 'Later' isn't good enough. When?"

Anger stiffens my shoulders, and I swallow hard. "VoiceAssist, close email. Shut down computer," I say. Pushing to my feet, I straighten to my full height and face my second in command. My friend. "When I'm goddamned ready to. Don't bring it up again."

"Dax," Ford reaches for my arm as I try to shoulder past him, and I jerk back, hitting the door jamb and losing my grip on my cane.

"Don't touch me," I growl. "And get the fuck out of my way."

But he doesn't back down. "You want a fight? Let's go."

TWENTY MINUTES LATER, I slam my locker door at Beantown Boxing and head for the ring. "Sal?" I call when the tip of my cane finds the steps. "You around?"

"Right here, Sergeant. You need help with your gloves?" As Sal's heavy footsteps thud closer, I fold the red and white monstrosity and hold up my hands. He tugs the boxing gloves over my taped knuckles and secures the wrist wraps firmly. "Been a while."

"Busy few weeks."

"You ready to get your ass kicked?" Ford asks as he claps his gloves together.

"Ready to take you down."

Sal wraps his thick fingers around my elbow and helps me into the ring.

I run my gloved hands across the ropes, getting my bearings. A few feet away, Ford clears his throat, and I scan the hazy, diffuse colors in front of me for his shadow. "On three," I say.

His countdown lets me know how far away he is, and I bring my hands up to guard my face. His first punch sails wide as I weave to the right, and I send an uppercut to his jaw.

"You going to forget about that damn phone call?" I ask as I take two quick steps back into the ropes. The corner of the ring gives me a point of reference, and I tuck and roll towards where I think Ford's standing, sweeping my leg out and catching him behind the ankles. He hits the mat with an *oof,* and I push to my feet and dance back until I hit the ropes again. "I'll call him. Eventually."

Ford lands a jab to my obliques, and I try to dart away, but he sidesteps me and grabs my shoulders. "I don't give a fuck when you call Ryker. But you've been a shitty boss and a shittier friend the past two weeks."

His knee rams my solar plexus, and I go down, coughing and sputtering. "What the hell does that mean?" Staggering to my feet, I raise my gloved hands and wait for him to give some form of audible cue.

"Fight now. Talk later."

Whirling around, I curse under my breath. How the hell did he end up behind me? I may be blind, but I'm fucking Special Forces. We trained for missions in near darkness. In some of the worst conditions imaginable. Learned how to echolocate. How to anticipate our opponents. And Ryker and I spent most of our time in Hell blindfolded, relying on our other senses to help us survive. *Pay attention, fucker. Get your head in the game.*

We spar until sweat drips into my eyes. And then, Ford lets loose with a barrage of jabs and crosses that drives me back into the ropes. "Enough," I grunt, dropping my arms. "You win." After a breath, when the heat from his body disappears, I add, "Today."

"You've got ten minutes," Ford says. "Then we're headed to the pub across the street, and you're going to listen. After that, do whatever the hell you want about Ryker. But you're going to hear me out. No interrupting."

"Fine."

I hear Ford slam his hands against the swinging doors to the locker room as Sal shuffles over to help me unlace my gloves. "Everything all right, Sergeant?"

"It will be. But how many times do I have to ask you to call me Dax?" When my left hand is free, I swipe it across my brow.

Sal chuckles. "Since I never made it out of the enlisted ranks, it's never gonna do any good. Looked like a serious fight."

As Sal hands me my cane, I shake my head. "He'll get over it." But...will I?

THE BAR'S quiet on a Monday evening. With my hand gripping Ford's arm, I let him lead me to a booth in the corner. After we both take a swig of our beers, Ford clears his throat. "We do good work. You know that, right?"

"We're the best on the eastern seaboard. What's this have to do with anything?" All I want is to finish my beer and go home. Try to eek out more than three hours in a row of shuteye.

"Losing Wren—"

"We didn't *lose* Wren. She's in Seattle. Not dead. And she still works for us."

He pauses long enough I almost ask if he's all right, but then continues, "How many times have you talked to her since she left?"

I don't know what I expected him to say, but the question takes me by surprise. "Maybe four?"

"And how many of those times did you ask about Ryker?"

Bristling, I start to peel the label off my bottle. "None. And he didn't ask about me either. We talked about work. About...how she likes Seattle."

"How she likes Seattle, but not how she's doing or the man she's in love with? The one she's living with? Bullshit. You'd have to purposely sidestep that minefield." His voice takes on the rasp of disbelief, and I slam the bottle down a little harder than I intend.

The temptation to just get up and walk out of here hits me hard, but I clench my hands into fists under the table and count to five. One of Wren's little tricks. Only for her, it helped her anxiety. For me...well, sometimes it stops me from laying into someone when I know they're trying to help. "That shit's between me and Ryker. You think I should go and chase the guy down? I won't do that. I can't."

"Not saying that at all." Ford shifts, the leather booth creaking under his weight. He's six-foot-ten—or so he says—and built like a linebacker. Sparring with him feels like going toe-to-toe with a tank. Ryker's the only guy I know who's bigger. "I'm saying every time you talk to Wren—and don't address the elephant in the room—you're hurting everyone. Her, Ryker...me, the rest of the office..."

"What the hell?" No amount of counting's going to settle my anger now. "We're friends, Ford, but I'm still the boss. If you have a problem with me—"

"I don't 'have a problem' with you, Dax. I'm worried." His voice softens, and the table rocks under my elbow.

Times like these, I miss my sight the most. My vision is limited to a diffuse haze and some very muted colors. Like someone smeared thick, dark grease all over a window. Something in front of me is darker than the brown wood booth, but flat, and almost two-dimensional. Right now, I wish I could see his eyes.

"You're not sleeping. Anyone can see that. And you're short with everyone. How long until one of our clients notices?" He pauses, then chuckles, almost to himself. "You know...most of the time, I forget you can't see. Wren wrote all those adaptive programs for you—hell, you're a better typist than I am."

"You have more than ten years on me, old man. I had to learn typing in school." It feels good to joke. But also...unfamiliar. How long has it been since I smiled? Or just...shot the shit with the men and women I work with? "Fuck."

"You get it now?"

I take a long swig of my beer, swallowing hard over the lump in my throat. "Yeah. I think...I do."

I don't open up. Don't share. Other than with my shrink—and I haven't seen him in two years. Ford...he's not just my VP of Operations and weapons specialist. He's my friend. And I can't remember the last time we went out for drinks after work and just...talked.

"You have time to grab a burger?" I ask as I return to peeling the label off my beer bottle.

He slaps the table lightly. "That's more like it."

2

_____

Evianna

Pushing back from my computer, I drop my head into my hands. "Why now?" The deep breath does little to stop my heart from threatening to burst through my chest like some alien parasite.

All morning, I've tried to find an explanation. Some reason for Kyle to violate his employment agreement. To make a copy of Alfie's code and send it God knows where. We're less than three weeks from launching the most advanced home security device the world has ever seen. And he has to do this *now*?

He's always been a model employee. A little dismissive at first —but so are a lot of guys in this industry. Until they realize I can code circles around them. And control their paychecks. Kyle got over himself after less than a week, and though every one of my team of fifteen programmers is top-notch, Kyle's the best of them.

Firing him this close to the finish line feels wrong. But the agreement he signed is ironclad. And Noah Goset—the CEO— won't stand for disloyalty. After four hours poring through the logs, hoping for some explanation, I admit defeat.

Buzzing Noah, I try to relax my jaw. If I'm not careful, I'll crack a molar.

"Yes?" His terse voice warns me he's about as stressed out as I am, and I force a deep breath before I respond.

"I need to see you. There's a problem with Kyle. Do you have a few minutes?"

He sighs. "I'm meeting with New England Insurance Services in thirty. You need me, get in here right now."

Silence blares over the line, and I lock my workstation, grab my tablet, and head for Noah's office at the other end of the bullpen. Beacon Hill Technologies takes up the top floor of one of the newer office buildings in the South End of Boston, and Noah and I have the two corner offices with the programmers working in a giant open space between us.

At his frosted glass door, I tap softly.

"Come in," he says.

Noah's blond hair sticks up in all directions as he pours over paperwork. His suit looks like he slept in it—and he probably did. We've all been working twelve to fourteen hours a day for months preparing for the launch of Alfie—our home automation and security device. If we pull this off, we'll redefine the entire industry. "Evianna, what's so important it couldn't wait until tomorrow?"

"This." I unlock my tablet and show him the logs. "Kyle transferred a copy of the code base to an off-site server five days ago. And a second copy last night."

His brow furrows, and he pages through the systems log. "He knows that's a violation of company policy."

"We just renewed our contracts last month in preparation for the launch. The lawyer you brought in was very clear about the need for complete confidentiality." I sink into Noah's guest chair and work my jaw back and forth, hoping to avoid the searing headache I usually get when I'm stressed out. "Tell me not to fire him. Please."

"I can't." Noah shakes his head. "Fucking idiot. If we get audited and this comes out, we're done for. Legally, we don't have a choice."

"Fantastic." The amount of sarcasm dripping from my tone could drown a small child. "I'll put security on standby to escort him out of the building."

"Do it. Is this going to put us behind on the final feature work and bug fixes?" Noah pushes the tablet back across the desk and holds my gaze.

"The rest of the devs won't be happy about picking up Kyle's slack. But we'll make it. A few extra catered meals the next three weeks, a couple more bottles of bourbon for the launch party, and they'll all pitch in."

"Then do what you have to do." His tone tells me I won't get anything more out of him, so I nod my thanks—not that he notices—and trudge back across the bullpen to my office.

Time to put on my "I'm the boss" face.

"KYLE," I say from my office door ten minutes later, "can you come in here for a minute?"

His desk is less than thirty feet away, and his eyes narrow as he rises and grabs his phone. "Sure, boss."

After I shut the door and slip back behind my desk, I fold my hands on the leather blotter to stop them from shaking. "Kyle, we have a problem."

"I knocked out those three bugs from yesterday," he says, then runs his hand through his jet black hair. "Checked them again this morning. No performance degradation at all."

"That's not what I'm talking about." I angle my monitor towards him and bring up the system logs. "You made a complete backup of Alfie's code base twice in the last five days. Want to tell me why?"

"I...can't." His pale cheeks redden, and he starts to fidget with the employee badge clipped to his belt loop. "But I'm the only one who has access to the cloud drive. The code's safe. I'm not doing anything that's going to hurt the company. I swear."

My heart aches. He sounds so sincere, but we have rules for a reason. And there's no legitimate cause for him to take code home with him. Not when he has access to the company's servers remotely. "Kyle, what you did is against company policy. The new employment agreements we all signed two weeks ago? We all read them. Noah brought in a lawyer to explain all the legalese. What you did is a fireable offense."

"What?" His brown eyes widen, and he leaps up to start pacing the room. "You can't fire me. You need me to finish Alfie. And I just wanted to...help."

"I don't have a choice," I say quietly. "I need your employee badge."

"No!" Kyle slams his palms down on my desk. "I've given this company two years of my life. Days *and* nights. Weekends. Holidays. This is bullshit!"

"The logs don't lie, Kyle. You know how sensitive this project is. You've done great work for us, but this...you *knew* this was against policy, and you did it twice."

"I was worried, Evianna. Something's not right with the code. I didn't want to say anything until I knew for sure, and this was the only way." Kyle's voice turns pleading, but there's still a hint of anger under his words. "I haven't shared the code with anyone. It's safe."

"There's nothing wrong with the code. All our performance indicators are just where they should be. Error rates far under benchmarks. Alfie's solid."

"Oh my God—" Something shifts in Kyle's voice, and he balls his hands into fists. "You know...don't you? You're part of this. Evianna, if you fire me, when everything goes to shit, you won't have anyone who knows how to fix these...*problems*. The launch will fail. And your reputation...the whole company's reputation..."

Sucking in a quick breath, I reach for the phone. "Stan, please send Security to my office."

"Security? Evianna, come on!" Kyle throws up his hands, and my heart starts pounding against my ribs. He's just a kid. Twenty-four at most, and probably all of one hundred and fifty pounds. But right now, he's looking at me like I just killed his puppy.

As soon as two beefy guys wearing dark blue suits enter my office, I open a secure browser connection with a few keystrokes. "Log in to your cloud storage, show me where you uploaded the code, and hard delete it. While I watch. No backups."

"Evianna, listen to me—" He lunges for my hand, but Jimmy, the older of the two security guards, grabs Kyle's arm.

"Easy there, kid. Don't do anything you'll regret," Jimmy says.

Fear creeps into Kyle's eyes, and his shoulders slump. "I wasn't going to..."

I nudge the keyboard closer to him. "Delete the files and hand over your access card. We'll have any personal effects at your desk sent to you."

I hate firing people. The betrayal in Kyle's eyes makes my heart hurt as I watch him navigate to a secure cloud server, enter a long string of letters and numbers, and show me the directory he created.

After I verify the size of the folder is the same approximate size as the data he transferred, I nod. "Delete it. And all the backups."

He turns off automatic data recovery, purges the directory, and empties the temporary trash files. "Satisfied?"

His sneer spurs the Security guys to take a step forward, but I wave them off. Kyle won't hurt me, despite his anger. God, he's the best damn coder I've ever met. I hate having to do this. "Yes," I say softly. "I'm sorry, Kyle. I didn't have a choice." Holding out my hand, I try to force some strength into my tone. "Your badge, please."

Grumbling something unintelligible under his breath, Kyle jerks his badge off his belt clip and throws it down on my desk. "Fuck you, Evianna. Fuck this whole company."

This time, the building's security guards won't be placated. Jimmy wraps his hand around Kyle's arm again. "Enough, kid. Don't make a scene. We're going straight to the elevator. Anything you need from your desk, you tell Laird here and he'll get it for you. Understand?"

Jimmy has a good hundred and fifty pounds on Kyle, and the kid nods, keeping his head down as Jimmy escorts him into the hall. After I shut my office door, I sink down onto the edge of my desk, my legs not quite steady.

Taking over as CIO for Beacon Hill Technologies three years ago allowed me to move back home to Boston from Silicon Valley. To take care of my mom for a while—until her condition progressed to the point where she needed round-the-clock care.

The brisk raps on my door force me to pull myself together, and I shake my head quickly to rid myself of the lingering feelings of doubt. I didn't have a choice. He broke company policy, and that's a fireable offense.

"Yes?" Before I can stand, the door opens a crack, and Ulysses peers in.

"Everything okay, boss?" The compassion in his almond-shaped eyes and his quiet demeanor are why I hired him a year ago as my administrative assistant. When this job threatens to steal the last of my sanity, Ulysses shows up with a cup of tea or a cannoli from Mike's Pastry shop. Or a sympathetic ear. Sometimes all three.

"No." With a dramatic sigh, I wave him in and wait for him to shut the door. "I had to fire Kyle."

"Well, I figured that out. *Everyone* figured that out." He moves to my little electric kettle and starts the water, then fixes me a cup of jasmine tea.

The soft, floral scents calm me, and I sink onto my little over-stuffed chair in the corner by the window. "I can't tell you why." When he frowns, I hold up my hand. "You know how tight our NDAs are. But let's just say it was so blatantly against company policy, I didn't have a choice."

As the tea steeps, Ulysses pulls up my calendar on my laptop. "You don't have anything for the rest of the day, Evianna. Why not go see your ma for a couple of hours? Then maybe the spa? You can come back tomorrow and pretend none of this ever happened."

"Maybe. After I talk to the troops. They need to know."

He checks his watch. "Okay. I'll call the Waxing Spa on Newbury and see if they have anything available tonight. They're open late. Now, drink your tea and have a little breather. Then you can make your announcement, stick around for questions for an hour, and be at your ma's by 6:00. 'Kay?"

"You're a lifesaver, Ulysses," I say as he hands me the mug. "What would I do without you?"

As he leaves, he offers me a small smile. "You'd overdose on coffee and snap."

He's right.

By the time I trudge up the steps to my brownstone—well, my mother's brownstone—I feel like a wet noodle. That massage was just what I needed. And my mom was having a good day. The new computer setup I got for her allows her to use her barely functional fingers to pick words and phrases off a large monitor so she can communicate. When she can no longer move her fingers, it'll track to her eye movements.

ALS—amyotrophic lateral sclerosis, also known as Lou

Gehrig's Disease—is terminal and insidious. First, she started to stumble. Then noticed weakness in her legs and muscle spasms. That was six months after I moved back to Boston, and two months ago, she lost the ability to speak. But her mind is strong, and even though there's no cure—yet—and I know she probably only has another year or so with us, she can still read, watch television, and now...send me emails and "talk" to me when I visit her every few days.

Tonight, she spent an hour telling me the story of her and Dad's first date. And how it ended with food poisoning and a trip to the ER. I haven't laughed that hard in weeks, and the joy on Mom's face...it makes all the long days worth it.

After a shower and a cup of chamomile tea, I slip into bed with my tablet to catch up on a few lingering emails before I try for a solid six hours.

The first message waiting doesn't have a subject, and I don't recognize the sender. CodeAnon01? What the hell? But as soon as I click on it, my heart starts pounding in my chest and I grip my tablet tighter.

Everything I did was for the good of the company, Evianna. EVERYTHING. And what do I get for it? Fired by the coldest bitch on the planet. You wouldn't even give me a chance to explain. I thought you cared about the company. I thought you cared about all of us. But all you care about is covering your ass. Whatever you're planning...it's going to fail. And everyone will know it's your fault. Noah never should have hired you. You don't deserve to work for a company like Beacon Hill. I hope you get what's coming to you.

My stomach pitches, and my tablet almost slides off my lap. My hands shake as I forward the email to our HR manager, Sarah, with a note.

"I thought you should have a copy of this for your records. He's angry and hurt, and I don't blame him. But in case he tries to break his NDA, we'll need an electronic trail."

Despite there being nothing I haven't heard before in the email, something about it unsettles me. Unable to deal with any more drama tonight, I go back for a second cup of tea, and this time, add a generous splash of bourbon to the cup. So much for all that post-massage bliss. Now, I'm more stressed out than ever.

Dax

FIVE HOURS. As my alarm blares, announcing the time, I'm tempted to grab my phone and throw it across the room. but I rely on it for everything: the color scanning app to help me get dressed, the saved number to the Sighted Companion Network if I get myself lost or need a guide to learn a new neighborhood, the optical character recognition technology built into my lightly tinted glasses that reads menus and signs for me.

At least those five hours were mostly continuous. Better than I've had in the past two weeks. Ford and I shot the shit over beers and a burger for three hours, and though my level of "opening up" could only be described as a shallow paper cut, when I got into the Lyft, something between us had shifted from confrontational to almost comfortable again.

My life depends on routines. The toothbrush in its precise place. My electric razor on the charger. The shampoo to the right of the soap. As I run a comb through my hair, I wonder if today's the day I'll work up enough courage to call Ryker.

The memories threaten as I sit by the door and pull on my

shoes. We came up together. Got roaring drunk together the day we put on our berets and patches for the first time. And for three years, I was his Warrant Officer, his second-in-command.

"Alpha Team! Move! Move! Get the fuck out of there!"

Ry's order comes a second too late. We're pinned down, and bullets pepper the rocks all around us, sending shards pelting our helmets and tactical gear. Dropping to my belly, I try to raise CENTCOM. "Alpha Team in need of air support. Now, now, now!"

"We're on our own," Ry mutters as he rolls over onto his back next to me. Digging into his pouch, he tugs out a grenade, pulls the pin, and counts to three before letting it sail towards the group of guys we thought were goat herders until they opened fire. "I counted seven. You?"

"Same. Ripper?"

Our Communications Sergeant grabs the radio out of my hands as the explosion rocks the side of the mountain. "Based on where that landed...five now," he says with a grin. The man's insane. Zero sense of self-preservation. I swear, he's only alive because he cares about the rest of us too much to do anything overly stupid.

I angle a quick glance through a crack between two rocks. "Two down, one...Jesus fuck. Make that three. The third guy is...well, spaghetti."

In seconds, Ripper's modified the radio to send out a morse code burst with our location. "Hold 'em off for another ten minutes, and we'll be sitting pretty on the chopper out of here."

"Sitting ugly, you mean," Gose says. "We're the sorriest looking sons of bitches in Afghanistan. Hab's covered in goat shit, for fuck's sake."

"And yet Ry still looks like he's modeling for an army recruitment poster. He's the prettiest thing out here," I joke. That earns me a punch to the arm, but I'm right. The fucker could model—if he wasn't always covered in dirt and tactical gear.

"Fuck you. Don't call me pretty." He jams a fresh magazine into his M4. "Ready?"

Checking my own mag, I nod. "I got your back."

I always had his back. And he had mine. Even in Hell. How can I be too scared to call him? I'm fucking Special Forces. No one can take that away from me. Even if I can't see more than vague hazy shapes and colors. I don't back down. I don't let shit scare me off. But calling Ry...I just can't. Not yet.

———

Evianna

I step off the T a little after 7:00 a.m. Noah and I have a meeting with the legal department of one of the largest insurance agencies in New England at ten, and my technical presentation needs to be perfect. If this goes well, we'll have letters of agreement signed with every major insurance company in the United States by the end of the week.

As I walk the last four blocks to the office, I mentally run through my slides. Alfie's origins. Her safety features. How she'll give the elderly—and their families—peace of mind. On the corner, I stop and let a group of early morning runners pass, and the longing hits me. Back in California, I used to run every day. Maybe...once we launch, I'll have time to start up again. Glancing down at the box of doughnuts in my hand, I stifle a snort. No exercise, doughnuts for breakfast, pizza for lunch...no wonder I've put on thirty pounds since I moved back to Boston.

"Evianna!" The angry shout startles me enough to send coffee sloshing over the rim of my travel mug. Kyle stumbles as he passes the last of the running group, and his eyes are bloodshot and half-focused. "We nnnneed to t-talk."

"Oh God, Kyle. You smell like the bottom of a tequila bottle. Go home. There's nothing to talk about." I try to sidestep him, but he grabs my arm and squeezes, hard. "Ow! Let *go*."

I'm not a tiny slip of a thing. Hell, I outweigh the kid. But his fingers dig in tighter, and tears spring to my eyes unbidden from the pain. "Kyle. This is getting dangerously close to assault," I say, trying to keep my tone low and measured—the exact opposite of how I feel. "Let go of me. Now."

"You're gonna...lisssten to me, Evianna. Or I'm gonna go public. Alfie's...broken and when people...find out..." He's dragging me towards the building now, and I scan the street, searching for someone—anyone—to help me.

Balancing my briefcase, travel mug, and a box of doughnuts for the bullpen, I'm not exactly in a position to wrench my arm free. With my stellar grace, I'd probably land on my ass with coffee all down my white silk blouse.

"If you break your non-disclosure agreement, Beacon Hill will sue you for everything you're worth. Alfie's not broken. She's perfect. Leave. Get the hell out of here, and I'll forget this ever happened. Please, Kyle. You're...a good kid who made a mistake. Don't let it ruin your whole life."

The box of doughnuts tumbles to the ground, followed by my coffee, and I claw at Kyle's fingers, prying them loose so I can take two quick steps back.

When Kyle lurches for me again, the building's security guard shouts a warning. "Hey! Leave the lady alone." He races over and puts himself between the two of us. "Ma'am? Is everything all right here?"

"Fine," I say, forcing strength I don't feel into my tone. "Minor disagreement with a former employee. Kyle was just leaving."

The security guard puffs out his chest as he turns to face Kyle. "Sir? I think you want to listen to the lady."

With a muttered curse, Kyle backs off. "You're gonna regret this, Evianna."

I DON'T KNOW how I manage to hold it together until our meeting with Revere Insurance Services is over, but as their lawyers rise and the lead council offers me his hand, I plaster a wide smile on my face.

"Thank you, Mr. Carter. Alfie launches in ten days, and your customers will have an exclusive opportunity to pre-order their units five days in advance. I'll be sure to send over test units for you, Mr. Limet, and your executive team this afternoon. Any problems, just give me a call."

The thin lawyer gives me a nod and a smile, but his grip is a lot like a wet noodle. Mr. Limet does a little better with the handshake, thankfully, but addressed all of his technical questions to Noah. My boss—and majority owner of the company—may be a great guy, but he doesn't know the tech like I do. And even after he corrected the lawyers twice, they kept addressing him and him alone.

Assholes.

"Evianna is the heart and soul of Beacon Hill Technologies," Noah says as he comes up behind me and slings his arm around my shoulders.

Great. Thanks for making me look like a token pair of breasts, Noah.

He continues as I grit my teeth. "Alfie's success is one hundred percent her doing, and we look forward to a long, and successful partnership, gentlemen."

As the two lawyers head for the elevator, I duck out from under Noah's arm, the headache brewing behind my eyes tapping an incessant drum beat only I can hear. "The 'heart and soul of Beacon Hill Technologies'? Where the hell did that come from?"

"It's true." He shrugs and holds the conference room door open for me. "Look, I know you don't want anyone to 'protect' you in this industry, Evianna. But those two were *not* respecting your talent. When we launch, it might be my name on the letterhead, but this is *your* baby. And I want to make sure you get all the credit."

"Then next time, don't call me the 'heart and soul' while you're treating me like your arm candy." I'm so over this day.

While Noah's right, Alfie *is* my project and my passion, he's never been so...complimentary before. Especially not in front of people. But then he had to go ruin it with that little gesture.

Dropping into my ergonomic chair, I set the meditation app on my phone, close my eyes, and try for five minutes of relaxation. But two minutes in, I shift, and my arm presses against the side of the chair.

"Ow! Son of a bitch." Any hope of meditating long gone, I shut off the peaceful music and shed my jacket. *Oh my God.* Four distinct finger bruises mar my upper arm.

Ulysses knocks as he enters, and I hurriedly shove my arm back into the sleeve. "Yes?" I ask, trying to force some calm I don't feel into my voice. "I *was* meditating."

"I heard you swear, Evianna. I know you weren't meditating. Not any longer. Is something wrong?" Ulysses braces his hands on the edge of my desk, leaning forward to give me the once over.

Flopping back in my chair, I shake my head. "Nothing a little time and some arnica won't fix."

"Explain."

After I tell Ulysses—in very vague terms—about the email and what happened outside the building this morning, he shakes his head and sighs. "Evianna, you should call the police," he says as he hands me a cup of tea.

"And have them do what?" He's a kid. A kid who lost his job because he did something stupid. He was drunk off his ass." I blow on the steaming liquid, my fingers finally steady around the ceramic pixelated heart mug. "Let it go. If he approaches me again, I'll call them."

IN THE DARK of my bedroom, the alarm blaring through Alfie's speaker sends my heart rate skyrocketing, and I bolt out of bed, trip over my discarded slippers, and fall to the floor with a bone-jarring thud.

"Alfie, quiet mode report," I whisper as I yank open the top drawer of my nightstand and fumble for the hunting knife I keep there. My hands shake, but I manage to unsnap the sheath.

The little gray device blinks once, then says in a muted voice, "Motion detected outside front door. Lock sensor tripped. Alarm activated. No current motion detected. Should I call the authorities?"

No movement inside the house, and whoever's outside either ran away or is at least standing still. I take a steadying breath as I creep closer to her screen. "No. Show live view."

The night-vision camera reveals only my empty doorstep, and I tap Alfie's screen to turn the alarm off. "Alfie, replay last five minutes of video."

With a glitch of static, the view changes and shows a skinny guy in a dark hoodie stumbling up to the door with a small bag in his hand. Just before he raises his arm, he looks up at the camera.

Kyle. Oh God. I'm the deepest sleeper on the planet. Plus, I had my white noise machine running. I didn't hear him pounding on the door. It's been two days since the incident outside the office, and though he sent me half a dozen emails, he stayed away. I thought...maybe he'd let it go.

"*Evianna, get your ass out here! Right now!*"

He gets angrier and angrier when I don't answer, finally using his shoulder to ram the door. But this house is over a hundred years old, and the door is solid. Three times he tries, then rubs his left arm, wincing.

"*You ruined me! I tried to call Lampster to get an interview with their dev team and they wouldn't even talk to me! The whole world is going to know what you did—to Alfie and to me!*"

I yelp when Kyle shoves something through my mail slot. The

brown paper bag lands with a heavy splat. Oh God. Did he seriously drop a bag of shit on my hardwood floor?

His final kick to my door sets off Alfie's external alarm—the one that woke me—and then he races down the street and out of sight.

"Alfie, show l-live view," I say over the lump in my throat. After one last check to make sure Kyle hasn't come back, I swallow hard. I have to go check the front door. And get that bag out of my hallway.

The trip down the narrow staircase to my living room feels like it's a mile long, but that's probably because every muscle in my legs is shaking almost uncontrollably.

Clutching the knife so hard my fingers hurt, I step over the bag, approach the door, and give the knob a yank. The old wood creaks, but holds. *Thank God.*

Still spooked, my heartbeat roaring in my ears, I flip on every light downstairs before I approach the brown paper bag. "Ugh. Gross." The odor turns my stomach, and I hurry back to my kitchen, grab my cleaning gloves and trash bags, and triple wrap the disgusting present before checking the back door camera.

The alley's clear, so I open the door and drop the bag on the stoop.

The adrenaline thrumming through my veins won't let me sit down, so I pace back and forth between the kitchen and my small office at the front of the house until I start to get chilled, then realize I'm only wearing a tank top and panties.

"Smart, Evianna. Walk around the house half-naked at 3:00 a.m.—holding a hunting knife. You probably look like a psycho." The thought makes me laugh, and I can't stop until I sink down onto my ass, the hardwood floor stealing more of my body heat. Wrapping my arms around my bent knees, I close my eyes, trying to center myself.

Breathe. Just breathe. In and out. Focus on your breath.

As I start the mantra for the second time, glass breaks, something crashes to the floor only a few feet away, and I scream as I scramble up and press my back against the staircase.

"Alfie, c-call 911!"

The device in my living room initiates the call, and I peer into my home office. "Oh, shit." Amid the broken glass, a large, misshapen brick rests on the floor, and the cool night air steals the last of my sanity as it swirls around the room.

4

Dax

At seven in the morning, my walk to the office is quiet. Only the hum of the traffic and the occasional horn interrupt the sound of my cane sweeping across the sidewalk. So much easier than trying to navigate through the crowds at rush hour.

Despite the size of Boston, the South End is all old neighborhood. Lots of small, narrow streets, cobblestones, trees. Lucy and I owned a house halfway between my apartment and my office, and I still remember how to get there. I loved that house. Loved her too—at least the young, naive love that hasn't been tested by fire.

She lives in Dover now. Remarried. Two kids. The life I thought I wanted. The life I'm too fucked up to have.

"Mr. Holloway," the security guard greets me as I enter the six-story office building on Albany Street. "Nice walk today?"

"A quiet one, Chester," I say as he calls the elevator for me. "Anyone else in yet?"

"Mr. Lawton, Mr. Moana, and Ms. Benew. You have a good day now, Mr. Holloway."

As the elevator *snicks* shut, I search out the three dots that mark the button for the sixth floor. As the car rises, my phone's mechanical voice announces a call as the device in my pocket starts to vibrate.

"Call from: Trevor."

I tap the earbud with a sigh as the elevator dings. "I'm literally ten steps from the office, Trevor. I'll talk to you in a minute." He starts to say something as I disconnect the call, but I'm already at the outer door and push through.

Right into a plastic, sticky wall that wraps itself halfway around me.

"What the actual fuck?" I snap as I try to extricate myself from what feels like tape. My glasses, my hair, my Bluetooth…shit. Even my cane is stuck to the damn stuff.

"Oh, God. Boss. I'm sorry," Trevor says from the other side of the tape.

"You do realize I'm fucking blind, right?" I let my briefcase slip from my hand as Trevor curses under his breath and starts pulling pieces of tape off of me, taking at least a couple dozen hairs with them. "Watch it, asshole."

"That's…uh…what I was calling to tell you," he says.

"Oh, shit." Ford's at my side in another two seconds and gently peels the tape from my glasses. "Trev, what the hell were you thinking?"

"That Clive needed payback for putting lube on my desk chair last week. I called Dax to warn him…"

"Thirty seconds before I walked into…what is this? Packing tape? It's not like I can see the damn stuff. No more pranks at the office. Period."

It takes another few minutes for Trevor and Ford to remove the last of the tape, then Ford presses my cane and briefcase back into my hands. I stalk into my office and slam the door.

My eyebrows are still sticky. Fucking pranks. I pinch the bridge of my nose as a headache threatens. Some days, the damage to my eyes, combined with the repeated concussions and side effects from long term exposure to parasites leave me with migraines and cluster headaches. Today's going to be one of those days.

Ford raps three times on my door. "Can I come in?"

"Do I have a choice?" I pull open my desk drawer and flip the lid on a plastic container of wet wipes. The damn things smell like baby powder, but that's better than feeling my eyebrow hair stuck together all fucking day. "Tell Trevor to clean that shit up and send out a company-wide memo. Anyone else tries a prank in the office again, they're fired."

As Ford shuts the door, he sighs. "I thought you and Ryker used to be your unit's pranksters."

"We were. But there's a big difference between lubing up a toilet seat so a new recruit sinks ass-deep in blue water and putting up a barrier into the office when *your boss is blind*. This is one of the only two places I ever feel completely safe, Ford. You know that. I will *not* let anyone take that away from me."

"Trev and Clive wouldn't do anything really dangerous. They're just having fun." The guest chair across from me creaks as he sits down. "You haven't called him yet, have you?"

"This again? Don't you have a job to do? The Aquarium's Executive Director isn't going to pay her bill if you can't give her some assurances her ex-husband is going to jail for a very long time." Crushing the wet wipe in my fist, I toss it into the trash next to me and boot up my computer. "I don't want to talk about Ryker, Trevor, Clive, or what a shitty boss I am. I'd rather pay the bills and keep the damn lights on for all the rest of you."

"I'll send out the memo," Ford mutters as he heads for my door. "Try not to be a total dick to Trevor when he briefs you on the embezzlement case he closed last night."

The walls shake as the door slams again, and I drop my head into my hands. The scent of baby powder clogs my nose, and I suck in a breath through my teeth. Fuck. How did I become the boss who has to be warned not to be an asshole?

"Just wait till Hab tries to put on his boots," Ryker whispers as he pulls me into a dark corner of the barracks. "Dude's gonna lose his shit."

I chuckle at the memory. Two quarts of lube—one in each boot—and it was half an hour before Hab could stand up without doing the splits. I used to be that guy. The joker. Now...

Shit. I don't know who I am anymore.

MY PHONE RINGS a little after noon. "Do you have time to speak to a potential new client, Dax? Ford isn't back from lunch yet." Marjorie, our receptionist, screens all incoming calls, and Ford normally handles the initial contact.

"Put it through." Time I started acting like a boss again. "This is Dax Holloway. How can I help you?" I ask.

"Mr. Holloway? I was told to ask for Mr. Lawton." The light, female voice on the other end of the line is hesitant, with an undercurrent of distrust.

Engaging my voice recorder, I lean back in my chair. "I'm the owner of Second Sight, Ms...?"

"Oh. I'm so sorry. Evianna Archer. I was told you...Second Sight...could help me when the police...can't."

Something in her tone raises the hairs on the back of my neck. "Are you in danger, Ms. Archer?"

"No. Um...maybe? I don't think it'll come to that. Not really. Kyle's a kid. I always thought he was harmless. But..." She draws in a shaky breath, then pauses for so long, I'm about to ask her if she's okay. "I shouldn't have called. This is silly. I mean...what are you going to do? Threaten the kid and tell him to stay away from me?"

"That *can* be effective. I take it you have a stalker?"

"Yes. One of my former employees. I fired him a few days ago, and he hasn't handled it well."

"Ms. Archer, stalking can range from mostly harmless to deadly. There's every chance yours is one of the harmless ones, but come to our office and meet with me and Mr. Lawton—Ford. Bring your police reports and any evidence you've collected. Consultation is free. If we think you have cause to worry, we'll tell you. If not, you've only lost an hour." Something in this woman's voice drives me to reassure her. To get her in here.

"Um, okay. Thank you for not...I don't know. For not laughing at me."

A burst of anger punches me in the solar plexus. This country's stalking laws are shit, and the police, for all the good they *want* to do, have their hands tied. "That's not what we do here. Ever. I'll need to send you back to Marjorie for scheduling. She's the only one who has access to everyone's calendar. But before I transfer you, I need to ask you to do something."

Evianna sucks in a shaky breath. "All right."

"Even though the police can't do much in these cases, if you feel in danger or threatened at any time before we meet, call 911. Can you do that?"

"I'm at work. We have excellent security. But...yes. If anything happens, I'll call them. Thank you, Mr. Holloway."

"Dax. You can call me Dax. I look forward to meeting you, Ms. Archer. Be safe."

Evianna

My hand shakes as I hang up the phone. But I have an appointment at Second Sight in an hour. I can do this. With another cup of coffee. Snagging my mug from the corner of my desk, I head for the coffee machine in the office's small kitchen.

"Hi, Barry," I say as our newly promoted lead programmer shuts the fridge door and turns with a can of Mountain Dew in his hand. "What's the mood out there today?"

He scowls. "You have to ask?"

My brows furrow and I take a step back. "What's that supposed to mean?"

Advancing close enough so I have to crane my neck to stare up at him, he gestures to the bullpen—and the very empty desk where Kyle used to sit. "You fired our lead, Ms. Archer. A month before launch. Sonia stayed until midnight last night. Parvin didn't go home at all."

"We're close, Barry. I know this was a hard blow, but—"

"A blow? You really don't get it, do you? Kyle understood what it means to code. How our minds work."

Bristling, I slam my cup down on the counter. "Watch your tone, Barry. I paid my dues in this industry. Alfie started from *my* code. You want to compare script success rates?"

"Bullshit. I'd win. Every time. You're only here because Mr. Goset needed a pretty face who could speak the language."

I swallow hard and school my face into a mask of calm. I can't let him bait me like this. I'm the boss. I need to set an example. And if I lose my shit now, I'll only confirm his prejudices. "You're walking a dangerous line," I lower my voice even more. "Noah may have hired you three months before me, but I'm still your boss. While firing you would put us behind, I won't tolerate disrespect. From anyone or towards anyone. Get back to work. Now."

Sinking back against the counter when he stalks back to the bullpen, I blow out a breath. *A pretty face.* My whole career, I've fought against that stereotype. Doing everything I can to hide my curves. Working harder and longer than all the men around me.

And yet, one comment can still send me back to my first job, where the lead developer backed me into a corner and threatened to fire me if I didn't start...*playing nice.*

Coffee splashes onto the counter as I fill my mug, and I

swallow the sob trying to escape. *Get yourself together, Evianna. You're the CIO for fuck's sake. And once Alfie's released, maybe it'll be... enough. Maybe you'll finally feel like...enough.*

MY HAIR'S A MESS, dark brown tendrils escaping my french braid as I rush into the six-story office building only a few blocks from Beacon Hill Technologies and scan the directory for Second Sight.

Once I'm on the elevator, I force out a deep breath and take a moment to compose myself, tucking a few strands of hair behind my ear, smoothing my pencil skirt, and stilling my trembling hands.

I can do this.

These guys are supposed to be the best. All former Special Forces, Rangers, and SEALs. One of my sorority sisters hired them a year ago to find her husband. He'd emptied her bank account and fled to Bali after the FBI hauled him in for questioning, suspecting him of selling government secrets to Russia. He was guilty as sin, but they managed to get her money back *and* collect enough evidence to prove she knew nothing about the spying.

At the reception desk, I offer my name, and a petite older woman with kind brown eyes shows me to a conference room and promises to return with coffee.

Oh wow. Two men rise as I approach, and my jaw drops open. The taller and older of the two wears a hint of gray at his temples and looks like he could bench press a car. The other man...black hair, glasses with reddish tinted lenses, and a strong jaw. A scar angles across his forehead, and his dress shirt molds to broad shoulders.

"Ms. Archer?" The older man extends his hand. "Ford Lawton. This is Dax Holloway, owner of Second Sight."

Ford meets my gaze, and doubt darkens his hazel eyes as he notes my Rolex, Coach briefcase, and dusky pink manicured nails. "Evianna, please. Thank you for meeting me."

Turning my attention to Dax, I try to cover my frown. Unlike Ford, he seems to look past me, but his grip is firm, and his voice holds a hint of a southern twang. "Have a seat, Evianna. Did you have any trouble getting here?"

"N-no. My office is only a few blocks away. I work for Beacon Hill Technologies." I unzip my briefcase as Dax cocks his head.

"I know that name. Some big home automation solution releasing soon?"

"We've barely started advertising, Mr. Holloway. I'm impressed."

He huffs—part snort, part laugh. "I've been following the development rumors for six months. Looking forward to picking up one of your units when they're available."

I shift into sales mode. "We launch in ten days with mass availability in two weeks if all goes well. I can set you up with a pre-production unit if you're interested. You'd still need to purchase the final product, but we're in beta testing now, and looking for testimonials."

The receptionist knocks and pokes her head in. "Coffee?"

As she sets cups of rich, black brew in front of each of us, I pull out copies of the police report and the dozen emails Kyle's sent me over the past few days. Fortified after my first sip, I slide the entire folder across the table towards Dax, but Ford's the one who pulls out the papers.

"Someone threw a brick at your window?" Ford lets out a low whistle. "And you were in the room?" As I nod, Ford lays the first paper in front of Dax. "Police report," he says quietly.

Dax sits up a little straighter, fiddles with his ear, then his glasses, and scans the report while Ford looks through the rest of the documents.

"So, you fired this...Kyle Devlin six days ago. And since then, he's been harassing you, both at the office and at home? That about summarize it?" Ford asks.

I nod, then find my voice. "Yes. He was in clear violation of company protocol. Our non-disclosure agreements are ironclad, and he knew long before he copied our code base that it was a fireable offense." Rubbing my arm where the bruises have almost faded, I sigh. "The first time I talked to him, he was practically pickled in tequila. But last night...err, this morning...he didn't look drunk."

"I don't suppose you have cameras outside your home?" Ford asks.

Dax arches a brow at his coworker. "I'd be shocked if she didn't. Knowing where she works."

Setting a small USB thumb drive on the table, I smile at Dax, but his expression doesn't change at all. He seemed so nice on the phone. Even when I walked in. But now, it's like he doesn't care at all. "Video from this morning."

Ford tucks the small drive into his pocket. "We'll take a look at this later, if that's all right?"

"Uh, sure." I take another sip of my coffee, unsure what else to say. "Until he threw the brick, I didn't consider him...danger-ous. I don't know what I expect you to be able to do, but—"

"Evianna," Ford says, "why don't you tell me a little bit about your company. Dax might know all about it, but I don't."

Setting the delicate cup back on the saucer, I fold my hands in my lap. "Alfie—the female version of Alfred...like from Batman? —is the next evolution in home automation. She's not just a digital assistant like the other devices out there. Alfie works with everything else in your home. Your thermostat, refrigerator, light switches, security system, digital calendar...everything."

Ford chokes on a sip of his coffee. "Like...a robot?"

"You have to listen to Wren more," Dax says. Resting his fingers on the top of the conference table, he slides them slowly toward one another until he clasps the mug. Odd ritual. But damn. His hands are twice the size of mine. Knuckles that look like they've been broken a time or two.

"Evianna?" he asks when I'm quiet for way too long.

"I'm sorry. I didn't sleep much last night." Swallowing hard, I hope the blush to my cheeks isn't too obvious. At least Dax didn't seem to notice me staring at him. "No, Mr. Lawton. Alfie isn't a robot." I pull out one of our spec sheets from my briefcase and show him her photo. "She's designed to sit on your countertop or on a bookshelf. With a video screen, she's eight inches in diameter. Without, she's only five."

"That makes your HomeAssist clunker look ancient," he says to Dax. "And you're launching in ten days?"

"Yes. I...I'm worried Kyle's escalating, but honestly...it's more than that. If he goes public—not that he'd get much sympathy since he clearly breeched his NDA, the press could tank our launch. And if that happens...we could lose everything. We have a multi-million dollar marketing campaign ready to go and testimonies from some of the biggest names in business. Based on our preliminary in-home testing results, we have LOAs with all of the major insurance companies—"

"LOAs?" Dax asks.

"Letters of Agreement." I look from Ford to Dax as they both cock their heads. "Contracts. The insurance companies will offer their customers discounts on their policies if they install Alfie devices in their homes. Our next phase of development will include a car unit that can monitor a customer's driving and give them a discount on their insurance if they practice safe habits like always using their turn signals, and avoid actions like stopping short or exceeding the speed limit on residential streets."

Ford whistles. "Sounds a bit...invasive."

Setting my mug down with a little more force than necessary, I ease back in my chair. "How much of your life is accessible online, Mr. Lawton? If you had to guess. What could I find out with a little searching on the dark web?"

"I don't know. My name, address, phone number, and birth-day? My military commendations?"

"Try your social security number, high school GPA, a copy of your birth certificate, all the plane tickets you've ever purchased, parking violations, credit score, and the results of your latest blood work."

Ford sputters, almost shooting coffee out his nose, and pulls a pressed, white handkerchief from his pocket, dabbing at his lips.

Dax chuckles. "Man. Wren's going to have a field day when I tell her how much of a luddite you are." He takes another sip of his coffee, then touches the saucer with his free hand before he sets the cup down. "I gave up on privacy a long time ago, Evianna. Not much choice in the matter." A roughness edges his tone, but in the next breath, he shakes his head and almost smiles. "We can offer you protection. One of our junior guys positioned outside your house at night, Ford or Trevor to accompany you to and from the office. And we'll look into this Kyle—what did you say his last name was?"

"Devlin." The hard knot in the pit of my stomach eases slightly, though I hate the idea of having a babysitter. Even if Ford is kind of handsome. "How much is this going to run me? And... in these cases, how long do people usually need...*protection*?"

"We don't come cheap," Dax says. "A deposit of five thousand will cover you for approximately ten days. That includes the nightly protection from 8:00 p.m. to 7:00 a.m., escorts to and from your office twice a day, and a thorough background check on Mr. Devlin."

Ford rests his elbows on the table, his lips pressed together in a thin line. "And once we get a better sense of Devlin, we might be able to *strongly suggest* he leave you alone."

"You mean..."

"Yes." The weight of Dax's reply hits me hard, and I stare at him, forgetting my manners. There's something mesmerizing about him. His eyes are unbelievably pale—or maybe that's just an odd effect from the tinted glasses—shiny, rough scars cover the tops of his cheeks, and a lock of black hair falls over his forehead. I want to brush it away.

"Evianna?"

Get a grip, Evianna. Stop staring.

"My apologies, Mr. Holloway—"

"Dax."

My cheeks flame. Not only is Dax staring at me, but now Ford's gaze hardens. Unsurprising since I'm ogling his boss. "I-I'm sorry, Dax. This isn't...anything I ever thought I'd have to do. I'm a computer geek at heart. I like my quiet office, my quiet house, and until this past week, I thought I was safe both places."

A sympathetic smile tugs at Dax's lips. "You'll be safe from now on. That we can promise you. Do you know what a burner phone is?"

Scoffing, I give him a look that could probably break glass.

"That's a yes, then," Ford says with a chuckle.

For a split second, confusion slides across Dax's face, but one breath, and it's gone. "Good. Get one. All communications with Second Sight should occur using that phone. Normally, we don't go to those lengths, but since this Kyle is a programmer, and you say he's highly skilled, extra precautions aren't a bad idea. Ford will be your liaison with the rest of the team. How often you communicate, and the level of protection you want from him—whether he stays hidden or is out in the open, that sort of thing—is between the two of you. However, here's my card should you need it."

He pulls a black business card from his pocket, and as our fingers brush, a burst of warmth settles in my core, and I smile at him. His expression doesn't change at all, and frustration edges my tone when I turn to Ford. "Thank you. I have to get back to the office for a meeting. When...uh, when do we start?"

Ford glances at his watch. "I'll have Clive follow you back to your office and home tonight. I have a few things to clear off my schedule, and Trevor's wrapping up another case this afternoon. Can you pick up a burner phone on the way back?"

"There's a drug store on the corner."

"Good. Text me the number when you get it. And try not to worry, Evianna."

I laugh for the first time in what feels like a week. "That's like telling a chocolate chip cookie not to taste good." The release of tension in my shoulders is so palpable, it feels almost like something snaps inside me.

As I stand, the two men rise, and I hold out my hand to Dax, wondering what the hell is up with his stone-faced expression. His hand hovers three inches from mine. Some stupid power move? *Jerk.* But my mother didn't raise me to be rude, so I grip his fingers tightly enough his brows shoot up, highlighting the odd scars on his cheeks and forehead.

"Is something wrong, Evianna?" he asks.

"Nothing. Good day, Mr. Holloway." Turning, I smile, and Ford inclines his head as we shake hands. "It was lovely to meet you, Ford. I'll text you with the burner phone number in an hour or so."

5

Dax

EVIANNA'S subtle scent lingers in the conference room, though my fingers may never be the same. And I don't understand why she said goodbye with such a hard edge to her voice.

As I head for the coffee machine—and my ill-advised third cup of the day—Ford's footsteps creek on the hardwood floors. This building is ancient, like many in Boston, and being able to hear my team coming is one of the reasons I feel safest here.

"Clive's following our new client back to her office," he says as he pours himself a cup. "Want some?"

"Yeah. What do think about her...her case?"

"I wish we had Wren for this one," he replies.

My phone vibrates at the same time as Ford's. *"New text message from Accounting. Subject: Evianna Archer,"* the computerized female voice announces in my ear.

Removing my Bluetooth, I tuck the receiver into my pocket. "She pays on time. And I keep telling you. Wren's not dead. She's in Seattle. They have the internet there. Hell, she emailed me this morning asking when we'd have something for her. Pull her in so we can wrap this up quickly."

"You don't like our new client." Ford follows me back to my office. "Why not?"

"She clearly doesn't like me. That handshake was—" Ford starts laughing, and I arch a brow. "You didn't think she was a little...confrontational at the end?"

With a final snort, Ford gets himself under control. "You're wearing your glasses."

"What's that have to do with anything? I needed the camera in the damn things to read me her police report. And I've had a low level headache for three days. They help with the light sensitivity."

"Look, I know you can't see yourself, but your glasses hide a lot of the scarring. And how pale your eyes really are. Evianna smiled at you a couple of times. You didn't respond. And when you held out your hand at the end? She was waiting for you to take hers. She doesn't know you're blind."

"And I came across as a total jerk?" Pulling off my glasses, I pinch the bridge of my nose. Tension bands around my forehead, and I blow out a slow breath. "Shit."

I want to ask Ford what she looks like. Something about her voice called to me. Soft, feminine, but with a hint of steel running through it. But she's a client, and even if she weren't...I'm too broken to expose anyone to my scars.

"I'll explain when I talk to her," he says, turning around so his voice echoes into the hall. "Clive's going to handle everything until I can line up Ronan or Vasquez for the night shift. She didn't want close contact. Those two know how to be unobtrusive."

"Don't." Sinking down into my chair, I tighten my fingers around the handle of my mug. "Don't tell her anything about me. It's not important, and I don't want anyone's pity. She doesn't have to like me. She's a client. One I probably won't talk to again."

"Whatever you want." Ford's phone buzzes, and he swears

under his breath. "Gotta take this, then I'm heading out. Catch you tomorrow."

I almost ask him to wait. I have to call Ryker back today, and I'm not ready. But I don't know what to say to the man who carried my broken, bleeding, and blind body out of the worst hell on earth, then helped me kill the asshole who put us there.

There's more darkness inside me than anyone knows, and I need to keep as much of it hidden as I can.

I'VE PUT off going home as long as I can. Well after six, the office is quiet. Even Trevor abandoned his dark cave and left. The guy hates daylight. As I step through the building's front door, the sounds of Boston comfort me. My vision might be limited to a dull haze, shadows and muted colors moving around me without context, but I can still savor the fresh air, the hum of traffic on my left, the scent of the pizza place on the corner.

With my cane sweeping back and forth across the sidewalk, I set off at a brisk pace. Two blocks later, I turn right and head down East Dedham Street. It's quieter here. Calmer. The magnolia trees bloom in mid-May, and while most people don't notice their subtle scent, I do.

Another six blocks and I'm almost home. When I rented this place, I hired a sighted companion to help me learn the neighborhood. There's a little Mom and Pop grocery store on the corner. A liquor store two shops down. My local bar between the two.

I know exactly how many steps it is from the corner to my building's front door. The short set of stairs to the landing. The keypad at ten o'clock. Chest level. Eight-two-five-six-zero-three. The buzzer grates, sending my low-level headache ratcheting up a notch.

Four flights of stairs. Thirteen steps each. I run my free hand along the railing as I climb. A right turn, and I try not to disturb my neighbors with my cane's scraping until I reach the third door on the left.

I stow my briefcase on its designated shelf, my shoes under the bench seat by the door, and my jacket on the hook. My routines are rigid. Never changing. If I set something down in an unfamiliar spot, I might never find it again. Or worse. I'll trip over it and end up on my ass.

Dropping down on the couch I've never seen, I run my hands over the leather. If I don't call Ry today, I'll lose my fucking nerve. But what the hell am I going to say to him?

My head pounds, the migraine making me lightheaded. Resting my head against the back of the couch, I try a few deep breathing techniques, hoping I can avoid taking a pill until it's time to go to bed.

Sleep has been an elusive bitch lately, and I doze off—only to wake to more pounding. This time at my door. "Coming," I call. "Who is it?"

"Ford."

Great.

He strides in, pauses, and says, "VoiceAssist: Lights on, sixty percent. It's after eight, Dax."

Shrugging, I head for the kitchen. The few people I let into my inner circle all know how to work around my blindness. How to turn on the lights in my apartment, how to describe a plate of food using clock time, when to touch me and when to leave me alone.

"Beer?" I ask with my hand on the fridge door.

"Sure." There's a strain to Ford's tone I'm not used to. He's one of the calmest guys I've ever met. Hell, the only time he's lost his temper in the past couple of years? The other day when we fought about Ry.

"What's wrong?" I pass him a bottle and head back to the couch.

He sinks down into the chair across from me with a quiet groan. "You're scary, you know that?" A swig of beer, and he sighs. "I thought I was hiding it pretty well."

"It's in your voice. Spill." With my arm draped over the back of the couch, I let the cold beer soothe my nerves. My phone is still on the cushion next to me, and I feel its presence. Like a physical weight that won't go away until I call Ry.

"Joey's missing."

"Joey?" I wrack my brain, unable to think of anyone Ford and I know named Joey. "Sorry, but who is he?"

"She." He rises and starts to pace, the angle of his voice changing with every few steps and his hazy form dizzying. "Josephine Taylor? The woman I was dating when I joined the marines?"

Bits and pieces of past conversations coalesce. "Don't you mean the woman who *dumped* you when you joined the marines?"

"Well, sort of. I mean...no." A pause, another hard swallow, and Ford clears his throat. "Her sister called me. No one's heard from Joey in ten days. She was working for Doctors Without Borders in Turkmenistan, and the whole group's just...gone."

"Shit. Turkmenistan's a war zone, Ford. If she got caught up in a local gang war, she's not missing. She's in a shallow grave somewhere."

I cringe as soon as the words leave my lips. *Get it together, you insensitive prick.*

"Don't you think I know that?"

Throwing up my hands, I try for apologetic, but given my track record lately... "Sorry. Is the CIA involved? Any demands for ransom?"

"The CIA won't investigate. Something about not wanting to upset the fragile peace in the region. Total bullshit. And Doctors Without Borders doesn't even know where the group was before they went missing. Their last known location was somewhere outside of Sayat, but they were packing up and preparing to head south. Once they found a good spot to camp, they were supposed to check in."

The leather chair squeaks quietly as Ford sits back down, and his voice is muffled, like he's leaning forward, elbows on his knees. "I can't just leave her out there, Dax. I owe her that much."

"You don't *owe* her anything. She couldn't handle dating a marine on active duty and she bailed."

"No. She didn't. Not exactly." Ford makes a low, frustrated sound in his throat. "She stayed with me for almost a year. We wrote letters, even talked on the phone a couple of times. But… then my squad got three days leave. Back home in San Diego. And I didn't call her."

Arching a brow, I huff out a breath. "So, let me guess. You were out with the guys, drinking until you were shit-faced, wearing your whites to impress the ladies, and she just happens to walk into the bar with her girlfriends to find you with a pretty little thing on your lap."

"I wasn't shit-faced. That came later," he says quietly. "Never touched another woman. Never even *looked*. All my mates were trying to hook up with anything that moved. Me? I just sat at the bar. Nursing a beer. For three fucking hours."

"Why?" I can hear the sadness in his voice, and while I'm still confused—and a little mad at him—he's one of my only friends. I can't…not listen. Even if all I can think about is Lucy. Her tears, sliding hot and fast over my hands as I cupped her cheeks the day I came home. How strange it felt to lie in bed next to her at night, wearing a t-shirt and pajamas to hide my scars. The day she left, telling me she couldn't stay with a man who hated himself.

Another sigh, and the angle of his voice changes again, almost bouncing off the ceiling. "It was Desert Storm, Dax. We were dropped in country after only six weeks of basic. The day before we got the news they were rotating us home…I killed six hostiles. After watching a target take out a public market. Kids.

Babies. Innocents. Joey didn't deserve thirty-six hours of me crying and asking her why."

"And did you tell her that?"

"Nope. I fucked up. Wrote her letters trying to explain, but she returned every damn one of them. Unopened. Eventually...I stopped writing."

A long swig of stout doesn't wash away the bitter taste of my own memories, but it gives me a chance to form a reply not colored by my own bullshit. "What are you going to do?"

"I have a contact in Uzbekistan—Nomar—who's trying to slip unnoticed into Turkmenistan. If so, he'll check out their last known location, retrace the route they were supposed to have taken. He'll contact me tomorrow."

"And then?" I don't have to ask. Ford's going after her. I just need to know when he's leaving.

"If there's a chance she's alive...I'm going to find her." His bottle of beer makes a hard *thunk* on the coffee table. "But that means I need you to find someone else to take over the Archer case. Or...at least run point on it with me until I hear back from Nomar."

I squeeze my eyes shut, then press the cold bottle of beer to my temple. The pounding in my head intensifies, and if I'm not careful, I'll be flat on my back with a migraine in half an hour. "There isn't anyone else. Ella's tied up on that embezzlement case. Trevor can handle the basic surveillance on days, and Vasquez at night with Ronan as backup, but Clive messaged me right before I left the office. His mom's about to have open-heart surgery."

"Fuck."

This time it's my turn to sigh. "First thing in the morning, read me in with what you have so far. If you need to leave, I'll run point with Wren until Clive returns."

We finish our beers in silence, and when I walk him to the door, he clears his throat. "I never stopped loving her, Dax."

"Then you'll get her back." I reach out and find his arm, squeezing once—about all the physical contact I'm willing to have—with anyone. "But until we know more, don't tell Evianna I'm involved. No need to worry her until we know there's something to worry about."

Confusion mars his tone, but he doesn't argue. "Whatever you say. I'll see you in the morning." He's halfway down the hall when his footsteps stop, and he adds, "Thank you."

6

Dax

Two hours later, after another beer, I pick up the phone. "VoiceAssist: C-call...fuck." After I punch the couch cushion, I try again. "Call Ryker."

One ring. Two. Three. My stomach clenches, and I'm about to hang up when his rough voice carries over the line. "Dax."

"Ry."

Silence stretches between us. God, I wish I knew what to say. "How's Wren?" I finally ask.

"She's...good. Any news from the Roxbury drug ring?"

I can hear the concern in his voice. No. More than concern. Love.

"They've been quiet. Ford called one of his contacts in Vice last week. Wren's safe, brother." The word slips out, and Ry's breath catches in his throat.

"Thank fuck." After a pause and a few murmured words, he returns to the line. "Dax, I...don't...I wanted to call...every damn day...but..."

"I didn't think you were coming back." The admission rushes

out before I can stop myself. And suddenly, I'm back there, huddled in the dark, dirty cell, my eyes swollen and infected, and so fucking scared I couldn't think straight.

"What?"

Memories tighten my throat. "After you escaped. Even with all those tricks you taught me, I never had your memory. With the fever...I was in and out. And after Kahlid...my eyes...I lost count of how many days—"

"Ten. Ten of the longest days of my life." After a pause, he blows out a breath. "I was so fucked up they wouldn't let me back out any sooner. One of the guards shot me twice before I snapped his neck. And when I got to the surface...I didn't know where I was. Crawled through the snow and dirt, fell halfway down the fucking mountain. When Sampson found me, he thought I was dead. Scared the piss out of him when I grabbed his arm."

I manage a choked laugh. I've only met the man a couple of times, but West Sampson's one of the calmest guys I know.

"He and Inara were part of a joint op to try and find us. The last one CENTCOM would authorize." His voice roughens, even more than his usual low rasp. "I fought them, Dax. Begged them to go back with me to get you out. But...we got attacked. Inara took a fucking bayonet to the thigh. And then I passed out and woke up in the field hospital two days later."

"Kahlid told me you'd been shot. Four times. Tried to get me to tell him how we'd planned to escape. Said he'd find you and take you to a hospital. I told him to go fuck himself."

This...despite the pain the memories still cause...this I can do. It's like a movie in my head. One that still has pictures. Unlike the rest of my life.

"Fucker lied. But twice was enough. Once in the leg. Another in my shoulder. If I'd moved faster, done...*anything different*...maybe..."

I take a long swig of my third beer of the night, needing the buzz of the alcohol to loosen my tongue and keep me from shutting down completely. "You got out. You couldn't have known... what he was going to do."

"When?" The question is no more than a whisper. "When did it happen?"

Dropping my glasses on the couch, I trace the chemical burns under my eyes. "I think...it was the second day after you got out. Maybe the third."

"I'm so fucking sorry, Dax." Ry's voice thickens, and it's so like the night he escaped, I'm back there in a heartbeat.

Three taps rouse me from my pain-induced haze. I struggle to open my eyes—not that it does me any good. It's pitch black inside my cell. The canvas our captors tack over the bars keeps us in the dark. Except when they bring us our infrequent meals or come to drag one of us away to be beaten or interrogated. Another series of taps, and I try to concentrate enough to piece together the words.

"We have to go."

Mustering what little strength I have left, I respond with five taps of my own. Our code for no.

I can't walk. Can barely focus. This is our only chance. Ry's only chance. Mine disappeared as soon as they broke my leg.

Another series of taps. He's not going—won't leave me.

"You have to. If not, we both die." *A combination of morse code and our own special language developed over fifteen months spent in this fucking place, the taps let us communicate without our captors knowing what we're saying. At least...we hope. We change things up every couple of weeks.*

"I will come back for you."

I want to laugh, but I don't have the strength. "Go, brother."

Brother. I can't tell Ry how much he means to me. Can't thank him for protecting me. For keeping me sane. For keeping me alive all the times I wanted to die.

Clawing my way towards the cell door, I dig my fingers around the edge of the canvas, forcing one corner up so I can stick my hand through the bars. The dim lights from the tunnel almost blind me, but

I wait until I hear a metallic click—Ry picking the lock on his cell with a shard of metal he shoved under the skin of his forearm weeks ago. How he didn't end up with sepsis, I have no idea. My leg won't last much longer. I can smell the infection, and the fever hasn't let up in days.

As a shadow heads for me, I snake my arm out and grab his ankle. His skin is cool. He's barefoot—we lost our boots months ago. Hell, Ry doesn't even have a shirt anymore. The last strip of it is tied around his left arm and the knife wound Kahlid gave him the last time they took him.

He reaches down and covers my fingers with his. "Stay alive, brother," he whispers. "Please. I'll come back for you."

"Hooah."

And then, he's gone. The tears I haven't let fall in fifteen months burn my eyes, but before they escape, I pass out.

"Dax? Say something. Yell. Tell me what a piece of shit I am. Tell me you never want to hear from me again."

"No." I clench my fist around the bottle until my knuckles crack, and I'm back in that cell. Sobbing as I listen to the only family I have leaving me to die. "I can't. I don't know how to do this. What to say. But...don't disappear again."

The hoarse sounds carrying over the line send me sliding off the couch and onto the floor, my head between my knees, beer in one hand, phone in the other. Ry's never broken down. Not once in all the years I've known him. Not even when they carved up his face.

"Never...fuck." He pauses, clears his throat, and then almost growls, "Never. I...I almost lost Wren in Russia, Dax. When they took her—it was like they took a part of me. The best part. The only part that mattered. If we hadn't been able to get her out, I was going to go into that fucker's fortress with enough C4 to blow a hole in the world."

Images of Ry—what he used to look like anyway—with packs of explosives strapped to his chest, back, arms, and legs flicker in my mind, and a rough laugh escapes as I swipe the back of my hand over my cheeks. "Sounds like something you'd do."

"Then Sampson and Inara show up spouting all this shit about family. I didn't want to hear it. Didn't..." His voice cracks, and when he continues, his words take on a quiet, reverent tone. "You're family. And...family doesn't disappear. I understand that now. I want to fix this, brother. Let me try."

The lump in my throat is now so large, I'm scared to even try to talk, but I have to. Because he's right. We're family. "Tell me," I rasp, "about Hidden Agenda."

"Started it not long after I left the army. Didn't know what else to do. I couldn't go back to teaching. Not looking...the way I do. Wish I'd had you with me. Your instincts. You were the best. Pretty sure you still are."

"You ever think about...Ripper? About what happened to him?" After our Communications Sergeant disappeared from Hell, Kahlid stopped limiting our torture to arms, legs, and torso —body parts that could be covered in any propaganda video. And he started in on Ry's face.

"One of Kahlid's men killed him," Ry says quietly. "Sampson's team captured three of 'em when we came back for you. Ahmed copped to it. Said he tossed Ripper in the hole and broke his neck."

We let a moment of silence pass for our fallen comrade. "Crazy son of a bitch," I mutter. "Probably jumped, yelling 'geronimo' the whole way down."

"Damn straight." He chuckles, clears his throat, and sighs. "Got three people on my team. Sampson, Inara, and a new guy— Graham. But... I fucked up, Dax. Big time. Had another guy for a while. Coop. Never took orders, went rogue in Colombia, and Sampson almost bled out. And we thought Coop had died. But the People's Army tortured him. And when he finally escaped, he came after Inara. Almost killed her guy."

"Shit. And...that's why you came back to Boston?" The realization that I never gave him a chance to tell me why he showed up after six years hits me hard.

"Yeah. Didn't know where else to go. You were the only person in the world I thought would understand."

"And I kicked you out." Draining the last of my beer, I let my head fall back against the couch cushions. "Tell me what happened."

By the time Ry finishes talking—about Hidden Agenda's K&R work, the mess with Coop, and how hard it was for him to go to Sampson and Inara for help, his voice is hoarse, and it must be well after midnight.

I run a hand through my hair, wondering when it got so long. "I almost didn't call tonight." The admission lifts a weight from my chest. "But...I'm glad I did."

Rolling my head from side-to-side, I cringe at the three loud pops. "I get migraines sometimes. What's left of my vision, the TBIs...I need to crash. But, maybe—"

"I'll call you in a couple of days?" The hope in his voice mirrors the emotion choking my throat, and I swallow hard before I can answer.

"Yeah. And maybe next time, you'll let me get a word or two in, asshole."

His deep laugh reaches one of the shattered pieces of my soul, and my eyes start to burn.

"Maybe I will, brother. Because I want to hear about Second Sight. About the migraines. About...what happened when I escaped."

"Give me a little time for that last one. But...keep asking."

"I promise," Ry says.

Wren taught us both that one. The importance of the word promise. When I hang up, the tension I've carried since he walked back into my life weeks ago, washes over me in a violent wave, and I drop my head into my hands and let it out in loud, choking sobs until there's nothing left.

7

Evianna

AT PRECISELY 7:00 a.m. the next morning, the burner phone on my counter vibrates.

Ford: I'm outside. Two blocks south. I'll be behind you the whole way to work.

Kyle didn't show last night, but he sent another series of increasingly angry email messages from several anonymous accounts. The last one warned me if I sent the cops after him again, I'd regret it. And he included a fun little animated GIF of a woman being stabbed through the heart. I sent it to Ford, but it's just one more piece of evidence the police can't do anything about.

I don't understand what he thinks I did. Besides firing him. And that's on him. Noah keeps telling me to ignore him and he'll go away, but I can't help feeling like there's more to this. Kyle never struck me as...unstable. Eccentric, sure. High maintenance. Had to have his electrolyte-enhanced water, ate Sweet-Tarts like they were all he needed for a balanced meal, talked to his code sometimes. But this is a side of him I've never seen.

My walk to the T station is surreal. When I turn corners, I catch sight of Ford. All six-foot-ten inches of him. With a brief-case in his hand, he looks like all the other commuters around me—except for his size and the way he's constantly scanning the crowd.

The phone vibrates again, and I stifle a snort as I read his message.

Ford: Stop looking for me. Act normal.

After I've swiped my fare card and make my way down to the platform, I respond.

Evianna: Being stalked isn't exactly "normal" for me. Neither is having a bodyguard. You try acting normal with a giant, lethal-looking dude following you.

Ford: Think of me as a really tall teddy bear. Who knows how to fight. Dax and Trevor are the lethal ones.

On the train, I scan through my email. Nothing new from Kyle, but one of our test machines is throwing errors every few minutes. Great. This is going to be a stellar day.

I nod to the security guard on my way into the building. Ford slips into the elevator with me at the last second and punches buttons for the second, third, and fourth floor. "Sorry. I needed to talk to you for a minute."

My heart skips a beat, and I swallow hard. "Is something wrong?"

"Not exactly. It's nothing to do with your case. But I have an emergency I have to take care of. You're not leaving the office today?" His hazel eyes carry a deep sadness, and a hint of something else, I think. Worry.

"No. It's crunch time. We're getting sandwiches delivered and it's all hands on deck. I won't leave until eight." I heft my briefcase strap a little higher on my shoulder. "Hell, if I didn't have to worry about scheduling with you, I might stay until midnight. But I can pack up at eight and finish up the night at home."

Ford nods and runs a hand through his sandy hair. "Okay. The Dunkin' Donuts right next door is open until ten. I have to coordinate with the rest of the team, but I'll send someone there at eight to meet you. I'll text you their photo once I figure out who's free."

The doors slide shut on the fourth floor, and the next stop is Beacon Hill. "Ford?" He meets my gaze, and I reach out to give his forearm a squeeze. "I hope everything's okay."

"Me too, Evianna. Thanks for understanding."

I leave him on the elevator, and my last glimpse of him ties a knot in the pit of my stomach. Things are definitely not okay, and I worry they never will be again. Not for him.

Dax

The three raps on my door aren't unexpected. "Come on in, Ford."

"I got the call." My visitor chair creaks as he drops down. "Nomar found four bodies outside of Batash. Two local bodyguards, one doctor, and an aid worker. All men. The others in the group were women. Joey, a twenty-four-year-old medical tech on her first oversees assignment, and a twenty-three year-old junior resident from Cedars-Sinai."

"And no sign of them?" Unease crawls up my spine. That area of Turkmenistan is known for sex trafficking, and if whoever attacked them killed the men, things for Joey could get dicey. Fast.

"No. But the locals told Nomar stories of their daughters going missing. Being taken to Basaga and then disappearing." After a pause, Ford swallows loudly. "Nomar's waiting for me at the Uzbeki border." Pain infuses his every word, and even his breathing sounds strained.

"Take Trevor with you. And...I'll call Ryker. If anyone's got Joey, he and his team...they can get her out."

"Dax—"

"I talked to Ry last night. Couple of hours after you left. This is what he does, Ford. K&R. Let me help. I can't...go with you. But I can do this."

"Let me get there first. Get the lay of the land. I'll take Trevor. He's got contacts all over the Middle East. But..." A sigh, and Ford scoots the chair closer. The scrape of the legs on the hardwood floor pierces the stillness of the room. "We were already under-staffed this week. And if I take Trevor, there's no one to watch Evianna. Unless you want to pull Ronan or Vasquez off nights."

Shit. He's right.

"Ronan's too green. He's only been with us for a month. He's fine as a backup to Vasquez, but not on his own. Not with a guy who's escalating to violence." I rub the back of my neck, trying to ease the stress gathered there. "You do realize asking a blind man to step in as bodyguard is fucking ridiculous, right?"

Ford's choked laugh breaks a fraction of the tension suffusing the room. "Maybe. But from the little bit of research I did last night, this Kyle's never been in trouble before—other than some stupid college pranks."

"So why is he threatening Evianna? People get fired all the time and don't go batshit crazy. Vasquez didn't see anything on watch?"

"Nope." Ford's phone buzzes. "Shit," he mutters under his breath. "Nomar arranged for transpo from Turkey. But I have to be there in thirty-six hours. I typed up the case notes first thing this morning. They're in your inbox."

I stand and skirt my desk, waiting for Ford's hazy outline to rise before I hold out my hand. When he wraps his fingers around mine, I pull him in a little closer so I have to tip my head up to have any hope of him seeing my expression. "Promise me one thing."

"What?"

"Don't go dark on me. Check in, and if you need help, you let me call Ry."

Ford wraps his other arm around me for a single breath and gives me a hard hug. I stiffen at the contact, but this is my friend, so I force myself not to pull away.

"Be safe," I say as he releases me and heads for the door. "And get her back alive."

"I'm going to try."

THE OFFICE FEELS EMPTY. Ford. Trevor. Wren. Clive. It's just me, Ella, Hailey, and Bastian, and they're all tied up on their own cases. Holed up in their offices. No client chatter. Even Marjorie's quiet. Down four people, I made the executive decision to close Second Sight to new clients for the next week.

Stretching my legs out under my desk, I pull out my phone. "VoiceAssist: dial Wren."

"Dialing...Wren," the calm voice says.

"Hey, Dax. What's up?" She's never sounded so...happy. "I finished scanning for those stolen photographs from the mayor's phone. Ford should have the final report in a couple of hours."

"Ford's...taking care of some shit." I don't know how much to tell her, except...they might need Ryker's help. "He and Trevor are on their way to Uzbekistan."

"What the flapjacks are they doing there?"

"It's a long story. But...they might need you...and Ryker." The words don't feel as hard to say as I thought they would. "If he's around, put me on speaker?"

"Just a sec." Rustling carries over the line, and then the connection clicks. "Okay, boss. We're here."

"Ry." This is harder. When we hung up the previous night, I felt like someone had wrung me out and thrown me from a fourth floor window. *Spit it out. Stick to business. You can do the friendship thing later.*

"Ford thinks his former girlfriend's been kidnapped in Turkmenistan," I say in a rush.

"Oh my God," Wren whispers.

Ryker clears his throat, "Sampson's out for another few days, but Inara and Graham and I can be there in twenty-four hours."

By the time I fill them in on the details I know and Ford's desire to investigate on his own first, I feel almost steady. Talking business—even if it involves my friends in danger, makes me feel...capable. I can't be out there with him, no matter how much I want to be. I'm too broken to save anyone again. But this, I can do. Coordinate. Make things happen.

"We'll wait, then," Ry says. "But if Ford can keep me updated —even through Wren—I'll make sure the team's prepped if we're needed."

"Thanks, brother."

Over the line, Ryker sucks in a sharp breath, and my chest tightens. In some ways, it's like no time's passed. And in others, there's still this huge chasm between us I don't know how to cross.

"*De oppresso liber*," he says, his voice rough. "We don't leave a man or woman behind. Ever."

"I wish I could be out there." The thought escapes on a whisper before I can stop it, and I scramble to change the subject. "Uh, Wren, there's something else I need you to work on while we wait to hear from Ford."

"Give us a minute, sweetheart?" Ry's question sends my heart rate shooting up. I don't know if I can have another deep conversation with the man yet, but the phone clicks off speaker, and then his voice rumbles in my ear. "You all right?"

For several seconds, I freeze and turn towards the windows, needing the warmth of the sun on my face. Something to remind me I'm free, alive, and not totally useless. But it's past five, and only shadows greet me.

"Dax? Answer me, Sergeant."

The order snaps me back to the present. "Yeah. Fine." *Be honest. Tell him. Stop hiding.* Except, I can't. There's only so much sharing I can handle in a twenty-four hour period. Only so much weakness I can admit.

"Bullshit."

"I should be going with him! Is that what you wanted to hear, Ry?" Slamming my hand down on the desk, I wince as a twinge of pain races up my arm. "With Ford and Trevor gone, I'm under-staffed, and so I have to tell a client she's going to be guarded by a fucking blind man for the next couple of days. How the hell am I supposed to keep her safe? I can't even see her."

"You beat the crap out of me when we fought," Ry says quietly. "You lost your sight, brother. Not your skills. Not your training. You still earned that patch, and no one can take that away from you. And if I had to go into a fight with you at my back, I wouldn't think twice."

"You'd regret it."

An edge returns to his voice, and suddenly, we're back to being strangers again. "Not a chance. Here's Wren."

"Well, that sounded like it went swimmingly," she says dryly. "I'm not even going to ask. Not today. But the two of you need to figure your bull-pucky out soon before I lose my mind. Now tell me about this other case."

8

Dax

SITTING at the small table with my coffee, I wait for Evianna at the Dunkin' Donuts outside her office building. With how we left things yesterday, I don't expect her to be happy to see me, but at least escorting her home will give me a chance to explain.

Explain what? That you're blind? That's supposed to fix everything?

All I can hear is Lucy.

"Dax! Are you okay?" She grabs my arm and tries to help me up. "What the hell were you trying to do?"

"Make myself a damn sandwich. You want to tell me why you decided to leave your shoes in the middle of the floor? You know I can't see them."

"I didn't expect you to get up. I'm not perfect, Dax. All these changes? Putting everything back in the exact same spot, always warning you before I touch you...not to mention the nightmares? Did you ever think about how this affects me?"

I couldn't tell her the truth back then. That I was so wrapped up in my own shit, too hurt, to afraid to even realize she was there most of the time. Even when she tried to help.

The bell over the door rings, and the scent of freesia envelops me. "So this is how your company runs things?" Evianna's voice holds a note of annoyance as she stops a few feet away. "Ford was supposed to text me and let me know who was meeting me here. He didn't."

Frustration stiffens my spine, and I sit up a little straighter. "Ford had an unexpected family emergency to take care of. If he said he was going to text you, he should have followed through. But I understand why he couldn't. And I'm sorry."

Evianna sighs, and her voice softens. "Will his family be all right?"

"I don't know yet." What the hell do I do now? Pull my cane out from behind my chair and stand up? Just say it? *Oh, by the way, you should know...I'm blind.*

"I need a cup of tea. Excuse me for a moment, Mr. Holloway."

"Dax," I call after her as clipped footsteps head for the counter behind me.

Her voice changes, so much so I think she must be smiling at the young clerk as she orders a cup of chamomile. When she returns, she drops into the chair across from me. The other day, I thought she had short hair. But today, with the light behind her, I think maybe...her hair's long. Dark brown.

"It's been an endless day of frustrations...Dax. I shouldn't have snapped at you. Thank you for coming."

The band of tension around my head tightens, and I pull off my glasses so I can pinch the bridge of my nose. Sometimes, that's enough to stave off the headache for a few hours. The movement jostles my briefcase, and my folded cane tumbles out of the side pocket and clatters to the floor.

Evianna gasps, and now she knows. What I look like—or think I look like—without the glasses, and why I didn't take her hand yesterday.

"Oh my God," she says, her voice muffling as she leans down and picks up my cane. "You're...blind?" Warm fingers brush mine, pressing the cane into my palm.

Jerking away—I don't like to be touched—and setting the cane on the table between us, I offer a single nod. "Yep."

"I'm... I'm sorry. I didn't know."

Gritting my teeth, I put my glasses back on. "I don't need your pity. I've done just fine for the past six years."

"Oh, for fuck's sake." She sighs, and a hint of exasperation tinges her tone. Hearing her swear is...refreshing. Like a crack in her armor. "That wasn't pity. It was an apology for my less than professional behavior yesterday. And a little shock. Either I wasn't paying attention during our meeting, or you're *very* good at hiding it. I mean...you read my police report. Or...I thought you did."

I try to ignore the pounding headache threatening as I tap my glasses. Coffee wasn't a good idea. "There's a small camera embedded in the frame. It works with my phone—optical character recognition? Reads me restaurant menus, street signs, police reports."

"I didn't know they came that small." She blows on her tea, sending a sweet aroma wafting over me.

"They do when you employ one of the best hackers in the world. And have enough money."

Evianna's light laugh carries a hint of strain, but this is progress. Hope that perhaps she won't fire Second Sight before I can find someone more...capable to protect her. "Touché. I did a lot of research on OCR technology for Alfie. I'd like her to work with more adaptive devices in the next version. It's...why I built her, ultimately. But she has to prove herself first." After another sip of tea, she clears her throat. "Have you...um...found anything in Kyle's...past? Or any evidence he might be truly violent?"

An overwhelming need to reassure her flares up inside me, and I barely stop myself from reaching across the table. Not that I know where her hand is. But what I have to tell her won't go over well.

"Evianna...we can't find him. I sent Ronan to his apartment this afternoon. His neighbor said she hadn't seen him in two days. The mobile phone on his account is off, and he hasn't used any of the email accounts tied to him since the night he threw the brick through your window. He's gone dark."

"Oh God. That...can't be good."

Running my fingers over my folded cane, I try to find the words that will make this okay. "It isn't anything yet. Good or bad. He could have left town. Gotten a new job across the country. Be on a two-day bender."

"Or he could be waiting at my house."

I haven't felt this...useless in years. "Evianna, I want you to know...in a couple of days, I'll have another one of my employees escort you to and from work. We're just short-staffed right now."

Someone starts shouting obscenities outside, I tense, and the table shakes as Evianna turns in her chair.

"What is it?"

"Shit. Sorry. It's just kids horsing around," she says with a little tremble in her voice.

I wish I knew what she looked like. Because right now, she sounds like she's about to crack. "Ford said you usually take the T home, but it's late. I have a car service I use. Let me call them. I'll ride with you, and by the time we get to your house, Vasquez should be there."

"Are you sure? I mean...I can call a Lyft. You don't have to—"

"You hired Second Sight to keep you safe. I know I'm not exactly who you expected. But as off balance as Kyle's been lately, we haven't found any evidence he's stupid enough to try anything when you're not alone. Besides," I try for a smile, even though I feel about two inches tall, "I'm pretty damn good with this cane."

Evianna

"Two minutes," Dax says as his phone vibrates on the small table between us. "The driver knows to identify himself when we get outside." He stands and unfolds his cane, and I curl my fingers around his elbow to guide him towards the door. But he pulls away with a half-hiss, half-growl. "Don't."

Backing up a step, I raise my hands. "What did I do?"

His free hand clenches into a fist at his side, and lines of strain bracket his lips. He's breathing heavily, and he shakes his head. "Never," he says, his voice harsh and rough, "touch a blind man without an invitation. Where's the trash can?" He fumbles for his coffee cup, and I'm so shocked, I don't even think.

"Over there."

"Evianna, do you think I have any idea where you're pointing? Try using clock time. It's the most reliable."

Heat crawls up my neck, flooding my cheeks. "To your right. Um, four o'clock? Ten feet."

With his cane tapping on the tile floors, he reaches the trash bins and manages to get his empty cup inside after the second try. Turning, he makes a beeline back to me. "Head for the car. It's a black SUV. I'll follow you."

I nod before I realize what I'm doing. "O-kay."

A black Toyota rolls up to the curb, and a uniformed driver hops out. "Mr. Holloway?" the driver asks as we approach, Dax only a foot behind me. "I'm Thomas with Transportation Unlimited."

"Yes. We're headed to 1846 Newland Place."

"Absolutely, sir." The driver opens the back door, and I'm so out of my element, I don't know what to do.

Holding out his hand to me, Dax sighs. "Show me where the door frame is."

When I do, his warm fingers don't flinch, and he slides into the back seat with ease and folds up his cane. I stay as far away from him as I can when the driver shuts the door and jogs around to the front of the car.

"Just to confirm, 1846 Newland Place?" the driver says.

"Yes. Thank you." My voice isn't steady, and I wish I could rewind the past twenty minutes and avoid Dunkin' Donuts completely. But we're trapped here now, and I don't know what to say to the man next to me.

"About before." Dax runs a hand through his hair, high-lighting a scar slashing across his forehead and one misshapen eyebrow. "I'm sorry I snapped at you. Reflex."

His face carries the weight of his apology, and though he can't see me, I think a hint of sorrow lingers in his ultra-pale blue eyes.

"Apology accepted. I was just—"

"Trying to help. I get it. Look, did you ever go to one of those haunted houses when you were a kid? The kind where they turned off all the lights and the employees had night vision?"

A laugh starts to threaten, and I nod. "Of course. My friends and I went every year in high school."

He shifts uncomfortably in his seat and stares—or appears to stare—out the window. "How scared were you when someone grabbed you in the darkness?"

"One year, I went with a new boyfriend, and I'm pretty sure I peed my pants. *That* relationship didn't last."

His voice is low. Quiet. So quiet the traffic almost hides his words. "My entire life is one big, hazy, haunted house."

"Oh." My gaffe sinks in, and shame keeps my voice to a whisper.

"If I need help, I'll ask. Then it's fine to take my arm. Or if you're really worried about me running into a wall or falling into an open manhole or something, warn me you're about to touch me." His voice is softer now, almost as if he's ashamed he has to ask for help at all.

We don't speak for the rest of the trip, and when the driver pulls over at the end of my block—a quintessential Boston neighborhood with no parking and a street barely wide enough for a single car—I thank him, scan the street, then turn to Dax. "I don't see Vasquez."

"Hang on." He tucks his Bluetooth in his ear and taps the button. "VoiceAssist: call Vasquez."

The call connects, and after a minute, Dax makes a frustrated sound—almost a growl. "You were supposed to be here ten minutes ago. I don't care if you got stuck behind a Duck Boat. You plan for these things. How much longer?"

When he taps his earbud again, the stress lines around his lips deepen. "Vasquez is still ten minutes away."

Pulling out my phone, I check Alfie's status. "My cameras haven't caught anything in the past hour. I'll be fine. It's still early."

I'm pretty sure my voice belies my words, though, because Dax reaches for his cane. "I'll walk you to your door. If you want me to stay until Vasquez shows up, I will."

Throwing open the door, I ease myself down. "Get out on this side," I say. "Otherwise you're—"

"Exiting into traffic? I know. Only been blind six years, Evianna. I remember how cars work."

As he slides across the seat, I huff out a breath. "I'm not *trying* to be a bitch, you know."

"I'd hate to hear you when you are, then," he mutters.

"You know what? Screw it. Stay in the car, Dax. It's all of a hundred feet to my door, and I have the best security system in the world. Thank you for the ride. If you're going to pick me up for work in the morning, I have to be at the office by seven-thirty."

I slam the door in his face, then stride purposefully towards my home. With every step, I realize how much I depend on my eyes. Avoiding the pile of dog shit next to the curb, stepping over the single cobblestone that's an inch and a half taller than all the others, knowing how close I am to my door and when to reach for my keys.

Even with this new knowledge, I'm still royally pissed off at Dax. I was trying to be nice. It's not *my* fault I don't know anything about being blind. The touching thing...that he's got me on. I see how stupid that was now. But warning him about the traffic? What the hell?

Closing my door, I breathe a sigh of relief. "Alfie, I'm home."

Those words are supposed to turn on the downstairs lights, and the unit should greet me by name, but everything stays dark. "Alfie. I'm home," I repeat as I turn the corner towards my home office.

Something slams into my back, the stale scent of cigarettes assaulting my nose, and before I can scream, a hand wraps around my throat, cutting off my air. He's on top of me, his bulk pressing me face down into the thick area rug covering my office floor. Something sharp digs into my cheek, and I buck and thrash, trying to dislodge him.

"Where is it?" my attacker hisses in my ear. "Give me the drive, and I won't have to kill you."

9

Dax

I sink back against the seat. What the fuck is wrong with me? Evianna wasn't *trying* to be insensitive. And I snapped at her.

"Dammit. I have to apologize. How far is it to her door?"

"We're six houses away. You want me to walk you there?" the driver asks.

"Yes." I unfold my cane as the driver comes around to take my arm, and he guides me down the quiet block. More magnolia blossoms, followed by the scent of roses.

"We're here," he says. "Three short steps to the landing."

As I'm about to knock, several thuds sound from inside. And...is that a muffled cry? Another sound, this one closer to a scream, sends my heart shooting into my throat, and I grab the driver's arm. "Go back to the car. If you don't see me come out this door in sixty seconds, call 911 and report a break-in with assault in progress at this address."

"Seriously?"

"Go!"

The driver's shoes slap against the pavement as he double-times it back to the car. Something big crashes in the front room. Wrapping my fingers around the knob, I burst through the door. "Evianna?"

A man's curse and Evianna's choked cry answer me. Fuck. I don't know what her house looks like, but someone's hurting her. Ahead and to the right, glass shatters, and I make my way down what feels like a short, narrow hallway.

The tip of my cane finds an archway, but before I can turn, someone rips the metal out of my hand, and I duck, hitting the ground with my knees and tackling a large, tank of a man, twisting at the last minute to send him to the ground. The scent of too many cigarettes burns my nose, and a not-so-solid gut breaks my fall.

"Dax! Go left!" Evianna wheezes, and I roll off the guy seconds before the cane slams against thick carpet. Scrambling to my feet, I squint, desperate for some hint of where he is. A shadow. A harsh breath.

The punch catches me in the shoulder, sending me stumbling back, but I pivot on my right foot and launch an uppercut into a stubbly jaw. A deep, male *"Oof"* is followed by another curse, and now I know where this asshole is. My jab-cross combo leaves my fingers sticky with blood, and the guy throws something heavy at me, a book or a box of some sort that glances off my shoulder as I bob and weave.

"You want to keep the rest of your teeth? Turn around and put your hands up." I don't know what the hell I'm doing. The guy tried to attack me with my own cane. If he's not a fucking idiot, he knows I'm blind.

Evianna whimpers behind me, and the sound distracts me just long enough for Mr. Stale Cigarette Smoke to ram my gut with his shoulder. I go down as he drives the air from my lungs, and crash into a warm, soft body that smells like freesia.

Heavy footsteps thud down the hall, and a door slams. Then...nothing but Evianna's raspy, shuddering breaths as she trembles under me. Sliding off of her, I reach out and find her shoulder, then brush her hair away from her face. "Evianna? Are you injured, darlin'?"

The endearment escapes from some unknown place as her silky locks slip over my fingers.

"He...he wanted...he was going to..."

Sliding my hands up her arms, I pull her almost into my lap, close enough to feel her soft curves against my chest. "Evianna. Are. You. Injured?"

My sharp tone gets her attention, and she sucks in a deep breath. "I...I cut my cheek on something. He...slammed my head against the desk. But...I didn't...black out." She coughs, takes a wheezing breath. "He tried to...strangle me. But I'm okay." Her body relaxes slightly, and fuck. Even with the adrenaline racing through me, I can't ignore how good she feels.

Get your head on straight. Assess the situation and get Evianna somewhere safe.

I tap the Bluetooth that's somehow still seated in my ear. "VoiceAssist, call Vasquez."

"Yeah, boss?" Vasquez replies after only half a ring.

"You better be fucking close. Get to the back of Evianna's building. Someone broke in and attacked her. He just left." Sliding my arm around her back, I worry at the sharp tang of blood in the air. "Can you describe him, darlin'? Did you see which way he turned when he ran out the door?"

"A couple inches taller than you. Solid. Kind of...fat? Dressed in black. He had...really dark eyes. Like...Johnny Depp really let himself go. Smelled like cigarettes. And...um...he went left. Uh...south." Her raspy voice tells me she's barely holding it together, but she still manages to give a damn good description.

"You get all that?"

Vasquez lays on his horn. "Got it. A block north of you now."

As soon as I disconnect the call, I help her up then take a half-step back. I need the distance to think. She's a client, for fuck's sake. But her breath hitches, and she grabs my wrist, then lets go like I just burned her. "I'm...sorry. Shit. I just needed—"

"Never touch a blind man without an invitation."

I'm an idiot.

"Come here, darlin'. Hold on to me as long as you need. But can you turn on the lights? I had my driver call the police. They should be here soon."

"The lights? How—?" She intertwines our fingers, holding on like her life depends on it.

"I'm not completely blind. Very few people are. I can tell light from dark. See a few muted colors. Where's the switch?"

"Alfie, turn on the downstairs lights."

Nothing happens.

"I...don't understand. Alfie controls everything, and I checked her alerts in the car. She was operating fine. Nothing on the motion sensors." Evianna hesitates, then bends down, never letting go of my hand. When she rises, she presses my cane into my free hand. "I can...there's a manual switch by the door."

My shoes crunch over a few pieces of broken glass as she leads me back down the hall, but seconds later, light floods the small space, with dark shadows I think are other rooms up ahead.

"What now?" she asks.

"We get you into a chair and you tell me how bad that cut is." I want to hold her, to have her pressed against me again, but she's shaking and breathing too quickly for my liking, and I won't take advantage of her. "Do you have a first aid kit?"

"Kitchen."

The one-word answer worries me, but Evianna hooks her arm through mine, guides me deeper into the house, and flicks on another light just before we step into a larger, open space. "You can sit," she says, her voice flat as she curls my fingers around the back of a chair. "I'll get..."

Years of training and service in the worst conditions in the world taught me more than I ever wanted to know about human behavior. Her tone, her cool skin, her mechanical movements... they all point to an impending adrenaline crash. "No. You're sitting down. Right now." Digging a clean handkerchief out of my pocket, I brace my cane on the table and take a chair across from her. "Show me where the cut is."

Her hand shakes as she guides me to her cheek. There can't be too much blood, as I don't feel any dampness against my fingers.

"S-sorry," she whispers as she starts shivering. "Don't know what's wrong."

"You're losing adrenaline. Fast. This is normal. Do you have something sweet? Coke, orange juice, lemonade? It'll help."

"There's juice. In the fridge." She starts to get up, but her knees must give out, because her ass hits the chair, and she grunts softly. "Dammit."

"Keep pressure on this and tell me where to go." When she hesitates, I sigh, and roll my eyes. "I'm blind. Not helpless. Unless your fridge is pear-shaped with a combination lock, or you keep your glasses stacked like a Jenga tower, I can make my way around a kitchen."

"Fridge is directly behind you," she mumbles, and in four steps, I find the handle.

"And the juice?" If I can keep her talking long enough to get some sugar into her system, she'll be fine. If not, I'm going to have some serious explaining to do to the police.

"Bottom shelf of the door. The carton."

"Boss?" Five knocks—Vasquez's pattern—follow the tense word, and heavy footsteps thud down the hall. "Your driver said the police are almost here. No sign of the perp."

I shake my head as Evianna sucks in a sharp breath. Vasquez needs to learn to be a little more sensitive. "Find a glass," I snap as I return to her side with the carton. But as soon as I sit down, she takes the carton from me.

"Don't need one."

My jaw drops open as she takes a couple of large gulps loud enough for me to hear. Shit. Something inside of me warms. I wish I could comfort her, but that's not why she hired Second Sight, and I don't do comfort.

The police knock, and I reach into my pocket for my PI license. "Tell them everything, Evianna," I say quietly. "And then I'll take you somewhere safe. You're not staying in this house tonight."

Evianna

My house isn't...mine anymore. My...attacker...tossed almost every room. Only the kitchen and downstairs bathroom were untouched. Two police officers spend over an hour taking our statements while a crime scene tech dusts for prints, Vasquez finds my first aid kit and presses a couple butterfly bandages to my cheek, and Dax sits stiffly, his hands on his thighs, his back ramrod straight.

The tension rolling off of him makes the knot in my stomach twist and turn, and even Vasquez brewing me a cup of tea doesn't help.

I need to get into Alfie's logs. Something's wrong with her. She should have caught the break-in. But I went through every single event she recorded—the mailman delivering my weekly allotment of junk, my neighbor's dog getting away from her and running up the steps, and a group of construction workers passing by horsing around. Nothing at the front or back doors to let me know someone broke in, and none of the window sensors went off.

But I can't concentrate on anything right now. All I want to do is sleep. Or cry. Anywhere but here.

"Ms. Archer, we're done," Officer Danvers says as she hands me a piece of paper. "Here's the report number. You'll be able to access this online in a few hours." Her partner heads for the door, and she leans closer. "You might want to stay somewhere else tonight."

"She's staying with me," Dax says. He hasn't uttered a word in twenty minutes, and my mug rattles on the table as his rough drawl startles me. "Secured building, not linked to her in any way."

The officer nods. "Perfect. Good night, Mr. Holloway. Mr. Vasquez. Ms. Archer."

As my front door clicks shut, I turn to Dax. "Um, I'm staying *where?*" I'm too tired to argue, really, but his presumption that I'll just go with him rallies me a bit.

"You *want* to stay here?" His brow arches, highlighting the burns on his lids. "Your call. I can sleep on *your* couch just as well as I can sleep on mine."

"And what if I want to be alone?" I don't. But his arrogance has sent me from a state of shock and exhaustion into anger.

With a heavy sigh, he pinches the bridge of his nose and closes his eyes for a moment. "If you want to be alone, Vasquez can take you to a hotel. But he'll be outside your door all night. You asked us to protect you. This is how we do it."

He removed his glasses sometime in the past hour or so, and now, I can see the damage to his eyes. It's like...he's wearing opaque ice blue contact lenses. His pupils are pale...almost gray. Yet his stare seems to bore right into me, and I wonder how he manages to almost always know right where my eyes are. "Fine. I need a few things first."

"Do you need Vasquez to go with you?" Dax asks as I start for the stairs.

I roll my eyes at him, the gesture only slightly less satisfying knowing he can't see me. "The police searched the whole house. I think I can manage to pack my own underwear."

Vasquez stifles a snort as I pass him, and Dax mutters something under his breath I can't hear. I can't decide if he's being sweet and protective or rude and patronizing. Yet, upstairs, seeing the mess my attacker made searching through my things, knowing he touched my clothes, my pillow, the jewelry box my father made for my mother...it's too much.

Sinking onto the floor, I cradle the antique wood box to my chest. The lid hangs from broken hinges, a tangled mess of earrings and necklaces peeking out from under the dresser.

I don't even realize I'm crying until Dax kneels next to me. "Evianna? Darlin'? You need to get out of here. Come back downstairs. Tell Vasquez what you need, and he'll find it." His warm fingers curl around my arm, brushing the edges of the box. "What's this?"

"All I had left." The words escape on a whisper, as if saying them aloud will somehow make them real. Make my last memories of my father fade into nothingness. Dax eases the box from my grip and runs his fingers over the intricate patterns on the lid, finding the broken hinges and the dented corner.

"Who made this?"

I can't tell him. Hell, I barely know the man. As he gingerly sets the box back in my hands, I peek up at his face. Grief deepens fine lines around his lips, furrows his brow. Despite the damage to his eyes, I see the pain there too.

"We'll find out who's after you." His deep voice, with a subtle hint of the south Boston hasn't yet dampened, makes me feel safe, and I sniffle loudly as I slide the broken heirloom onto my dresser.

"I always felt safe here." A fresh cascade of tears tumbles over my cheeks, and Dax eases himself down and urges me to lean against him. "If he could bypass Alfie..."

"Evianna, look at—or...never mind. Just listen." Staring at the floor, he continues. "Nothing we do tonight is going to find this guy any quicker. You're hurt and exhausted. Pack a bag. Whatever you need for a couple of days. Vasquez is guarding your laptop. In the morning, call in sick, and we'll figure the rest out then."

"I...can't. We're so close to launch." Swiping the back of my hand over my damp cheeks, I sniffle loudly. "I have to—"

"Stop." Dax rests his hands on my shoulders. "What's the worst thing that'll happen if you don't go in tomorrow?"

I don't have an answer for him. Just more tears. I hate crying. Feeling like my life is out of control. Hate that I don't feel safe in my own home.

"Evianna, let's get up now. Okay? Get your things together so we can get out of here." Dax supports me with his hand on my arm as I push to my feet, and for a second or two, we're close enough I feel his breath on my cheek. He smells like rain and something spicy and woodsy. I wish he'd put his arms around me. I felt safe when he held me earlier. But a moment later, he picks his way over the clothes scattered along my bedroom floor and waits at the door.

Ten minutes later, Dax follows me down the stairs. He didn't say a word as I packed three days' worth of clothes, my toothbrush, make-up bag, and my mother's pearl ring. The only thing I have left that's not broken.

The ride to his apartment passes in silence, Dax staring straight ahead while I let my gaze drift over the lights of the city. Why couldn't I have overlooked Kyle's infraction? Or...just ordered him to delete the files and let him keep working. Maybe then...I'd still feel safe. Instead, I'm being driven halfway across town to stay with a man who both terrifies and reassures me.

"We're here, boss. Had to double park. Door's at twelve o'clock." Vasquez gets my bag out of the trunk while Dax weaves between two parked cars and up three steps to a dark blue door. "Ronan's watching your house tonight, ma'am. I'll be out here."

For a brief second, I wonder if Vasquez really would take me to a hotel and stay outside the door all night long. But then Dax calls my name, and I realize I don't want to be alone.

10

Evianna

"VOICEASSIST, ALL LIGHTS ON, SIXTY PERCENT," Dax says as he opens his door and gestures for me to enter.

Spartan. That's the only way to describe the space. Plain, beige walls, undecorated. A leather sofa underneath the window, two matching chairs opposite with a utilitarian coffee table in between.

"Bedroom's off to the left." Sinking down onto a bench by the door, Dax toes off his shoes and tucks them under the dark wood before placing his briefcase, his now folded cane, and his keys on the adjacent table. "You should get some rest. I just need to get a pillow and blanket for the couch."

I follow him into his private space, dropping my duffel bag next to the bed as I run my fingers over the perfectly straightened duvet. I don't think he lives here as much as he exists here. No personal touches. Everything's black or gray or dark brown.

"I can take the couch," I offer. "This is your home, and I appreciate you...uh...taking me in for the night."

"You're getting the bed." With a blanket tucked under his arm, he heads for the nightstand, but before I can warn him, he trips on my duffel bag and goes down, one knee slamming into the bed frame with an audible crack. "Fucking hell," he growls as he struggles to his feet.

"Oh God. I'm so sorry." Rushing over to him, I try to help, but he yanks his arm away. Tears burn my eyes—again, and I'm so sick of crying, the sensation carries me even closer to the edge of another breakdown.

His chest heaves, the white button-down shirt straining across his pecs. "Rules," he spits out, grabbing my hand and limping into the bathroom, tugging me along with him. "Anything you touch—*anything*—goes back in the exact same spot." Pointing at various items, he continues. "Toothpaste. Shampoo. Soap. Mouthwash. Tylenol. Everything has a place. A very precise place. Swap the Tylenol with the Imitrex or the shampoo with the toothpaste and I'm in a world of hurt. You understand?"

"Y-yes." The realities of his life crash down on me, and I realize what a huge deal it is that he's even willing to have me here.

But he's not done. Leading me back towards the bed, he gestures to my duffel bag. "Nothing on the floor. Ever. Shoes go under the bed. All the way." Back out in the main room, he nods at the carpet. "See the tape?"

Small, white Xs rest under each of the chair and table legs. "Yes."

"I can't. They tell my housekeeper exactly where to put the furniture when she moves it to vacuum. One inch off, and I'm going to trip and crack my head open."

"I get it," I snap. "I'm sorry. This is all new to me. Being stalked. Being attacked in my home. Knowing someone...blind. Taking the bed of a man I've only just met while he sleeps on the couch. I'm scared and tired and fucking up all over the place. And my mistakes could hurt you." My anger morphs into something more, something dark and terrifying, and tears tumble down my cheeks faster than I can wipe them away.

"Evianna—"

"No. You're right. I need to know all this. I'm going to move my duffel bag and let the office know I'm working remotely tomorrow. Or...today, I guess, since it's after midnight. Can I...uh...use your toothpaste? I think I forgot mine. I'll make sure it's put back properly." If I have to face this man in front of me for another minute, I'm going to break down, and that's already happened once tonight.

"Use whatever you need." His voice is softer now, almost apologetic, but I don't care. I trudge off to the bedroom, put my duffel bag on the bed, and sink down with my tablet.

The bathroom door closes, and water runs as I send a company-wide email.

I have a minor emergency to deal with today. I'll be working from home, but will call in for the status meeting at noon.

I'll catch hell from Noah, and I'm sure Barry will find a way to get a couple of digs in during the meeting, but Dax is right. There's no way I can go into the office.

Now that I'm no longer in imminent danger, all my various injuries make themselves known. Closing the bedroom door, I strip out of my sweater and wool pants. A fist-sized bruise below my ribs looks to be the worst. But as I take off my bra, I brush a swollen, painful spot on my back where I think I landed on my power strip. Pulling on my tank top makes my entire torso ache, and I slip into a pair of yoga pants before grabbing my toothbrush.

By the time I open the door, all the lights are off, and the apartment is completely silent. The bathroom mirror reveals the bruises around my throat, and I collapse against the counter, suddenly aware how close I came to dying.

His hands squeeze my throat, and he yanks me up a couple of inches before slamming me back down to the floor. "Where is it, bitch?"

"I...don't...know," I wheeze, barely able to get the words out, "what...you're—"

"Evianna?"

Dax. Oh God. Help me!

Safe. I'm safe. In Dax's apartment. His bathroom. Shit. On the floor, my arms wrapped around my knees. "Get up, Evianna. Brush your damn teeth and go to bed. In the morning, you'll figure out what to do."

My little pep talk gets me to Dax's bed, and his scent surrounds me. The few minutes he held me after the attack, I felt safe. Safer than I've felt since this whole mess started.

I wish he'd hold me again. Just long enough for me to take a deep breath. To get my head clear. But I can't ask, so I bury my face in a pillow to hide my sobs.

Dax

Well, you fucked that right up, Holloway. Couldn't just explain it to her? Had to yell at a woman who's just been attacked, her home violated?

Punching the pillow, I turn over. I didn't tell Evianna I sleep on the couch all the time. Six years after escaping Hell, and there are still some nights I can't stand the softness of the mattress.

Searing pain lances through my temple, and I sit up with a hiss. Fucking migraines. The Imitrex leaves me fuzzy, and Evianna needs me at my best in the morning, so I head for the bathroom to grab a couple of Tylenol. Closed in the darkness, I tentatively feel for the toothpaste. In the perfect spot. I'm not surprised.

I stick my head under the faucet for a mouthful of water and toss the two pills back, hoping they're enough.

As soon as I crack the door, I hear it. Her muffled crying from the bedroom. Shit. I can't just ignore her pain. Not when some of it is on me.

"Evianna?" I reach the end of the bed and ease a hip onto the mattress. "What can I do?"

"I-I'm...f-fine," she stutters. "Go...away."

Sucking in a sharp breath at the tone in her voice, I'm back in Hell. Huddled against a wall in the darkness, praying for some sign I'm not alone. Every day. Every night. All the times they kept us separated. Whenever they made us watch one of our fellow prisoners die. The pain wasn't the worst of it. Shit. Not even losing my sight was as bad as the fear no one would find us. Hear us. See us ever again.

I know what Evianna needs. The same thing I needed every fucking day.

To know she's not alone.

"Do you trust me?" Sliding closer, I pat the bed until I find her arm wrapped around a pillow, and rest my fingers against her cool skin.

For a moment, silence blankets the room. I pushed too hard. But then, she whispers, "Yes."

"Scoot over."

"Dax, I don't want...I hardly know you." Despite her protests, she wriggles to the other side of the bed, and when I get under the covers, she holds her breath.

Lying on my side, my back to her, I tuck my arm under my head. "Get yourself comfortable so you can rest your hand against my back or my shoulder."

Confusion colors her tone. "What? How's that supposed to help anything?"

Choking back a laugh, I pull the blankets a little higher. In a t-shirt and pajama pants, most of my scars are covered, but my forearms are enough to scare small children. "You telling me you want me to kiss you?"

"No! Shit. I just met you."

"Yet here you are, in my bed."

"That was *not* my choice. And you're an ass."

Her huff makes me smile and wish I could see the indignation on her face. I know she's soft. Real curves. Silky hair. Dark brown, I think. Pale skin. "What color are your eyes?"

"Brown. Now are you going to tell me how this is supposed to make me feel better?" After a shaky breath, she settles, and I keep quiet, waiting to see if she really does trust me enough to do what I asked her to do.

The sheets rustle, and then warm fingers rest against my shoulder blade.

"Keep 'em there, darlin'. All night if you need to. You're not alone. Whatever happens tomorrow, we'll deal with it together. But for tonight, just know you're not alone."

Evianna's shudders slowly taper, and I close my eyes, hoping this isn't one of the nights I wake up in a cold sweat, screaming. The world starts to fade away when I hear, "Dax?"

"Yeah?"

"How'd you know?"

"Know what?" Careful not to spook her, I shift onto my back, and her hand moves with me, coming to rest on top of my shoulder.

"This. It's like...you're real. And touching something— someone—real...I can't describe it," she says with a little sigh.

"It grounds you."

"Yes." Her fingers move a little lower, closer to my heart. "Is this okay?"

Say no. Turn back over.

But the warnings in my head don't stop my lips from moving. "It's fine."

"So...you do this with all of your hysterical clients?" Her voice carries a teasing tone under the exhaustion.

"No," I say with more force than I intend. An intense emotion warms my chest, a desperate need to reassure Evianna that she's...special. "You weren't hysterical. And I've never brought a client here before."

"Oh." She edges closer, her warmth seeping into my hip. "At my house...how did you know I was in trouble?"

"I was coming to apologize to you. I was...an ass in the car. I heard glass breaking. And you tried to scream."

"You don't need to apologize. I...I think he would have killed me if you hadn't been there." A shudder wracks her body, and I ache to put my arms around her, but settle for covering her hand with mine. "You can be an ass all you want. You saved my life."

"Don't." I have to put a stop to this. If I let the darkness inside me escape, it'll destroy this woman I might already care for—even though we've only known one another for two days. "Don't make excuses for me, Evianna. I know how I acted."

The few minutes I spent holding her after the attack soothed an ache I've lived with for so long, it felt like it was a permanent part of me. But in the middle of her hallway, feeling her soft curves pressed against me, her breath tickling my neck, fingers digging into my sides, I felt...whole. The ache is back now, stronger than ever.

Get over yourself. You'll never be whole again, and if you keep this up, sooner or later, she's going to learn just how broken you are and she'll never look at you the same way again.

Her other hand brushes my upper arm. "Why are you so hard on yourself? I wasn't exactly the picture of empathy and understanding either. You're human, Dax. You're allowed to have a bad day."

"It's not a bad day. It's..." *More. Everything.* "This is who I am."

"Is that really what you think?" She scoots a little closer. "An ass would have ignored my crying and gone back to the couch. You *are* a mystery, though. I've never seen anyone move like you do. You fought like you could see. And then...you knew exactly what to do. You...care. Even though you don't want anyone to know it. That's who you are."

Evianna's fingers tighten on my arm for a brief moment, but I don't move. If I do, I'll say something I can't take back. Soon, her breathing slows and her entire body relaxes.

It's enough. This one night. This is enough.

But...is it? She needed me to ground her. Now...she's the one grounding me.

11

Dax

I'M SURROUNDED BY FREESIA. The delicate petals brush my cheek, and I swear I can see the damn things. White and yellow and pink and purple. The colors swirl together in my mind, and the subtle scent invades my broken soul.

And then, Evianna sighs.

Oh, shit. She's in my arms. In my bed. I fell asleep with my hand on hers. But sometime in the middle of the night...one of us moved. She's curled against me, my arm draped over the generous curve of her hip.

She'd whimpered. And I'd slid closer. Whispered to her. Held her. And apparently I'd never let go.

I try to slide my arm away, but she stirs and her fingers flutter on mine. But then, she gasps and her entire body tenses.

"Evianna, relax. You're safe." Her heart thuds rapidly against my chest, and she fights to free herself from my hold. "It's Dax. Listen to me, darlin'. You're at my place. Remember?"

"Oh God." With a shudder, the tension leaves her body, and

she burrows deeper under the duvet, closer to me, if that's possible. "I didn't know where I was. I'm sorry..."

With my arms crossed over her chest, I rest my cheek against the back of her head, trying to ground her. She's wearing some sort of tank top, and her arms are bare, the skin soft and supple, and fuck, she smells so good.

And then fear sets in. If she looks...if there's enough light in the room...she'll see the scars all along my forearms. Though I've masked some of them with what Ford tells me are intricate tattoos of skulls, the Special Forces motto, *De Oppresso Liber*, and parts of the Boston skyline, there's no hiding what I am.

A blind, broken monster.

"You apologize too much," I murmur.

"Can't help it," Evianna says with a shrug. "After so many years apologizing for who I am and who I want to be, it's kind of second nature."

Anger flares up, hot and bitter. "Who the hell made you apologize for who you are?" If they're still in her life, they might get a visit from Ronan. Or from me.

"I'm a woman in a position of power at a major tech company. Do you know how rare that is?" She turns her head slightly, and we're almost cheek-to-cheek.

Any closer, and I'm going to have to start reciting financial reports in my head to stop my dick from making its presence known. "Not really."

"I had to work my way up from junior coder to CIO. Even with a masters in computer science engineering and an MBA. Through a dozen companies, overt harassment, not-so-subtle comments on my looks, my breasts, my...well, the c-word. A lot of the men felt...threatened, I guess."

"Anyone at Beacon Hill? After last night, we know Kyle's working with someone. Could anyone else at your job have it out for you?" All business now, I almost forget the pain in her voice. Until she blows out a long, slow breath, and I realize I'm being an ass again. "Anyone who'd say that to you isn't a man, Evianna. Not one who deserves his dick, anyway."

She laughs, bumping her shoulder back against mine. "That's a new one. Doesn't deserve his dick. I'm going to have to steal that."

From the living room, my phone blares, "Text message from: Ronan."

"I need to check that. Stay here. I'll start coffee in a few minutes." Letting go of her is the last thing I want to do. So why do I rush to get out of bed?

Because this can't last, idiot.

My right leg aches as I take my first step, one more reminder of just how messed up I am, and I limp into the other room to snag my phone from the table by the door. "VoiceAssist, play last text message."

"No movement at client's house overnight. Headed to suspect's apartment now, then to catch some Zzzs for a few hours."

"VoiceAssist, reply to Ronan."

"What do you want to say?" the computerized voice asks.

"Confirm. Be back online by 5:00 p.m. and check in."

In the bedroom, I hear Evianna talking to someone—probably her boss from her tone, asking about the team, whether the latest performance numbers are in her inbox, and using a bunch of technical jargon I don't understand. Taking the opportunity to put a little distance between the two of us, I close myself in the bathroom. My routines keep me sane. Brush my teeth, run a comb through my hair. Wince as one of the bruises from that asshole last night makes itself known.

So much for the routine.

"Dax?" Evianna knocks softly. "Can I get your wi-fi password?"

When I open the door, the dim light seeping through the curtains highlights her dark-haired shadow, and she takes a quick step back.

"Sorry, I didn't—"

"Evianna, stop apologizing. I mean it." Using her close proximity as an excuse to touch her, I rest my hands on her upper arms as I ease myself around her. "Come with me to the kitchen. I'll write the password down for you."

With her head turned away, she stammers, "I'll, um, be right there." And a few seconds later, I hear the water running. Maybe I'm not the only one worried about morning breath.

In the kitchen, I pull the bag of coffee from the cabinet, the measuring cup from its precise place in the top drawer, and fill the coffee machine.

"Can I...help?" Evianna asks from a few feet away. My fingers close around the handle of the pot, and I turn slowly, unsure if she'll approach or wait for my invitation.

"You could fill this with water, then add it to the machine and turn it on. I don't have a lot of food here. But there are granola bars and yogurt and apples—or I can call and have groceries sent over."

"Dax," she stops after she turns the coffee maker on, "I...if you could see me, I'd put my hand on your arm and tell you it's okay. Coffee's fine. You've done so much for me already..."

"VoiceAssist, lights on, sixty percent," I say. It's been so long since I *wanted* anyone to touch me, I don't know how to ask. But if I don't show her who I am now—what I look like in the light— when I finally do work up the courage, the rejection will be that much harder. "You sure about that?"

"About what—oh." The uncertainty in her voice fades away as I hold out my arms. I only have a vague sense of what they look like. Memories from the last time Kahlid beat the shit out of me before he blinded me. But deep, jagged scars cover my right arm, and on my left, burns. Cigarette butts, a wimpy little blowtorch that still felt like it was melting my flesh from my bones, and more lye. Parts of me feel like sandpaper. Others, like a topographical map of the Rocky Mountains.

The coffee maker sputters, the first drops of black gold hitting the pot with a hiss, and I turn away, my hands not altogether steady as I open the cabinet and withdraw two mugs.

"I'm going to touch you, now. Okay?" Evianna whispers from behind me.

I'm not sure I can answer, so I nod as I set the mugs down, and her warm fingers skate over my forearms. "Will you tell me what happened?"

"Not a good story." I can't move. If I do, I'll break this spell, this perfect moment where a woman I'm starting to care for seems to...want me. Or...at least isn't repulsed by me.

"I feel like that's probably the understatement of the century." Pressing closer, she wraps her arms around my waist and leans into me. "Maybe the millennium."

A laugh scrapes over my dry throat. "You could say that."

We stay fused together until the coffee finishes, and Evianna slips around me to pour two mugs. "I still want to know. And you promised me coffee in bed. So come on."

As her soft footfalls recede into the bedroom, I'm left with a raging hard-on and no fucking clue how she can see me...any part of me...and not run away. But as she calls my name, I give up searching for a reason, and follow.

12

Dax

As I hover at the bedroom door, Evianna pats the bed. "I'm on the far side. I didn't leave anything on the nightstand."

The words I want to say won't come. The ones that say she's adapted to me, to sharing space with a blind man, faster than anyone I've ever met. The ones that tell her how much I do—and don't—want to have this conversation.

Setting my coffee down, I sit on the edge of the bed, facing away from her. "You sure?"

The sheets rustle, and I can feel her warmth at my back. "I'm sure." After a long pause, she clears her throat. "I don't know what this is, Dax. Maybe I'm still reeling from last night. Maybe you're the only person who's made me feel truly safe in...years. Maybe it's...nothing. But I want to get to know you. And whatever happened," she skates her fingers over a deep scar on my forearm, and I don't flinch this time, "is part of you."

"It's all of me," I say.

Evianna huffs and scoots back against the headboard. "Doubtful. I think there's a lot more to you than your scars."

Cupping my mug, I rest my elbows on my knees. "I'm Special Forces, Evianna. Or...I was. Five years as a Warrant Officer—second in command. There were twelve of us. Once."

The scent of the coffee helps keep me in the present, and I take a sip, trying to decide how much to tell her. The sanitized version or the whole fucking thing. "We were headed up into the mountains to meet with a group of villagers friendly to U.S. Forces. But some wet-behind-the-ears private didn't encrypt his radio transmissions. The Taliban knew right where we were going to be."

"Oh, shit." Evianna shifts so she's sitting next to me, close enough for me to feel her warmth seeping into my left side.

"We fight until there's nothing left, Evianna. That's what they drill into us every fucking day until we're worthy of calling ourselves Special Forces. I speak six languages. I can—could—look at the stars in the middle of the desert and know exactly where I was. We learned to read micro-expressions. Subtle shifts in a person's tone of voice. In their breathing. Heart rate." I hold out my hand, and Evianna gives me hers. Pressing my index finger against her pulse point, I almost smile. "You're a little worried, darlin'."

"Tell me the rest."

With a subtle snort, I drop her hand. "It ain't pretty." Yet, she doesn't pull away, so I take another sip of coffee and try to swallow the massive lump in my throat. "They took five of us. Hab. Ripper. Gose. Ryker. And me. Hab died the first week. He never saw Hell. But the rest of us... They kept us in a wood and cement block building off and on for a couple of months, moved us around from time to time. Beat the shit out of us, tried to get us to talk. Then, some Taliban asshole—Kahlid—decided we had it too easy."

Her breath hitches, and I think she curls her body inward a bit, but I can't comfort her. Not right now. "Hell Mountain was a system of caves deep under one of the peaks in the Hindu Kush.

They'd dug out a dozen cells. Three deep pits—they'd throw us down there and leave us until we were dangerously close to dying from dehydration. And every few days, Kahlid would send for one of us."

By the time I tell her about Ripper's disappearance, the coffee's gone, and I'm sitting on the floor. "Fifteen months. They had me and Ry for fifteen months. Broke us in every way possible —but we never talked. Never gave up a single secret. Whenever we could, we tapped out short messages to one another on the walls. Came up with an escape plan. And then, they broke my leg. A few days after that, Kahlid took a hot dagger and burned the shit out of my thigh. The infection was killing me. So Ry...he went alone. Killed two of the guards. As payback," I gesture to my eyes, "drain cleaner, I think. Never saw the bottle."

Evianna slides down to the floor next to me, her knees drawn up to her chest. "How'd you get out?"

"Ry came back for me. Along with six SEALs and a Ranger regiment. And when they got me out, they buried Hell under two tons of rubble."

For what feels like an hour, but is probably only a few minutes, we sit in silence. Then Evianna takes my hand and brings my arm over her shoulders. When I don't pull away, she shifts closer, easing herself onto my lap and wrapping her legs around my waist.

"What are you—?"

"Hush." Her breath ghosts over my cheek, the scent of coffee lingering and mixing with freesia. And then her lips are on mine. Hesitant, she keeps the pressure light, but the feel of her, the way she molds herself to me, and her taste awaken something in me I thought died a long time ago.

Tangling my fingers in her hair, I pull her closer, drinking her in as I capture her bottom lip, then trace my tongue along the seam until she parts for me. My hand molds to her ass, then I slide my palm all the way up to the nape of her neck. I don't ever want to let her go, and from her soft, desperate moan, she isn't interested in stopping either.

"Call from: Wren. Call from: Wren."

Evianna breaks off the kiss, then buries her face against my neck. Her breathing isn't steady, and her arousal fills the air around us. "You're not broken, Dax. You're anything but broken."

I wrap my arms around her, my eyes burning as she offers me the only thing I've wanted for six long years.

Understanding.

13

Evianna

DAX'S PHONE announces a second call from Wren, and he eases me off his lap. "I have to get this." His rough voice—and the bulge tenting his pajama pants—tell me I wasn't the only one to feel that kiss down to my toes.

Following, I ask, "Who's Wren?"

"Second Sight's computer genius. You'll like her, I think. You speak the same language." Phone in hand, he tucks an earbud in his ear and taps it. "Wren? Is something wrong?"

I can't hear her response, but Dax curses under his breath. "Hold up a second. Evianna's here with me. I'm going to put you on speaker. VoiceAssist, switch audio playback to speaker. Okay. Go ahead."

"Um. Hi. Evianna?" The voice on the other end of the line is soft, a little hesitant.

"Yes. I can hear you. Hi."

"Well, I've been searching the traffic cameras around—wait. Are you two somewhere with a computer?"

"I have mine, yes. I was just about to hook it up to Dax's wifi."
Well, an hour ago.

"Dax's...oh." The shock in her voice makes my cheeks flush,
and Dax shakes his head, almost to himself.

Shit. Think before you speak, Evianna.

"What do you need, Wren?" Dax runs a hand through his
black hair with a sigh.

"Can we...uh...video chat? Since Evianna's there, I can share
my screen and show her what I found. She might be able to help
me figure out where to go from here."

Dax's shoulders slump, and he presses his lips together for a
second before answering. "Fine. Can you give us thirty minutes?"

"Sure, boss. You connect—or have Evianna connect—when
you're ready."

The call clicks off, and I almost reach for Dax's hand, but stop
myself. "You're upset. I shouldn't have told her I needed your wifi
code. I'm—"

Before I can apologize, Dax slides his arm around my back
and he's kissing me with such desperate need, I can barely think.
He backs me up against the living room wall, caging me with his
arms, and I let him take. Everything. Anything he wants, he can
have, as long as he keeps kissing me.

But as my knees threaten to buckle, he breaks off the kiss, his
chest heaving and his arousal pressing against my hip. "Stop.
Apologizing," he grits out.

"Well, if you're going to do that every time I try...that's not
very good motivation for me, now is it?"

His brows furrow for a breath, and then he laughs. My God.
When he leaves the dour, tortured look behind, he's magnificent.
I see the man he used to be—before the scars around his eyes,
the slash across his forehead, his crooked eyebrow. But I also see
the man he is now. Older. Wiser. Sadder. And a hell of a kisser.

"Tell me the plan. Why did we need thirty minutes?" I curl my
fingers around his side, trying to keep him close to me as long as

possible. If he's planning sex, he's got another thing coming. We're going to need a lot more than thirty minutes.

"I don't want Wren to see me...like this." He holds out his arms, then drops them as he steps back a foot. "I need a shower. A cold one. The wi-fi code is on the counter. I'll be out in ten minutes, and then the bathroom's yours."

He doesn't give me a chance to reply before he strides down the hall and closes the door with a hearty *thump*. Even through the damage to his eyes, I know what I saw there. Fear. The broken, scared, terrified soldier is back, and I don't know if he'll let me in again.

Dax

The cold water does little for my hard-on. Unsurprising given how long it's been. I skip shaving. My hands aren't completely steady. Not after telling Evianna about Hell. And kissing her. Twice. But if we're going to be in this apartment together another night—and there's no way I want her staying anywhere else— there's one very important thing I need to do.

Running a comb through my hair, I wonder what the hell she sees in me. I know pity when I hear it. And her voice carries none of it. Running a hand down my pecs, I feel the burns. The scars. As I towel off, my leg aches. Two surgeries, and there's still an odd depression in my right quadricep from the infection that almost killed me.

I wish Ford weren't halfway around the world. I could use a friend right about now. If for nothing else, than to tell me what Evianna looks like. How far out of my league she is.

Cracking the door, I listen, hoping I can get into the bedroom and get dressed without her seeing me.

"Where are we on the authentication loop bug?" Evianna

asks. "It's number 32789. Barry, that was on your plate as priority zero."

"Done," the clipped male voice replies. "I checked in the hotfix this morning."

"What about the perf mon issues? I still see spikes. Who's got the bandwidth to take this on?"

I close the bedroom door quietly and head for my closet. Everything's arranged in precise order. Jeans, black pants, khakis. White long-sleeved dress shirts, followed by blue and black, then the long-sleeved Henleys. I can discern some colors, but most are a muted blur. So I stick to the basics.

By the time I pull on my socks and head out to the living room, Evianna's done with her conference call. "Mind if I shower?" she asks as I drop down onto the bench and pull on my shoes. "Are...you going somewhere?"

The uncertainty in her tone raises a lump in my throat. "Just down to the corner store, darlin'. This little Mom and Pop joint. They make damn good egg sandwiches, and you need to eat something. You want bacon, ham, or tofu?"

Standing, I hold out my hand, and when she wraps her arms around me, I press a kiss to the soft skin of her neck. "You're safe here, Evianna. The building's secured, and I'll lock the apartment door. But if you want me to wait, I will."

"Bacon," she says quietly. "And some sort of sparkling water?"

"Anything you want, darlin'. Anything at all."

THE WALK TAKES me less than five minutes, but once I duck inside the shop, I freeze. The reality of what I'm about to do hits me square in the chest, and it's hard to breathe.

"Dax?" Mrs. McClary asks from the cash register a few feet away. "You okay, son?"

Great. Why couldn't it have been her husband manning the

store today? "Can I get two bacon and egg sandwiches? And a bottle of sparkling water?"

"Two? Sure. Anything else?" Mrs. McClary fiddles behind the counter, and bacon starts to sizzle in a pan. "You're looking a little tired."

"I...do need something else. I don't suppose Ollie's here, is he?" Running my fingers over the strap on my cane, I hold my breath.

"No, hon. He's out picking up this week's vegetable order." With a little groan, Mrs. McClary shuffles out from behind the counter, and in the light from the window behind her, I think she might have her hands on her hips. "What do you need?"

Fuck. I can't avoid this. And same-day delivery won't be fast enough. Plus, there's the whole problem of navigating online shopping. Some websites are compatible with my VoiceAssist software, but others... There's a reason I pay my housekeeper to keep my fridge stocked.

"Condoms."

"Any particular kind?" Without any fanfare, she heads down one of the aisles, as if I just asked her for a stick of butter or bottle of antacid.

Hoping I don't knock anything over with my cane, I follow her footsteps until they stop. "I...don't know. Shit. This was a mistake."

"Dax, hon. You've been coming in here for almost five years now. And in all that time, you've never ordered two sandwiches. Never looked so...happy either. Though you need more sleep. So, you want plain, ribbed, flavored, studded, multi-color, or these ones that say 'warming' on them?"

Fuck. "Plain." *And for the love of God, don't ask me any more questions.*

"Got 'em. That bacon should be about done. Come on now. You want to take my arm?"

I don't think I could walk straight if my life depended on it, so

I wrap my hand around Mrs. McClary's elbow and let her lead me back up to the register. Ten minutes later, after she's toasted muffins with cheese and fried eggs, I head back to my apartment with a box I never thought I'd have to buy again hidden in my jacket pocket.

14

Evianna

WHEN I EMERGE from the bedroom, Dax has breakfast sandwiches plated on the small dining room table along with more
coffee and my sparkling water. He's staring at his phone, his Bluetooth blinking in his right ear.

"Hey. Those smell fantastic."

"VoiceAssist, cancel," he murmurs before he pulls the earbud
out and tucks it in his pocket. "Eat. You must be hungry. Then
we'll call Wren."

Yep. Mr. Tall, Dark, and Terse is back. But, he came with food,
so I'll forgive him—for now. Because as much as I don't want to
be a bother, I've subsisted on doughnuts and pizza and sub sandwiches for the past few weeks, and I'm half-starved. Also, horny
as hell. But that's obviously going to have to wait.

"Do you cook?" I ask as I sit down next to him.

"A little. Basic stuff."

The first bite of the sandwich tastes like heaven, and a little
moan escapes before I can stop it. "Oh God. This is fantastic. This
is from a grocery store?"

"More like a neighborhood institution. McClarys' Stop N' Shop has been here for thirty years. Same owners. They do takeout containers of lasagna at night." Dax carefully reaches for his coffee cup, his fingers gliding across the table top before he finds it.

"Can I ask you something...uh...I don't know...overly personal?" My cheeks heat, but I want to know everything about this man, and I suspect he won't just tell me.

With a sigh, he sits back in his chair. "I piss sitting down. That what you wanted to know?"

"No!" Though honestly, I probably would have wondered eventually. "Forget it. Despite how fantastic that kiss was, it's clear you don't trust me not to hurt you." Huffing into my coffee, I take a long sip and try to stop my eyes from burning. "We can call Wren whenever you're ready."

Dax pushes to his feet and strides into the kitchen where he braces his hands on the counter and I think I hear him counting. When he reaches ten, he blows out a long breath and turns back to me. "I haven't spent this much time with one person in years."

"What's that supposed to mean? None of your friends ever ask you questions? Like...was it hard to learn to use your cane? Or...I don't know...why are your eyeglasses tinted? Or here's one. Have you dated anyone recently? Though the answer to *that* question is clearly no because you're spectacularly bad at conversation."

"What do you want from me, Evianna?" Dax stalks out of the kitchen and yanks off his glasses. "My glasses are tinted because I get migraines and these help with the light sensitivity. Learning to use the cane was easy. Learning how to navigate without being able to see more than shadows? That was terrifying. Still is. And I don't really *have* friends." Dax's hands shake as he puts his glasses on again, and a muscle in his jaw ticks. When he rubs the back of his neck, I can see the scars around his wrist as the cuff of his Henley rides up. "As for dating...I haven't been with anyone in six years. Not since my ex-wife decided she couldn't handle living with a blind and broken man with severe PTSD."

Pushing back from the table, I approach slowly. "Can I touch you?"

My question must shock him, because he snaps his head up so he's staring right at me. Or at least, it feels that way. "Why would you want to?"

"You're serious, aren't you?" I start with his biceps, feathering a light touch up his arms to his shoulders. "You really don't think anyone could possibly care about you."

Dax squeezes his eyes shut, the gesture pulling at the burn scars on his lids. "Most people who come into my life...bolt pretty damn quick."

"Maybe that's because you don't let them in." I rise up on my toes and wrap my arms around his neck, then ghost my lips over his. "And maybe I'm not like most people."

"Evianna," he whispers, "you are definitely *not* like most people."

My breath stutters, and I take a step back. If I push him too far, he'll shut down, and as much as I wish we could spend all day just...talking, there's still the small matter of someone trying to kill me. "We need to call Wren. But...you should be careful, Dax. You're going to give me the impression you care."

DAX HAS me set up my laptop on the coffee table, and we sit close together on the couch while his phone reads me Wren's number. As the call connects, I almost smile. She looks just like she sounds. This little slip of a thing, red wavy hair, and a nervous smile. "Hi. Um...boss, you okay? You look...I don't know. Wiped."

"Fine."

The single word answer doesn't leave her any room for follow up, and she frowns. "Well, then, Evianna, I'm glad you're there," she says with a tiny huff. "I'm going to share my screen as I fill you in. I hacked into the traffic cameras all around your house for the half an hour after you were attacked, and couldn't find any evidence of the guy."

The small bit of hope burning inside me fades as the split screen shows my house in the dark and her smiling face. Wait. Why's she smiling?

"But since we don't know when he broke in, I couldn't match up anyone with a before and after. So, I went back to searching for information on Kyle. Those emails you forwarded, Dax, were extremely helpful. The first two were put through a handful of email anonymizers. Like one on top of another on top of another. Those might be untraceable. Even for me. But once the emails started turning more...violent? I'd bet the farm someone else sent them."

"You don't have a farm, sweetheart," a deep, raspy voice says from the background.

"I could get one. Then bet it. Shut up. I'm working." Wren grins and throws a pillow off screen. "Sorry about that. Ry's going a little stir crazy with no jobs to do."

With a snort, Dax drapes his arm over the back of the couch. "Unsurprising."

I don't know what's going on, but whatever it is, Wren gets herself under control and pulls up the first email that actively threatened my life. The little animated graphic of a woman being stabbed with a bloody knife makes me shudder, and Dax sits up a little straighter. "What is it?"

"That email had a rather...violent graphic in it," I whisper.

"So, this message was sent from a pathetically easy-to-hack account. The original source was the Boston Public Library on Boylston. The fifth email was from the same account, but the idiot was sitting at a coffee shop on Newbury. Using his own computer."

Her excitement is infectious, and I grin as she shows me the backtrace. "Tell me you know how to spike him." Even as the words leave my lips, Wren arches a brow in a "*you can't be serious?*" expression. "Sorry," I say with a laugh. "I just don't meet many women who geek out over this shit like I do and speak my language."

"Oh, we're going to be friends, I think. This guy was outside the Boston Public Library *and* the coffee shop." The split screen switches to another traffic camera view, this time during daylight hours. With a shot of a guy who looks like Johnny Depp went on a year-long bender. I suck in a sharp breath and grab Dax's knee.

"That's him. I think. It was dark and I was a little...terrified. But I think that's the guy."

Wren's expression sobers, and she leans closer to the screen. "I can find him, Evianna. It might take me a day or two, but I'll have his driver's license, date of birth, and mother's maiden name before long."

"Good work, Wren," Dax says. "Keep running searches for Kyle. Even if he's not directly responsible for the attack on Evianna, he's still got some sketchy behavior to answer for."

"Will do. Now...about your security logs?" She scribbles something in a little notebook next to her, then looks right at me. "You need help figuring out why your system didn't tell you about the break-in?"

"Can I get back to you on that? I wanted to start searching last night, but I wasn't really...able to focus. As soon as we're done, I'm going to start debugging." I don't want anyone else poking into Alfie's code...yet. Because even though Dax trusts this woman— and so do I—Alfie's my baby. No one knows her better than I do.

"Sure. I'll be working all day, and you know how to get in touch with me now. Or just go through Dax. Either one." She glances behind her and nods. "Boss, you have another minute? Ry's here, and we were wondering if you'd heard anything from Ford."

I start to get up, but Dax grabs my hand and tugs me back

down next to him. Tension rolls off of him in waves. On screen, the biggest man I've ever seen sinks down next to Wren. The difference between the two of them...he has to be almost seven feet tall, and half of his face looks a lot like Dax's arms. Ry. This is the guy he told me about. Ryker.

"I pulled Royce and Cam in for some electronic detective work," Ryker says, his voice deep and raspy. "Searching for any mention of Americans up for sale on the dark web. Any update on your end?"

"It's only been twenty-four hours. I doubt Trevor and Ford have even left Turkey." Dax's fingers tighten on mine, and I look between the man on screen and the one next to me, wondering what the hell's going on between them that Dax didn't want me to leave.

As if Ryker's just noticed I'm there, he blinks hard, his blue— or are they green?—eyes focusing lower than Dax's face. Our hands. "Evianna, right?"

"Y-yes. Did you say...'for sale'?" Turning to Dax, I sputter, "Ford...he said...a family emergency. This...what the hell sort of emergency is this?"

"Someone Ford cares about went missing in Turkmenistan," Dax says quietly. "She was with Doctors Without Borders."

"Turkmenistan is a hotbed for human trafficking, Evianna." On screen, Ryker leans forward, his elbows on his knees. Thick ropes of scar tissue wind up his forearms, along with ink so dark, I can't make out all the designs. "If Joey or the other two women are listed for sale anywhere, we'll know about it. I'd feel a lot better if you told me to go to Turkey, though."

"Not yet. If you show up and Ford's not expecting you, it could derail whatever infil plans Trevor put in place. Hang tight for another twenty-four hours. After that, if I haven't heard from him, I'll give you the green light. Tell me what you need from me— how much—and I'll make it happen." Dax tightens his grip on my hand, and a vein throbs at his temple. "And...thanks, Ry. I... owe you one."

"No, you don't. You don't owe me a damn thing. Ever."

A moment I don't understand passes between the two men, and then Dax nods. "Thanks, brother. I'll be in touch."

Wren hangs up the call, and Dax sinks back against the cushions. "Don't ask, Evianna. Not...yet."

With a sigh, I give his hand one final squeeze. "Not yet. But soon." He's not going to get away with hiding much longer. Not if I have anything to say about it.

15

Dax

"No. It's not safe." I fiddle with my earbud, turning it over and over in my fingers. "You're staying here."

"Excuse me? *I'm* staying here? I don't think so." Evianna slams the lid on her laptop and stalks into my bedroom.

I shouldn't follow, but she's like a drug. One I don't think I can ever quit. Touching her, being close to her, talking to her—even when she's mad at me—fills a hole inside me I've lived with for way too long.

"Evianna, we don't know anything about the asshole who attacked you." I sink down next to her on the bed, and skim the tips of my fingers along her cheek underneath the bandages. When she winces, I curl my my hand around the back of her neck. "You could have been killed."

"Don't you think I know that? I'm the one who couldn't breathe when he had his hands around my throat. I'm the one who was shoved into a bookcase so hard I have bruises in the shape of the spines on my back." Her voice cracks, and she pulls away.

"Fuck, darlin'. You should have told me." I slide closer, frustration lending an edge to my tone. I can't take care of her. Can't see where she's hurt, if she's tired, happy... "Do you need a doctor?"

"I'll be fine. As long as I can figure out why Alfie didn't tell me about the break-in. Why she wouldn't turn on the lights or call the police. And the only way I can do that is if I go into the office."

"You have your laptop. Why can't you do the work here?"

The duvet rustles as she stands. "Because I need an Alfie unit. Preferably two of them. Cables. And a second machine. It would be even better if I had *my* Alfie unit. But I can remote into her and pull the logs—if I'm at my office. I can't do that from here. Our software prevents it."

Dropping my glasses on the bed next to me, I rub my eyes. The migraine from last night hasn't hit full force, but it's still threatening. And I can't take anything but Tylenol. Not if we're leaving the apartment. Hell, not if we're staying here either. My defenses are down. That's the only explanation for losing control and kissing her this morning. For that new box of condoms in my nightstand drawer. The one I hid there while she was showering.

"Dax? My office is safe. No one's going to try to kill me in the middle of the day with twenty other people right outside my office door. I'm going whether you want me to or not. I'd rather you take me."

The quiet determination in her tone carries an undercurrent of something I can't put my finger on. Warmth. Tenderness, maybe. And right now, I'm not sure there's anything I wouldn't do for her. "Fine. We'll go. But you have to promise me one thing." I reach out for her hand, and she curls her fingers around mine.

"What?"

"Once I drop you off, you don't leave your office until I come back for you. No running down to the Dunkin' Donuts for coffee. No quick trips to the drug store. Do not get onto the elevator until I tell you I'm in the lobby. Okay?"

"I promise. Now can we go?"

"No." Pulling her back down next to me, I fumble for her other hand. "A few weeks ago, Wren asked for my help. Her brother OD'd on heroin, and she was convinced it was murder. I...didn't believe her. Thankfully, Ryker did. He saved her life. More than once."

"But she's okay, right?" Concern and worry fight for control of Evianna's voice, and she tightens her fingers on mine. "I mean... she and Ryker are together."

The ball of self-hatred I carry around with me every day crashes against my chest. Sure, Wren and I talk regularly. But... never about Russia.

"Dax?"

Breathing in Evianna's scent, I pull myself back to the present. "Wren taught me the importance of promises. She risked her life because of a promise. Almost died because of a promise. And... fell in love with Ry...because of a promise. Because to her, promises are everything. When I ask you to promise me you won't leave your office, I'm not using the word lightly."

Evianna squeezes my hands. "I promise. I won't leave without you."

"Then I'll call a car."

———

EVIANNA HAS her seat belt unbuckled before the car rolls to a complete stop. "I'll call you as soon as I'm ready to go," she says and gives my hand a squeeze.

"Wait. I'm going to walk you to the elevator." I slide out after her, ignoring her protests. "It's not because I don't trust you. Or even because I think there's danger. But I need to know the layout of your building. How to get in. Where to go. In case I need to get to you."

I'm not lying. But I'm also not ready to leave her yet.

"Okay," she says with a hint of reluctance to her voice. "Tell me what to do."

"Don't take my arm. How far are we from the north corner?"

She hums for a moment. "Five car lengths or so. And we're directly in front of the door. Maybe twenty feet away."

"What type of door is it? Sliding? Revolving?"

"Double door with big brass handles."

Sweeping my cane in front of me, I start walking, the scent of freesia on my right side. Once indoors, I stop and reach for her arm. "Okay, tell me what you see. Use the hands of a clock as a reference."

"It's a big lobby. Maybe thirty feet to the elevator at, um, eleven o'clock. The security guard's desk is behind us at seven o'clock. Another door to the outside at three o'clock that opens onto the side street."

"Now look around for places someone could hide." Evianna's never been stalked before. I need her to understand the potential dangers. A little shudder runs through her, and I squeeze her arm. "Go slow, darlin'. Really think about it."

Bright sunlight streams from the windows, and her shadow moves around me as she takes a few steps in each direction. "There's an alcove in front of the bathrooms at two o'clock. The stairwell—right next to the elevator—has a small glass window in the door, so I think someone could probably see out without being seen unless it's dark outside. If the security guard's not here, behind his desk. There are two couches off to the left, at nine o'clock. Though, anyone hiding behind them would be visible from the street."

Holding out my arm, I wait for her to step into my embrace. Fuck. She feels like heaven against me. All soft curves and warmth. Sliding my hand up her back, I find the subtle swelling from her bruises, and she stiffens slightly until I whisper my apologies and shift my fingers lower. "Any time you walk into a new room, look for the exits first. Then, pick out the hiding spots. Know what's around you at all times."

"You do this every day, don't you? I mean...as much as you can?"

Her words sting, but she's right. Most of the time, I have no idea what a room looks like. Not really. Shapes. Shadows. A blur of color when the lighting's just right. When I don't respond, she curses under her breath. "Shit. I'm sorry, Dax. I didn't mean—"

"What did I tell you about apologizing?" This time, I press a gentle kiss to her cheek. "I know my limitations, Evianna. And no. I don't like them. But three surgeries didn't fix me, so this is how I'm going to stay. And to answer your first question...yes. I was trained to do this. Infiltration, sedition, extraction. For almost a decade, this was my life. And even blind, I can't—and won't—turn off those instincts."

"You're not broken. You don't need to be...*fixed*." Her breath ghosts across my cheek, and, my God, I want to press her against the nearest wall and ravish her. But she has to get to work, and I have to find Kyle.

"Remember your promise, darlin'. And call me when you want to leave." Before she can say another word, I turn and head for the door, knowing when I get to my office, there's one very important call I have to make before I do anything else.

THE OFFICE IS QUIET. Ella is busy with her cases, Clive is with his mother, and Ronan and Vasquez are off duty. After I make myself a fresh cup of coffee, I pull out my phone. "VoiceAssist, call Ryker."

He picks up on the second ring. "Is it go time?"

"Calm the fuck down," I say, the urge to chuckle roughening my voice. The man has the patience of a gnat—unless he's on mission. "Going a little stir crazy?"

"No." After a pause, a frustrated growl rumbles over the line. "Maybe. Hang on." A door closes, and he lowers his voice. "I don't want to leave Wren. Like...ever. But other than the five hours a day I train at the warehouse, I don't have anything else to do."

"Five hours? No wonder fighting you felt like battling a tank."

Now it's his turn to bark out what sounds like it might be a laugh. "And I lost, remember? I need to up my game. I just talked to you two hours ago. What's up?"

"I need you to do something for me."

"Anything."

Ryker McCabe doesn't exaggerate. Or lie. Unless the mission calls for it. If I asked him to jump on a plane right now, he'd do it. Or told him I needed Inara, Sampson, anyone he had out here to help, he wouldn't think twice. But this...I don't want to admit how broken I am.

I take a long sip of coffee before I can force myself to spit the words out. "I need to know what Evianna looks like."

Silence. And then...laughter. A deep, rolling laugh I haven't heard in more than six years. "I knew it!" Ry says after he gets himself under control.

"If you're going to haze me over this, I'll hang up right now. I already feel like shit for even asking."

That sobers him up. "I suck at this, dude. And does it matter? She's...beautiful. Dark brown hair, kind of long. Curvy. Probably five-foot-six? Pale skin. She looked tired. So did you. Pretty sure I saw something else too, though."

"What?"

Ry snorts. "You're falling for her."

I don't respond. How can I? He's right. Even though I don't understand it. "I've known her three days."

"Doesn't matter. Want to know when I started falling for Wren?"

Rubbing the back of my neck, I blow out a breath. "Yeah."

"After she was attacked outside her apartment. When she

came to, she started saying shit like flippin' flapjacks and spit-snacks. I had her halfway out the door headed for the hospital when she told me that was how she cursed. That was the start of it. Right then."

"I haven't dated anyone since Lucy. There isn't one single reason Evianna should want to be with me." Fuck. Saying the words makes it real, and suddenly, I'm back in the hospital, my therapist trying to teach me how to eat without being able to see the plate in front of me.

"Bullshit."

"Ry—"

"I mean it, Dax. You remember what I looked like the last time you saw me? What those fuckers did to my face? Hell, my entire body?"

"I didn't fare a whole lot better, you know," I spit back.

"Yeah. I do. I carried your ass out of there. But that's not my point. The scars...I get someone being able to look past them. Took me a while to realize Wren didn't care a bit what I looked like, but that was a hell of a lot easier to accept than the rest of it. This conversation we're having? Before her, it never would have happened. Even with you. I've worked with Inara for more than three years. And before that shit with Coop, we'd never said more than a couple of sentences to one another outside of a mission. I didn't know a damn thing about her other than her abilities. And Sampson...shit. The man found me half dead and buried in the snow and I couldn't have told you if he had any family. Or how old he was. Or anything beyond his Krav Maga skills and what SEAL team he was on. *That* was the wall Wren saw right through. Hell, she did more than that. She knocked it down with a battering ram. The right person...you let them in because if you don't, you can't breathe. Can't even *think* about existing without them. So, answer me one question. Is that how you feel about Evianna?"

I don't hesitate. "Yes."

"Then tell her." Ry lowers his voice even further. "Do it pretty damn quick, too. Because if things go according to plan, around New Year's, I need you out in Seattle. And if you're still pining over this woman, you're going to be a pretty fucking grumpy best man."

16

Evianna

My hopes of making it from the elevator to my office without anyone seeing me are foiled when the doors slide open and Noah's standing at the desk chatting up our receptionist.

"Evianna? I didn't think you were coming in—oh shit." He takes me by the shoulders and looks me up and down, finally brushing my hair away from my cheek and sucking in a sharp breath. "Are you sure you should be here?"

Extricating myself from his overly solicitous hold, I force a smile. "I'm fine, Noah. Just a home improvement project gone wrong."

"What happened?" Before I can take another step back, he wraps an arm around my shoulders and starts to lead me to my office.

Jerk.

"I was trying to fix a shelf in my kitchen. And I couldn't see the can in the back corner. Next time I'll get out the step stool."

Ulysses gives me the side-eye, and I shoot him a pleading look, but Noah has me in my office and shuts the door before my poor assistant can even get up. He doesn't release me until I'm sitting in my chair and he's taken my briefcase off my shoulder and dumped it unceremoniously on the floor.

"You should go home. Relax. Everything's under control here."

I stand, throwing my shoulders back to try to look taller than I am. Noah has a couple of inches on me, but when confronted, he usually backs down. "I can hold my own against a can of chicken noodle soup, Noah. And your little overprotective gesture out there was both condescending and undermining."

He frowns, the move highlighting his pale, flabby cheeks. "I just wanted—"

"Stop." Holding up my hand, I put some space between us as I head for my little tea kettle. "I know you mean well. But it's hard enough being a woman in this industry, let alone the CIO. And when you put your arm around me and treat me like a wounded bird, the rest of the team sees that."

"This again?" He rolls his eyes. "You're respected here, Evianna. By me, by the devs...by everyone. Accepting a little help isn't going to change how people see you. Being a bitch will."

He's halfway to my door when I finally form a comeback, but before I can get the words out, he turns. "Barry tells me we'll hit zero bug count by Friday morning. I spoke to the building manager. The floor above us is empty until next month. We can use it Friday night for a three hundred dollar cleaning fee. If you don't need Ulysses today, I'd like him to work with Cyndi to pull together a ship party. All of Beacon Hill's employees and their plus ones."

"Fine. Take him." Too tired to continue to fight with Noah, I flip the switch on the little electric kettle as he slams the door. "Prick."

Before the tea kettle dings, a knock breaks the silence, and I try to pull my hair back over my cheek. "Yes?"

Ulysses comes in with a box tucked under his arm. "You okay? That was way out of line."

"Fine. He means well, he's just a relic from when the world was a different place, and sometimes...he forgets things have changed." Pouring the hot water over a bag of jasmine tea, I sigh. "You're on party planning duty today. Go talk to Cyndi."

"My favorite." There's enough sarcasm in his tone to make me laugh when he plasters a fake smile on his lips. "But first, this was just delivered for you. Want me to open it?"

"Who's it from?" I eye the plain brown box, suddenly worried. What if it's...dangerous?

"Some guy named Ronan dropped it off." My brows shoot up, the motion tugging on the cut on my cheek, and I gesture for him to open it. "Huh. Is this one of the beta testing units?"

Oh my God. Dax woke up Ronan to retrieve my home Alfie unit. "Um, yes. I'm just going to run some diagnostics on it."

Ulysses cocks his head, his brown-eyed gaze boring into me. "You sure? Look, I know Noah was out of line, but you *do* look tired."

"Nothing a couple of cups of tea and some debugging won't cure."

The look he gives me says he knows I'm full of shit, but he doesn't press. "Okay. You need anything else before I go try to keep Cyndi from running amok with the party planning and hiring a clown and a face painter?"

"Just some peace and quiet," I say with a chuckle. "Cleaning up the mess I made took half the night. And I still have one bug on my plate to track down before we can declare this code shippable."

"Whatever you say. But..." Ulysses pauses with his hand on the door handle, "you sure it was a can that did that to you? If that little creep put his hands on you—"

"Kyle didn't do this. I swear. Now, shoo. Oh, and can you send a beta unit here?" I pass him a Post-it note with Dax's office address on it.

"On it." With a final frown, he slips out the door.

Lifting my home unit carefully, I cradle it in my arms. She's been sitting in my living room for six months. Doing everything for me. Monitoring my security cameras, ordering my groceries, turning my lights off and on whenever I ask. Booking airline tickets and rental cars. Reminding me of doctor's appointments, holidays, taxes. Heck, I depend on her to play music for me when I'm sad or lonely.

"I'm going to figure out what's wrong with you, Alfie," I say quietly as I plug her into my computer and launch her system diagnostics. "You're going to be just fine."

If only I believed that.

THREE HOURS LATER, all I have to show for my work is a raging headache. I've gone through my entire stash of Post-it notes, and I'm no closer to finding out why the unit failed.

Every muscle in my body protests when I push to my feet. "Shit," I hiss. Maybe I should have let Dax take me to the hospital. My shoulder throbs, and I rummage around in my briefcase for a bottle of aspirin.

The office walls feel like they're closing in on me. I need more Post-it notes. And coffee. And to look at something besides lines and lines of letters and numbers that tell me nothing.

In the supply room, I snag two more packages of my favorite sky blue sticky notes, and I'm about to head for the coffee machine when I trip over a box on the floor and land hard on my knees. "Dammit," I mutter. For a moment, Dax's face flashes behind my eyes. The shock and confusion as he hit the floor. I can't believe I didn't think about picking up my bag. Of course he wouldn't see it.

I admit, I kind of miss him. I felt safe around him. No one would come after me here. But unease still crawls along my spine at every unexpected noise. Every loud cheer from the bullpen. Every *ding* telling me about a new email message.

"Get up," I whisper. "The sooner you figure out this mess, the sooner you can get out of here and maybe...we'll finish what we started this morning."

Grabbing the box, I realize what's in it. All the junk from Kyle's desk. Little vinyl toys, a small LEGO replica of the Starship Enterprise, his coffee mug—with a bit of mold in the bottom, *ugh* —and a ratty old notebook with loose pages. I can't leave the mug to grow legs and walk out of here on its own, so I snag it with two fingers and lift it gently. But one of the notebook pages sticks to the bottom.

Proc 28t29

Access codes???

Security protocol ZetaEpsilon

Who?

Kyle's notes don't make any sense. We don't *have* a security protocol ZetaEpsilon. Alfie's security subroutines are named for superheroes. What access codes? Every command sent from Beacon Hill's servers to Alfie devices relies on the most sophisticated encryption money can buy. There are no *access codes*.

Kyle was onto something. Something...bad. All of his rantings. Asking me how I could compromise her like that.

Could he have found something in Alfie's code? Something I didn't see? And then...shit. I ignored him. Over and over again. No wonder he threatened me. I have to figure this out. Throwing the moldy mug back into the box, I snatch up the notebook and clutch it to my chest.

As I round the corner, I run smack into Noah. Literally. Several of the notebook pages slip from my grasp, and Noah bends down to pick them up. *Please don't look at them.*

Thank God, he's still ticked off from earlier. "Might want to watch your step, Evianna," he says flatly. "Oh, and we're starting the party at 6:00 p.m. tomorrow"

I toss a quick "thanks" over my shoulder as I rush back to my office. I have to figure out what Kyle knows. Or...knew. I just hope there's enough in this notebook to point me in the right direction.

17

Dax

MY PHONE VIBRATES on the desk. *"Call from: Wren."*

"Tell me you have something." The headache I've had since yesterday turned into a full-blown migraine around 2:00 p.m., and my right eye throbs in time with my heartbeat. Flashes of light mar my limited vision, though at least the nausea subsided quickly.

"Your guy's name is Louie Stein. Thirty-one years old. And he's basically a ghost. His driver's license expired three years ago. No bank accounts, credit cards, leases, loans, or mortgages in his name."

"Where is he, and why is he after Evianna?" I lay an ice pack over my forehead as I lean back in my chair.

"No fudging clue," she mutters, and the sounds of typing carry over the line. "But he can't hide from me for long. He has a private mailbox in Watertown—one of those places that let you pay an extra fee to remain anonymous—and I'm hacking into their system now. Also the traffic cameras around the store. He's got to have a bank account, a cell phone, or *something* I can trace. I just need a place to start."

"How can I help?" I have to do something. Sitting in my office while Evianna's in danger makes me want to punch the walls, but I can't surveil her building. Can't watch traffic camera footage, can't even go clean up her house.

"I'll find him, Dax."

Pain skitters up my arm as I slam my hand against the desk. "Dammit. That's not what I asked!"

"Whoa there, boss. I'm working my apples off on this—"

"Fuck." I drop my head as my eyes burn. "I'm an ass."

"You're human." Her voice softens. "And...you care about her. You're allowed to be...a little overprotective. Pretty sure Ry would have me cocooned in bubble wrap if he could."

For a minute, neither of us speak. Fingering the scars at my wrist, I straighten my shoulders. "How are you, Wren?"

"What?"

I put that hesitation in her voice. "After Russia...I never asked. Are you...okay?"

She clears her throat, and when she replies, there's a little wobble to her tone. "I'm mostly good. There are days I'm not sure I'd make it without Ry. I miss Boston. But...it wasn't home anymore. Not without Z."

"I should have believed you."

"Dax—"

"I never met your brother, Wren. For me to judge him—it was wrong. I *know* you. I trust you. And I let my own shit get in the way."

"You were there for me—for us—in the end."

Wren's computer beeps, and I flinch at the high-pitched noise. The ice pack isn't doing shit for my headache, so I drop it on the desk, followed by my glasses, so I can rub my eyes.

"Holy snackcakes," Wren says. "I found Kyle. He gave a fake name, but he was arrested this morning. Public drunkenness.

Then tack on resisting and assaulting an officer. He…uh…
urinated on the statue of Paul Revere."

"He still in custody?"

"Oh, heck yeah. He's not going anywhere. Not with the assault
charge. He was booked under the name Jack Simmons." Wren
rattles off the precinct address, and I commit it to memory.
Maybe I can do something after all. "I'm going to try to get in to
see him. Find out if he had anything to do with the break-in at
Evianna's."

"Just…be careful, boss. This case…there are too many layers.
Why would someone try to *kill* Evianna over a thumb drive? A
thumb drive she doesn't know anything about. This is the age of
the geek. I might be one of the best, but there are probably a
couple dozen other hackers in the world who could break
through her company's firewall and take whatever they wanted.
Something doesn't feel right."

"I survived Hell, Wren. This case isn't going to do me in. I'll
contact you tonight."

Having a purpose leaves me so fired up, I don't even wait for
her to say goodbye.

———

THE POLICE STATION is a bustle of activity, and the various conversations, shouts, and random noises leave me a little disoriented.
The migraine's fading, but not fast enough. Standing just inside
the entrance, I wait, cane clasped in both hands in front of me,
hoping for a little assistance.

"Can I help ya'?" The thick, Boston accent booms from just
ahead and to my left, and I carefully edge forward until my cane
hits the front of a tall desk.

"Yes. I'm here to see Jack Simmons. I'm his lawyer. Matthew
Jones." Sliding my fake ID across the smooth wood, I try for a
half-smile.

"No shit? You like Daredevil or somethin'?"

Because that joke never gets old.

I shake my head as I push my glasses up so the guy can see my eyes. "No, Officer...?"

"Officer Bushman. You must get that a lot, yeah?"

"You have no idea." Trying to affect a bored, bitter tone, I lean against the desk. "Listen, the kid doesn't know I'm coming. He can't afford me, but his pop picked up the tab."

"He's still awaiting arraignment. I can get him in a room for ya' in the next ten minutes. Have a seat and I'll call ya'."

My ID slides back under my fingers, and I nod my thanks. "Where are the chairs?"

"Oh. Sorry. Turn around and they're at your two o'clock." In the next breath, Bushman starts yelling at someone behind him, and I take a seat.

"VoiceAssist: Text Wren. Message Content: At the station. Anything you have that can help me get him to talk, send it over."

A few minutes later, she replies.

"He got away with the fake name because his prints aren't on file anywhere. I'm checking the dark web for any evidence he's used the Jack Simmons alias before, but so far, nothing. He has a mother in St. Louis, and a brother out in California."

That might be enough leverage for me to get the kid to talk. That is, if he's not behind this whole fucking thing.

"Matthew Jones?" A bored, male voice calls out my alias, and I push to my feet.

"Right here."

Heavy footsteps approach to my right. "I can escort you back to the interview room, Mr. Jones. I have your visitor's badge here."

Once I clip the temporary badge to my jacket, the man clears his throat. "Can I assist you?"

"Yeah, sure." I'm too tired and still a little dizzy from the migraine, so I let the guy take my elbow in a feeble grip and escort me down the hall, around a corner, and into a room that smells of sweat, stale coffee, and fear.

For a moment, I hear Ripper screaming in my memories, but in the next breath, I realize there's no awful stench of shit and too much aftershave that always surrounded us in Hell.

"Simmons, you're goddamn lucky," the man says after he's pulled out a chair for me. "Your daddy sprung for something better than the public defender."

"I didn't—"

"Stop, right now," I snap, slamming my hand down on the table. "Don't you say another fucking word until we're alone. You understand me, son?"

Kyle sputters for a moment, and the officer who escorted me in here leans in. "He's cuffed to the table, Jones. You need us, you bang on the door."

"Who the hell are you?" Kyle asks when we're alone.

"A friend. Maybe. If you tell me what you know about Beacon Hill Technologies." I pull out my voice recorder and place it on the table between us.

"No way, man. I'm not talking to you. I don't know shit about any technology anything. And I don't want a fucking lawyer. Get out of here." Desperation roughens his tone, and something hits the table. His head, I think.

"Kyle—"

"Shut up. My name is Jack, asshole. Are you *trying* to get me killed? I'm safe here. No one knows—fuck. How did you even find me? Oh shit, shit, shit."

"My associates are extremely good at their jobs, *Jack*." I reach across the table, fumbling for Kyle's cuffed wrist. He flinches as I wrap my fingers around his bony joint. "The cops don't know your name. And I won't tell them. As long as you answer my questions." Punctuating my words by pressing two fingers against a trigger point along the bone, I let him feel the sharp pain for half a second before I release him. "What do you know about Beacon Hill Technologies and who's trying to kill Evianna Archer?"

"P-please," he whispers. "Get out of here. I c-can't help you, man. They'll kill me. If you found me, they will too. I'm dead already."

The kid's terrified, but the rasp to his words—he'll crack if I can just find some common ground. Something he cares about more than himself. "Who's after you? I can get you protection. You, your mom, and your brother."

"Oh shit. Officer! Officer! Get me the hell out of here!" Kyle starts pounding on the table, and a moment later, the door bangs open. "This asshole doesn't represent me. I don't want to talk to him. Take me back to the holding cell."

"You're refusing representation?" the tired voice of the guy who brought me in here holds a hint of shock, but he shuffles forward, keys jingle, and Kyle's chair scrapes against the floor. "Your loss."

As Kyle brushes past me, I grab his arm, lean in, and lower my voice. "Last chance, kid. Tell me who's after Evianna."

"Tell Evianna I'm sorry," he whispers, "for ruining her fancy sneakers."

18

Evianna

I KEEP EYING MY BRIEFCASE, dying to take out Kyle's notebook and flip through it, but the past couple of hours have been one interruption after another after another. Noah, Barry, Sanjay, Una... Every one of the developers has needed me to sign off on their bugs, and though I have my Alfie unit plugged in under my desk and scan through her logs every chance I get, I'm no closer than I was this morning to finding out what happened.

A power surge tripped her circuits around 5:00 p.m. yesterday, and that might have been why she didn't record the break-in. But why didn't she report the power surge? There's no logical reason.

The burner phone I tucked in the pocket of my jacket buzzes. "Dax. Oh God. I'm so sorry. I didn't even realize what time it was. I can pack up and be ready to go in ten minutes."

"I'll be in the lobby."

The call cuts off before I can reply, and the harsh edge to his voice worries me. He sounded...stressed? Frustrated? Worried? All of the above?

Once I pack up my laptop—and check, yet again, that Kyle's

notebook is still tucked safely into the pocket of my briefcase—I stare at my Alfie unit. Should I bring her with me? I can't really do anything with her at Dax's. I need to be on-site to get into the guts of her code. But leaving her here doesn't feel right either.

In the end, I unplug her and stow her in my file cabinet. I wouldn't put it past Barry to sneak into my office and take her—just so he can show me up and figure out what's wrong with her before I can. Jerk.

I don't make it three steps out of the elevator before Dax is at my side. "Let's get home," he says.

"Wait." Glancing around at the empty lobby—it's well after 7:00 p.m. and even the security guard's gone for the day—I pull him over to the couches in the corner. "There's no one here. Can we talk for a minute?"

"Did you check the potential hiding places you told me about this afternoon?" He arches a brow, his slight drawl the only thing that keeps his words from sounding like he's a complete ass.

With a sigh, I shake my head. "No. Not all of them. Wait here?"

"You did *not* just ask me to let you go off alone when you admit there might be danger." Grabbing my hand, he pulls me to my feet. "Take me around the lobby and check everywhere."

"Fine," I grumble. When I've checked the bathrooms, the stairwell, and behind the couches, I drop his hand. "Satisfied, Mr. Overprotective?"

"Yes." The corners of his lips twitch slightly, and God. He's got that whole damaged, ruggedly handsome vibe going on, and I just want to go back to his place and tear his clothes off. If I weren't still worried for my life.

"I found something today." Sitting, I pull one of the pages of Kyle's notebook out of my bag. "Can you do the thing...with your glasses? So you can read this?"

Dax taps the Bluetooth in his ear twice, then presses a tiny, black button on the upper right corner of his glasses before holding a hand out for the page.

"What does P-R-O-C 2-8-t-2-9 mean?"

"I have no idea. But this is Kyle's. There's a whole notebook full of random words, bits of code. It's going to take me days to get through, but I couldn't risk reading much of it in the office."

Dax scans the rest of the page, the letters and numbers, partial subroutines, rantings and nonsense. "Evianna, this could all be nothing."

"I know. But it could also be *something*. I want to go to Kyle's apartment. You can...um...get us in there? Wren said he'd disappeared." I can't believe I'm asking this man—this former soldier—to commit a potential felony. But I *know* I'm right. There's something Kyle knows, and if I can get into his place, maybe I can figure it out.

"She found him." Dax takes off his glasses and rubs his eyes. Under the scars, dark smudges bruise his skin, and when he drops his hands, strain is etched in deep lines on his face. "He's in prison."

"Oh shit. For what? Did he try to hurt someone else?" My heart hammers in my chest, and I clutch Dax's forearm, my fingers digging into the corded muscle.

He covers my hand with his, and the contact settles me. "No, darlin'. He...*wanted* to get arrested. He gave them a fake name, and when I went to see him, he refused to talk to me."

"You w-went there? And they let you talk to him?" I don't understand any of this. Why would Kyle *want* to go to jail?

"Well, they let Matthew Jones, Esquire talk to him." A weak chuckle rasps over Dax's throat.

"You're a lawyer?"

"No, darlin'. But any PI worth his salt has a couple of fake IDs. Just in case. Plus, keeps my name off of any official paperwork. Dax Holloway has Top Secret security clearance, and some of the shit we have to do to help clients would get that taken away damn quick."

Oh. I'm not sure why I'm surprised. From the start, he and Ford offered to...*threaten* Kyle if he didn't leave me alone. I should be upset, but instead, I'm thankful someone's on my side.

"He didn't say anything? Kyle?" I fiddle with the strap of my briefcase, unable to take my eyes off the papers tucked in the side pocket.

"He said one thing. And I don't know what the fuck he was talking about. As they took him back to the holding cell, he said, 'Tell Evianna I'm sorry for ruining her fancy sneakers.'"

"My what?"

"That doesn't mean anything to you?"

"No."

Dax shakes his head and curses under his breath. "The kid was scared. But he sounded lucid."

"So...can we go? To Kyle's apartment?" I can't help feeling like there's something there.

Withdrawing his hand, Dax's relaxed posture turns rigid again. "No. I can't protect you if anything happens. We're not going. I can send Vasquez when his shift starts in a little over an hour."

"Can't the three of us go? Vasquez won't know what he's looking for. I don't know that I will either, but unless Vasquez has some secret tech skills you haven't told me about... Have you eaten? We could grab dinner and wait for him."

When he doesn't immediately agree, I slide a little closer. "Kyle may not be a danger to me, but whoever is...what if they're looking for the same thing we are? Something that ties all of this together. I *know* this notebook means something. But the few pages I looked at in my office read like nothing more than crazy, fragmented ramblings. I know Kyle. Or...I knew him. He's neither of those things."

"Do you expect me to just let you walk into a dangerous situation unprotected? You hired us to protect you, Evianna. You go to work, and you go back to my place. That's it. And never alone."

"I *expect* you to treat me like an adult. Vasquez will be available in an hour. And we need to eat anyway. No one's going to try to kill me in a restaurant. That would be insanely stupid. So call Vasquez and have him meet us somewhere, and then we can check out Kyle's apartment afterwards." I hope the strength I've forced into my tone convinces him. I don't know why I feel like there's something at Kyle's, but...I know there is.

"You're not going to leave this alone. Are you?" Dax says with a sigh.

"Nope."

He taps his Bluetooth. "VoiceAssist, text message to Vasquez. Message reads: Meet us at Nona Guiseppe's at 8:00 p.m." After a pause, he continues, "Send message."

"Nona Guiseppe's?" I ask when he tucks his phone back into his pocket.

"Italian place I know. Private and discreet. It's only a couple of blocks from here. Let's go so I can tell the driver I don't need him any more tonight. If we can get the booth in the back, you can tell me more about what's in this notebook."

19

Dax

I DON'T KNOW why I'm doing this. Taking Evianna to a restaurant?
Is this...a date? Or a business dinner? I know what I want it to be.
Her scent calms me. When I offer her my elbow—not for her to
guide me, but just to have her close—something stirs inside me.

"What...do you do?" Evianna asks as we turn down Washington Street. "I mean...Wren hacks into traffic cameras and runs
facial recognition and stuff. Vasquez and Ronan are
surveillance?"

"They're in training. Vasquez joined us four months ago.
Ronan, two. In a year, they'll be taking on their own cases. Protective details, investigations."

She's going to ask me how I can contribute to a company that
depends on being able to *see* your target. My head throbs, and I'm
clenching my jaw so hard, I feel like someone's driving a metal
spike through my skull.

"What about you?" Evianna gives my arm a squeeze and
presses herself a little closer to me.

"I...keep things running. Pay the bills." I know she expects more, but I don't feel like justifying my entire existence when all I want to do is get her back to my place and lock her in so she'll be safe. Though, if I do, will *I* be safe? From her?

We don't speak again until we're seated in a booth in the back, and the young-sounding server has brought us two glasses of Chianti.

"You do more than pay the bills," Evianna says quietly. "Why won't you admit it?"

"Because I stand out enough as it is. I don't feel like explaining my skills to every potential client, then hearing the disbelief in their voices when they question me."

"I'm...just like every other potential client?"

I curse under my breath at the harsh edge to her tone. "Dammit. You know you're not."

"Then talk to me."

After the server takes our order—two spinach lasagnas—I settle back against the vinyl booth. "What do you know about the Special Forces?"

"Um...you're highly trained? You do things no one else can or will? Like the SEALs or the Army Rangers?"

I fight a smile. "Frogmen don't have anything on us."

"Frogmen?" Her light laugh settles me.

"That's what we call the SEALs." A sip of wine helps loosen my tongue, and I drape my right arm over the back of the booth. Evianna settles closer to me, and I touch my nose to her hair. I might never be able to get enough of her. "Special Forces training is...different. We're not always the most capable. A SEAL sniper might beat one of us on the range every day of the week. But we're the most adaptable. We blend in. We're trained to assess a situation and diffuse it. To work with the locals. Most members of my—" my voice cracks, "—detachment spoke at least six languages. We study micro-expressions, local customs. We blend in."

"I had no idea." Respect infuses her tone, and she shifts—I

think to pick up her wine glass. "So...what do you do for Second Sight? Besides paying the bills?"

"I listen." After another sip of wine, I search for a way to explain how I do what I do. "I was trained to hear the truth in someone's voice." Turning towards her, I slide my hand up her arm to her shoulder, finding a thick lock of hair I let slip through my fingers. "When you're overwhelmed, your voice gets this raspy tremble. When you're aroused, the tremble turns...husky. Most people wouldn't be able to tell the difference between the two. I can."

"So, what am I feeling now, soldier?" Her breath ghosts over my cheek, and I'm about to answer when her stomach growls.

"Hungry."

Evianna bumps her shoulder into mine. "Big mystery there. So this listening thing..."

"That's why I go to all the initial client meetings. We occasionally find people who want to hire us for illegal practices. I can tell. It's in how they tell their story. The words they use. Someone who's lying will use the same words over and over again. Their story won't change. A person telling the truth naturally varies the language when recounting the same facts over and over again. It's human nature."

The server delivers our lasagna, and I clench my hands under the table. After six years, I shouldn't be so fucking embarrassed about asking for help. "Evianna, can you...um...describe my plate?"

Her breath stutters for a moment—and even after a few days, I know this means she's confused. "It's...a rectangle of lasagna with two slices of bread and a small dish of olives."

"Pretend the plate's a clock," I manage through clenched teeth.

"Oh. Um...the lasagna's at nine. The olives are in a tiny bowl at two. And the bread is criss-crossed at...um...they're diagonal from three to six. Is that...?"

"Fine." I find my fork without too much trouble and scoop up a piece of pasta so I don't have to continue this conversation. It's so hot it burns the roof of my mouth, but I don't care.

"Dax?" Evianna asks softly. "I'm going to touch you, okay?"

I don't respond, instead fumbling for a piece of the bread, but my hands aren't steady and the bread tumbles off the plate. Evianna's fingers brush the top of my thigh. "Got it. I'm putting it at the top of the plate. Twelve o'clock."

I nod my thanks, but then she returns her hand to my leg. "Don't, Evianna. This...this was a bad idea."

"Dinner? Dax, I know you can't really *see* me, but you've had your arms around me. You know I'm not...a supermodel. And I haven't eaten since this morning. Dinner is always a good idea."

Her self-deprecating laugh hints at her insecurities, and mine fade into the background. "You're...perfect."

"Hardly." With another laugh, this one decidedly sad, she links our fingers. "I'm carrying an extra thirty pounds. At least."

"Don't put yourself down, Evianna. Not around me. Not ever." Sliding my arm around her, I appreciate the generous curve of her hips. "You're brilliant. And capable. But...that's not all. You think about other people. About their needs. And you do it effortlessly."

"You're a puzzle," she says quietly. "One I want to solve."

I don't want to let her go, but if this goes on much longer, I won't be able to walk away from this woman. Easing back, I pick up my fork and manage to scoop up a halfway decent bite of lasagna. "A puzzle?"

"Yes. You're almost like...two different people. The Dax who's protective, who makes jokes, who seems to actually like people, or at least...likes me. And then there's the other Dax. The one who hates himself. Who thinks he's damaged. Worthless. The one who's ashamed to be who he is." Evianna picks up her wine glass and her voice muffles slightly. "I wish I could convince that second guy he's every bit as worthy as the first one."

"Boss?" Vasquez says as we exit the restaurant. "Ten o'clock. Got the Land Rover today."

I slide into the backseat after Evianna and turn to face her. "Are you sure about this? Vasquez can go on his own."

"I'm sure. Kyle was a good kid. I hired him. He was my top developer. But I looked at his stats today. For the past three weeks, his bug resolution rate fell to almost nothing. He started assigning his work to the other devs so he could spend all day, every day, combing through the code. But I don't know what he was looking for." Evianna slips her hand over mine. "We need to get inside his apartment, Dax. Please."

With a sigh, I tell Vasquez to head for Kyle's, then link my fingers with hers. This is a bad idea. Going somewhere I've never been? With a woman I have...feelings for?

But if we can't find out who's after her, it won't be long before I'll have to hand her protection over to someone else. And then... will she still want me?

The fifteen minute drive to Kyle's apartment passes in silence, and when Vasquez opens the back door, I climb out and hold out my hand for Evianna's. I don't want to let her go. Not now. Not when I don't know how much longer I have to be close to her.

Kyle lives on the third floor, and this building doesn't have an elevator. Instead, the cast iron stair rails wind around the center of the building. Vasquez's footsteps echo on the floors, and Evianna holds my free hand.

A door opens behind me, then shuts a second later, but I swear I heard a muffled groan.

"Shit. Boss...that was the guy. Louie," Vasquez says. "He just shoved somebody into a stairwell down the hall and started for the street."

"Go! Get him!" I wrap my arm around Evianna and urge her up the stairs. "We're getting into Kyle's apartment right now."

Up another floor, and Evianna squeezes my hand. "His door's right here. But...it's locked."

From the pocket of my jacket, I withdraw a pair of black gloves, tug them on, then pull out my wallet.

"What are you doing?"

"Picking the lock." The tiny kit fits in one of the credit card slots in my billfold, and I break it apart, holding up the thin metal pieces.

After I find the key hole, it takes me less than a minute to open the door.

"You're...scary," Evianna says.

I lace our fingers together. "You're my eyes, darlin'. And you have to see *everything*. Do *not* let go of my hand, no matter what. Anything out of the ordinary, you tell me immediately."

20

Evianna

DAX PUSHES THE DOOR OPEN, and I stare. "Oh my God."

"What?" His fingers tighten on mine. "Evianna? You're my eyes, remember?"

His sharp tone pulls me out of my shock. "It's been...uh... tossed. Be careful. The floor's a mess." I take two steps forward, then use my foot to shove the fallen coat rack over. "Stay right behind me and I'll make sure there's a path."

Transferring his hand to my waist, I shuffle forward a few steps.

"Don't touch anything. Fingerprints," he warns.

"Um, can I have one of your gloves?"

After he's passed me one of the thin black gloves, I reach down and pick up Kyle's broken laptop. "They took the hard drive out of his computer. And I think stomped on the screen."

"What do you see? Just stop and look around. Is there a pattern? Anywhere the damage is...concentrated?" He's tense, the rigid muscles of his chest pressing against my back.

Scanning the small living room and tiny kitchen, I try to

figure out what might be important. "The couch cushions are ripped open. There's a desk in the corner. The drawers are halfway across the room—and empty. One of them's broken—again, like the guy slammed his foot down on the particle board.

"So he was angry. Start there."

A few feet at a time, we make our way to the desk. A down jacket's ripped open, and my steps kick up feathers. Dislodging his hand from my waist, I give his fingers a squeeze. "I need to move around a little bit to see what's here. I won't go more than arm's length."

He blows out a breath, nodding. "I don't like this, darlin'. Be quick."

Every time he calls me darlin', I melt a little. The hint of the south, the tenderness...I could get used to hearing him call me darlin' every day. With a shake of my head, I focus on the mess in front of me as I sink to my knees.

"There's another notebook here. From the office. Same brand. A bunch of pages are missing, but some have writing on them."

"Take it with you."

I tuck it under my arm. "The rest is mostly junk. Pens, paper-clips, a checkbook. Normal stuff."

"Where's the bedroom?" Dax holds out his hand, and I let him pull me up. "To the left?"

"Yes. How did you...?"

"Shadows. A dark one in the shape of a door. And I can hear the hum of the fridge in the other direction."

I close my eyes, and he's right. The fridge makes a low, droning sound to our right. "I never would have heard that."

"But you hear it now, right?" With his hand on my waist again, he follows me. At my confirmation, he continues. "The whole 'super hearing' thing is a myth. My hearing isn't any better than yours. But I pay more attention to it."

"They tore up the mattress," I say quietly. "Pulled it right off the bed. The sheets are in the corner. Nightstand overturned."

"Take a minute, darlin'. Breathe. You're gettin' overwhelmed."

His palm slides around to my stomach, and he keeps me cradled against him as I force a few deep, calming breaths. "Anything here look...personal? Like it would mean something to Kyle but to no one else?"

"I...I don't know. We worked together for two years, but I'm not really sure I knew him at all." The realization hits me hard. "I thought I was a good boss. That...I cared about my team. How can I not know...?"

Pulling away from Dax, I take a slow tour of the room. Clothes are strewn on every surface, the hangers in the closet empty. The small dresser is on its side. And in the corner... "What the hell?"

"Evianna? Talk to me," Dax says sharply.

"It's an old...answering machine. Like...from the 80s." Something tickles the back of my mind. "What did Kyle say to you when you left the jail?"

"Tell Evianna I'm sorry I ruined her fancy sneakers."

"Oh my God. *'Janek's little black box is on his desk between the pencil jar and the lamp.'*"

"Huh?"

"Sneakers. It's a movie. It's *the* hacking movie everyone watched in the 90s. We had a movie night at the office last year to celebrate the first units going into testing. Kyle's too young. He'd never seen the movie before. But he loved it. Told me he watched it half a dozen times on his own. And in the movie, the secret was hidden *in an answering machine.*"

I grab the machine, searching for a catch, anything that might open it. Dax cocks his head, sniffs a couple of times, and turns. "Evianna, I need your eyes. What's behind that door? Closet or bathroom?"

As soon as I touch the handle, I smell it. Blood. "Bathroom." The weathered door swings open, and I stifle my choked cry. "There's...a lot of blood. Like...spattered on the sink, the floor. A pool by the cabinet."

"We're getting the fuck out of here right now," Dax growls and reaches for me. "Tell me you didn't touch anything with your bare hands."

"N-no. Nothing. Well...the answering machine. But—"

"That's coming with us. Get us back into the hall. Wipe down the apartment door handle. You touched it before I picked the lock."

His harsh words, more orders than anything else, help me focus, and I grab his hand, leading him back through the remnants of Kyle's life. As soon as the door's locked with us on the other side, I use my sleeve to wipe down the knob. "What now?"

"Down to the car." He taps his Bluetooth. "VoiceAssist: Walkie-talkie mode. Contact Vasquez." After a moment's pause, he snaps, "Vasquez! Where the fuck are you?"

Despite not being able to see the stairs, Dax practically sprints down them, and we spill out onto the street, no response from Vasquez. "Somewhere public. Lots of people. Do you see anything?" He tightens his fingers around my elbow, the pressure keeping me focused.

"There's...a bar across the street."

"Get us there. Vasquez, where the fuck are you?"

Two steps away from the dimly-lit bar, Dax stops. "Thank fuck. We're across the street. Get to the car. We'll meet you there."

Wrapping his arm around me, he buries his face against my neck and takes a deep breath. "He's on his way. Someone jumped him and started beating the crap out of him until a store owner yelled for the cops."

I can't believe this is happening. Someone might have died in Kyle's apartment. One of my bodyguards was just attacked, and I'm carrying an answering machine. An *answering machine*. This is my life now? Why?

Dax helps me into the back seat of the SUV and holds me

close. "No more going anywhere but work and my place," he mutters under his breath as Vasquez guns the engine and peels away from the curb. The junior bodyguard with the smile and slight accent has a busted lip, a rapidly swelling eye, and he groaned as he got into the car.

All because of me. And some mystery Kyle got himself involved in that threatens to kill us both.

My eyes burn, and—keeping the notebook and answering machine tucked between us—I hold onto Dax like my life depends on it. Because right now, I think it does.

Dax

Stupid. How could you have been so stupid?

In my arms, Evianna shudders once, and I rub her back. After we get back to my place, we're not leaving until we find this asshole.

"I'm sorry, boss," Vasquez says from the front seat. "I don't know when he doubled back behind me. The first hit caught me in the lower back. Then he started in on my head. If that deli owner hadn't started shouting..."

"After Ford gets back, you're going through surveillance training again." The SUV wavers, like Vasquez just flinched with his hands on the wheel. Shit. I need to be better at dealing with people. "You didn't screw up, Vasquez. Anyone who can hide from Wren for more than an hour is a pro. Call Ronan and have him relieve you. Make an anonymous call about a loud fight inside Kyle's apartment so the police investigate the blood—and the break-in—then get yourself patched up. We're not leaving my place tonight."

The Land Rover coasts to a stop. "We're right in front of your door, boss. You want me to walk you up?"

"No. Just wait here until Ronan shows up. Make sure your comms are on, and stay alert." Unfolding my cane, I climb out of the back seat, then hold out my hand for Evianna's. Her fingers are chilled and stiff, but freesia surrounds me as she presses to my side.

An odd scent lingers in the stairwell. One I've smelled before. It gets stronger the closer we get to my apartment. "Evianna, stay behind me."

"What is it?"

"Maybe nothing." *Yeah, right. And I'm the Easter Bunny.* Outside my door, I pause and listen. Everything's quiet. Running my fingers over the door jamb, I don't feel any signs of forced entry, but there weren't any obvious ones at Kyle's either.

The rasp of my key is loud enough to make me cringe, and I extend my arm to protect Evianna as I shove the door open. Wood cracks against wood. I sweep my cane across the carpet, and hit something. Something that shouldn't be there.

Fuck. Fuck, fuck, fuck. "Voice Assist: Walkie-talkie mode. Vasquez, get up here right now." I turn and wrap my arm around Evianna's shoulders and rush her back towards the stairwell.

"Where are we—? Oh God. Your apartment," she whispers as she casts a glance over her shoulder. "How did they even find you?"

Vasquez's heavy foot steps pound up the stairs. "Boss?"

"My apartment's been compromised. Clear it." As Vasquez draws his gun and flips the safety off, Evianna gasps. "It'll be all right, darlin'."

"No. They found me here. Or...they found you. And I don't know which is worse."

I rest my forehead against hers as Vasquez confirms my apartment's empty. "Neither do I."

21

Dax

BETWEEN VASQUEZ AND EVIANNA, I have a pretty good idea what my apartment looks like. It's a fucking disaster. The only place I ever feel completely in control, and now...I can't take more than three steps without stumbling over the broken pieces of my life scattered around me.

Somewhere in my periphery, Vasquez says, "Get here as soon as you can." Then, a moment later, "Ronan's on his way, boss. You sure we shouldn't bring the cops in?"

"I don't want anyone else in here. Bad enough I don't know where a damn thing is anymore. The police will just make it worse. It's a secure building. You didn't see any signs of forced entry."

"What can I do?" he asks. Between Louie jumping him and this mess, the poor kid is beside himself.

"Clear paths. Bedroom, bathroom, kitchen, couch. Just shove things out of the way so I can get around. And find me a damn duffle bag."

"Where are we going?" Evianna's voice cracks, and I wrap my

arm around her waist. She's shaking, and I curse under my breath. I don't want to go anywhere. If I were alone, I'd stay here. In the dark. With my pistol.

"Hotel."

"They'll be able to find us," she whispers. "We can't use credit cards, can't show our driver's licenses…"

"Unless whomever they sent here is *extremely* good, that won't be a problem. But I need your help, darlin'." Pulling her closer, I bury my face in her hair and lower my voice. "When Vasquez is done in the bedroom, I'll show you."

As if on cue, he passes by us. "There's a path to the bed and to the closet. And a duffel bag on the pillow."

"I'll…help you pack," Evianna says. After she's shut the bedroom door, she turns to me. "What can I do?"

"Come here." I don't trust myself to take more than a step or two in any direction, and my entire body is one raw nerve. Her warmth settles me, and her soft curves take my thoughts off the mess and onto what I'd hoped would happen in this room tonight. But now…we have to get somewhere safe.

"Dax? You're scaring me."

Fuck. Get your shit together. "Sit down for a minute. I need to move the nightstand." The small oak set of drawers slides easily on the carpet until it hits pieces of something—my broken lamp from the sound. But after I clear enough space—or what I hope is enough—I sink to my knees. "Does anything look out of place here?"

"No. Hell, there isn't even any dust. Your housekeeper is amazing."

"This part's all me." Curling my fingers around the baseboard, I yank it off the wall with a quiet snap. The plastic bag is still in place, and carefully, I ease it from the little hidey-hole and lay it in Evianna's lap. "Open it. Pull out the packet with three paperclips."

"What is this?"

"Something I hoped I'd never need." After I put the base-board back into place and feel around so I can position the nightstand on the duct tape Xs on the floor, I ease up next to her. "I don't trust very many people, Evianna. Ford and Wren are the only other people who know about that bag in your hands."

"This is... Oh my God. Passport, government-issued ID, credit cards...a Dunkin' Donuts card? Oliver Russell? This is...fake... right?" Despite her voice being only a soft whisper, there's still a tremble to her tone.

"That bag has six different identities. Oliver's just one of them. He has a clean social security number, a good credit score, bank accounts, and a job working for the Boston Public Library."

"Holy shit."

"Every member of Second Sight has a handful of fake IDs. But these...Second Sight's relocation expert doesn't know about them. I had a friend—one of Ryker's guys, a former Navy SEAL—get these together for me a few years ago."

"This is all...my fault." Evianna sniffles once, and her voice muffles. "Your place...having to use one of these IDs...if I'd never come to you, none of this would have happened."

Sliding my fingers into her hair, I pull her close and crush my lips to hers until she melts against me. "Shhh, darlin'. None of this is on you. And if you hadn't come to me—"

"He would have killed me last night," she whispers.

Taking the packet with Oliver Russell's identity, I tuck it into my jacket pocket. "Put the bag in the bottom of the duffel, then help me piece together some clothes that match? I don't want to stay here any longer than we have to."

———

RONAN DRIVES us to the Fairmont. They're known for their discretion, and Oliver has a computerized history here, even though

I've never used this ID before. Evianna hasn't said a word since we left my apartment, nor has she let go of my hand.

"Where do you want me, boss?" Ronan asks when he pulls up to the curb.

"Call Wren. Have her hack into the security cameras here and monitor the feeds for any sign of Louie or Kyle. Then get yourself a room at the Westin across the street. Clean credit cards only. Keep your phone on and stay awake. We'll check in by eight tomorrow morning."

Adjusting the ball cap to shield my eyes, I get out of the back seat and wait for Evianna to take my arm. To anyone on the street, I hope I look like I can see. "You okay, darlin'?"

"Uh huh."

She's not, but she's holding it together well enough. "Just remember your cover and we'll be fine, *Sierra*." I don't have a fake ID for her, but for the hotel's records, she's now my wife, Sierra Russell.

Less than fifteen minutes later, we're in a corner suite on the top floor of the hotel. "Wow. This is...wow. Noah and I went to San Francisco a few months ago to meet with West Coast Allied Insurance, and he booked us a five star hotel. And it wasn't anywhere near as nice as this."

"Oliver has a long and completely fabricated history with the Fairmont. Wren had to help me a little with that." Unfolding my cane, I start to map the room. Desk, dresser, master suite bathroom, window—where I pull the drapes closed—bed, and then, Evianna's next to me, and I could care less about where the nightstand and television are, because she's all that matters.

"You got two bedrooms," she says, and the hesitation in her voice cuts right through me.

"Darlin', I asked for a quiet room on a high floor. I didn't say anything about two bedrooms. This was probably all they had for a walk-in VIP." Wrapping my arm around her shoulders, I pull her against me. "There's no way in hell I'm leaving your side tonight."

As if our sleeping arrangements were the only care she had in the world, she melts into my embrace, but a breath later, she's shaking in my arms. And then her tears soak into my shirt. "My entire life is falling apart, Dax. Everything I've worked for...I thought...I had a plan. Release Alfie. Start working on more adaptive tech to go with her. Wait for Noah to retire and then take over the company."

I reach out my free hand, find the edge of the mattress, and ease her down next to me. "You'll still do all of those things, Evianna." Every instinct I have warns me not to say the next two words, but I have to. "I promise."

"Don't say that. You can't say that. Not after tonight. How did they even find you?"

She's too distraught for me to go into the various theories that have been bouncing around in my head for the past couple of hours. But I have my suspicions. Mostly involving someone hacking into the police department's computer system.

"Wren will figure that out tomorrow. For tonight, we're safe. Ronan's still a junior PI, but he's the best we have when it comes to spotting a tail. And he's right across the street. By now, Wren's hacked into the security cameras all around this building, and if there's even a hint of anyone suspicious around, she'll let us know. We're safe here, darlin'. And...I want to hold you. All night."

I want a lot more than that—and as I shift closer, my cock presses against her, and Evianna draws in a sharp breath. "I... uh...need to brush my teeth. And take off my makeup. I'll be right back."

Fuck. She's not ready for this. Hell, she probably doesn't even want me. A few kisses are one thing. Seeing me naked, covered in scars...no one would want that. While she's in the bathroom, I find the duffel bag on the desk and rush to change into a t-shirt and pajama pants. She won't have to see any more of me than she already has, and I'll tuck her in and let her fall asleep before I climb into bed next to her.

It's better this way.

Yeah, right. I should tell that to my cock. Or more importantly, my heart.

"Dax?" Evianna calls from the bathroom. "Come in here?"

Feeling along the wall carefully, I make my way to the now-open bathroom door. "What is it?"

"Give me your left hand."

The hell? But I do as she asks. I think I'd do just about anything for her.

She tugs me forward gently, and once I can feel the sink pressed against my stomach, Evianna guides my hand to a shelf in front of me, and my fingers brush against a tube. "In order: toothpaste, shaving cream, razor, Imitrex, and Tylenol. All the way on the right, there's a toothbrush holder. Yours is in front, mine's in back." She keeps her hand over mine, tracing the wall until I feel the cool marble counter under my palm. "Soap dish is right next to the sink, and there's a bar unwrapped. Behind the sink, two tiny bottles of mouthwash. I moved the hand cream bottles into the drawer since they're the same damn shape."

It's not better this way.

I don't know what to say to her. In less than ten minutes, she's gone from a woman I care for to...a woman I could easily fall in love with. Or...maybe more. Maybe I've already started to fall.

22

Dax

"You remembered. All of it." Everything's in the same order I kept it at home.

Her self-conscious laugh does things to me I don't understand, and she pulls her fingers from mine. "I tried. I wasn't sure about the medicine bottles. Do you...need anything else? Towels are on the rack behind you—"

"No, darlin'. Wrapping my arms around her, I hold on until I'm no longer worried she's going to see me break down in a very unmanly way. But...though my employees and the few people I count as friends are always helpful, solicitous, and nonchalant about assisting me, they've known me for years. Evianna? Days.

"I'll just be a couple of minutes. Make sure your briefcase is under the bed. When I'm done, I'll secure the suite's door *and* the door to the bedroom. I want everything critical in the room with us."

"Okay." She pulls away slowly, her fingers sliding over my obliques, and fuck. My cock feels like it's about to explode, and

I'm suddenly worried about coming in my briefs like a goddamned teenager.

Brushing my teeth helps calm me down, as does reciting all the information I memorized on Oliver Russell. Date of birth, address, phone number, credit card pin...over and over again. By the time I've locked the door to the suite and wedged a chair underneath the handle, I'm almost calm. Well, my dick is almost calm. My heart is hammering against my chest so hard I'm worried I'm going to crack a rib.

Snagging my own briefcase from the desk in the main room, I dig into one of the pockets. There. If I'm wrong about this...about how she feels...I might never risk myself like this again, but saying a silent prayer, I tuck three of the condoms into the pocket of my pants.

The bedroom smells like her already. Freesia and fresh rain. The door locks with a *thunk*.

"What side of the bed?" Evianna asks. "Last night...you just—"

"For tonight? Closest to the door." I realize my mistake as her breath stutters. "We'll be fine, darlin'. It's...training more than anything. Always be prepared and all that shit." Feeling my way over to the bed, I pull back the sheet and blankets, and slide in next to her.

"Isn't that like...the Boy Scouts' motto? You were a Boy Scout?"

My laugh sounds more like a choked cough—that's what happens when you don't find much use for the sound for a few years. "Nope. I was...not the greatest kid. Ran with a bad crowd in middle school. My dad lost his job when I was seven, and we moved to a pretty dangerous housing tract outside of Charleston. I was damn lucky I was a fast runner. Otherwise, I probably would have landed in juvie before high school."

"I...no. That's not you." Under the blankets, she reaches for my hand, her fingers cool.

"Not anymore. Saw a friend—well, a kid I thought was my friend—steal from a corner store when I was eleven. The little old woman who was at the register tried to stop him, and he pushed her hard enough, she hit her head." I rub the back of my neck as the memories of that day play like a movie—the only kind of movie I can still see. "I wanted to help her, but he told me I was stupid and left me there. I ran too, but I called 911 from a pay phone a few blocks away. When my dad found out, he beat my ass for 'being such a little shit.' Not too soon after that, he drank himself to death. But that ass whooping scared me straight."

"What happened to her?" Evianna asks, though the hesitation in her voice tells me she's scared of the answer.

"She was fine. Lots of blood, but I went by the store a week or so later, and she was back behind the counter." Bringing our joined hands to my lips, I brush a kiss to her knuckles. "I've never told anyone that story. Not even Ry."

Evianna slides closer, and her free hand cups my cheek. "Take these off," she says as she traces the frame of my glasses. "The light in here isn't too much, is it?"

A hard swallow, and I force out a "no" and set my glasses on the nightstand.

The pad of her thumb traces the scars from whatever chemical they poured into my eyes. Her breath tickles my cheek, and then her lips are on mine.

Kissing her...it's like coming home. To a home I never knew I wanted or needed. Hesitant at first, she waits for me to take control, and I do, threading my fingers through her silky locks and angling her head for better access. Tracing the seam of her lips, I wait for her to open for me.

When she does, I let my tongue tangle with hers in bold, sweeping strokes, and the purr low in her throat tells me I haven't completely forgotten how to kiss a woman.

The first hints of her arousal scent the air, so sweet, I ache to taste her. But when she grasps the bottom of my t-shirt, my entire body tenses, and I pull back, panic dredging up all the ways I've played this scenario out in my head. And all the ways it could end —very badly.

"Turn off the light?" I wheeze.

"No." Evianna straddles me, and fuck, she feels so good with her sex pressed against my cock. "Not unless it's hurting your eyes."

I can't lie to her. Hell, that's the first thing they drill into you in Special Forces training. You *do not lie* to your team. Ever. And Evianna is absolutely my team. "You don't want to see me."

"Can you read minds?" she asks with a little huff. "Because I'm pretty sure as observant as you are, that's *not* one of your many talents. So you have no idea what I do and don't want to see." Wriggling her hips slightly, she chuckles, the low throaty sound making me even harder. "Well, okay. Maybe you know a little bit about what I want. But if you think for one minute you need to hide from me, then maybe...maybe...we shouldn't..."

The strain in her voice breaks me, and I strip off my shirt in one fluid move. Then, hold my breath.

She's not saying anything. Why isn't she saying anything?

I'm about to reach for my discarded shirt when her lips press to one of the deeper, thicker scars across my right shoulder. Her fingers trace an uneven line of raised flesh, badly healed, along my side. "One day, I want you to tell me about some of these. If you can," she whispers just before her teeth graze my ear lobe.

"I remember...every one of them." Desperate to feel her, to have her chase away the ghosts that have haunted me every day for more than six years, I fumble for her waist, finding her curves wrapped in cotton. "What...are you wearing?"

"Tank top. Sleep shorts," she says, a hint of confusion in her tone. "Why?"

"Just because I'm blind, doesn't mean I can't imagine."

Molding my palms to her sides, I slide my hands up close to her breasts and skim my thumbs over the hard points of her nipples.

"I need to feel you, darlin'. Can I...?" Tugging at her tank top, I hold my breath until she raises her arms. Her scent envelopes me as I peel off the tight material, and in the hazy blur before me, an expanse of cream—until she wraps her arms around herself tightly.

"Dax," she whispers. "I haven't done this in a long time..."

"Do you want me to stop?"

"No...I'm just...scared. I don't understand how I can feel this much..."

Starting at her shoulders, I skim my hands down to her wrists and gently unwind her arms. "Maybe we don't need to understand it. Maybe...we just feel." Easing her down onto the pillows, I brush her hair away from her face. I can't get enough of her taste, and I start with gentle kisses to the corner of her lips.

Her skin is so soft, and her nipples scrape against my chest as I angle my body over hers. When she smoothes her hands down my back, I tense as she feels the hundreds of scars cross-crossing my shoulders, but her hips shift under me, and she keens softly.

The curve of her jaw tastes like rain, and the smell of freesia is concentrated behind her ear. I nuzzle the tender skin, biting down until she whimpers and shudders. "Dax..."

The single word carries so much emotion, I can't answer her. Instead, I kiss my way down her collarbone to her breasts. Her nipple rises up to meet my lips, teeth, and tongue, and my God, if she keeps whimpering, I'm going to lose control. But I want this to last.

Her stomach quivers as I continue my trek south, and when I reach the waistband of her sleep shorts, she tenses. "Trust me, darlin'."

"Uh huh." The thin fabric slides down her hips, and I bury my nose in lace.

"Fuck, Evianna. I need to taste you." Her panties rip under my fingers, and then she's bared to me, curls tickling my cheek as I press gentle kisses to the inside of her thighs.

This...I never thought... I wish I could see her face. See her eyes go hooded and dark before her release, but without the visual, I can simply feel. Taste. Listen. Swiping my tongue gently through her folds, it's all honey and slick heat.

She's so wet, so ready, but I can't get enough. She's going to come more than once tonight if I have anything to say about it. My fingers dig into the soft flesh of her hips, and as I continue to torment her little bundle of nerves, her thighs start to tremble.

"Dax! Oh God. Right there!" With one last flutter of my tongue, I score my teeth over her clit, sucking gently, and she flies apart, her hips undulating, her heels driving into the mattress as she claws at the sheets above my shoulders.

Every pulse of her release sends more of her arousal flooding me, and I drink her in until she's panting, unintelligible whimpers tumbling from her lips.

"Easy now, darlin'. I've got you." Crawling up her body, I gather her into my arms, and she buries her face against my neck. "Hold onto me."

"Don't let go. Don't ever let go," she whispers, and by God, I want to promise I won't. Ever.

"Kiss me."

Evianna tips her head up, her hair cascading over her shoulders. And for a second, I can almost imagine her smile as she whispers, "Only if I get to take those pants off you."

Lying back, I try not to tense as she flicks open the button at my waist. "Trust me, Dax."

With a nod, I blow out a breath. "My leg's..."

When she tosses the pants to the bottom of the bed, she makes a soft, "oh" sound, and then her fingers trail from my briefs down my thigh. "Later. You'll tell me that story later."

"Later. Kiss me." I can still taste her, and when she straddles me, a smile curves the lips that press to mine. Her tongue sweeps into my mouth, like I'm water after a year in the desert, and my dick strains against my briefs, so close to where I want to be. "Pants," I half-growl as I push myself up, one hand at the small of her back, the other fumbling for my discarded pants.

"Dax?"

"Protection." The foil packets crinkle in my grip, and I toss them onto the pillow as I roll her over. Kneeling between her spread thighs, I yank my briefs down, freeing my cock. I'm so hard, my balls are already tight, and when she wraps her fingers around my shaft, I groan. Numbers. Baseball stats. Anything. *Just let me last long enough to make her come again.*

"Evianna...fuck. I...it's been too long."

"We have all night," she says as her thumb brushes the tip, the drop of pre-cum, and then makes a lazy circle all around the crown.

In the dim light from the bedside lamps, I can almost make out the shadow of her arm, and I'm not ready for just how fucking hot it is when I hear her suck on her thumb, hear the *pop* as she releases it, and then taste us, together, when she kisses me.

"Inside me, Dax. I need you." The foil packet tears, and her deft fingers roll the condom over my length.

She's so fucking tight, and I slide home an inch at a time, letting her get used to me, while I plunder her mouth, pinch her nipples, and tell her just how perfect she is. Until she wraps her legs around me and urges me deep.

"Fuck. Oh God, Evianna. I won't last." With a groan, I lose myself to another deep, languid kiss and start to move inside her. Each stroke sends me closer, and every muscle in my body begs for release.

Reaching down between us, I swipe my fingers through her slick folds, and when I pinch her clit, she screams my name, and I can't hold on. My hips thrust faster, harder, and as her inner walls pulse around me, what's left of my vision goes white, my heartbeat roars in my ears, and I finally let go.

Evianna

My muscles feel like Jell-O. I'm not sure I can do much more than lie here. But...why would I want to do anything else? Dax is wrapped around me, one arm under his head, the other snaked around my stomach, holding me close under the luxurious sheet and fluffy duvet. One of his legs is draped over mine.

His warm steady breathing tickles my shoulder blade, and I wonder if he's fallen asleep. But as if he can read my mind, he stirs and presses a kiss to my neck. "You all right, darlin'?"

My laugh sounds strange, my throat a little raw. "I don't know."

As if someone lit a fire under the mattress, Dax sits up, patting the bed until he finds his shirt. "I'm...sorry. I should get dressed. Check in with Wren—"

"Dax. Stop." Curling my fingers around the black cotton in his hands, I still his jerky movements. "What are you apologizing for? That was the best sex of my life. You're...amazing."

His ruddy skin flushes a deeper shade, making the pale scars on his chest, cheeks, and around his eyes stand out, and I reach for him, cupping the back of his neck and pulling him down next to me. Tangling our legs, I let my gaze trail slowly over his body, trying to memorize every muscle, every scar.

"What are you doing?" he asks, uncertainty roughening his tone.

"Admiring the very naked man in bed with me." Despite my lack of muscle control, the idea of a second round—and maybe a third—makes my heart beat a little faster.

Dax tries to pull the duvet higher, but I stop him. "For a Green Beret, you have some serious confidence issues, soldier. You're...built. Like seriously." Trailing my fingers over his eight pack, I follow one of the deep *v* lines down his hip to his leg. "Tell me about this?" I ask as I find the two inch long divot in his thigh.

"Not a good story," he grits out, and his body tenses, but I squeeze just below the scar, and he sighs heavily.

"For the first six months, the asshole in charge of Hell worked us over every couple of days. Thought he could still break us. Used us all against one another." He shudders, and I reach up to cup his cheek, but he stops me, links our fingers, and rolls over, tugging me with him so I'm pressed to his back. "His name was Kahlid. Not long after we were captured, Hab...he was already half-dead. Sepsis. He didn't have long. Maybe a few days left. So Kahlid used him to try to make us talk. Tortured him in front of us. When that didn't work, he slit Hab's throat as we watched. Gagged and cuffed to the wall."

"Oh shit." I can't manage more than a whisper, and Dax swears under his breath.

"Don't ask me the rest, darlin'."

"You don't have to protect me from your past, Dax. I want to know." Pressing my lips to his shoulder, I try to offer him whatever strength I have.

"Somewhere around month eight, Kahlid realized we were never going to break. But he couldn't just let us go. Or even work a prisoner exchange. He'd tortured us too much. The military would have shot him dead the second they saw the shape we were in. So he got mean."

"Slitting Hab's throat in front of you wasn't mean?"

A rough laugh escapes, and he shudders. "Not to him. Insane fucker." After a pause, he rubs his leg. "We were malnourished. And the shit they fed us...? Intestinal parasites. The whole damn time. A few weeks before we'd planned to escape, Kahlid broke my leg with a metal pipe."

Squeezing his hand, I say nothing, afraid he'll shut down.

"Then...he took a blowtorch to my skin. Doesn't take much for a wound to get infected in those conditions. Ry set the bone, but I was in bad shape. It's...why I couldn't escape with him. Why I was still there for..." He brings my hand to his lips and sighs. "Damn thing never healed right. Doctors said I was maybe a week away from losing the leg completely."

As if a dam has opened, one he can't stop, Dax's words pour our now, faster and fainter. "I wonder every day...why I lived. Ryker...he protected me whenever he could. But he couldn't stop them from killing Ripper or Hab or Gose. Ripper was...the worst. One day, he just disappeared. Kahlid never told us what happened to him. We'd ask, and he'd just laugh. For five months before the end, we wondered. Didn't find out what happened to him until I talked to Ry the other day. One of Kahlid's men threw him into the hole and he broke his neck."

He swipes at his eyes and continues. "I remember every scar, Evianna. Ryker...he has this insane memory. And he taught me all the tricks. I...don't forget. Anything. I can't."

I wish I could comfort him. Take away even a fraction of his pain. Instead, all I'm doing is causing more. Doubt creeps in, and I roll onto my back. Now, it's my turn to hide. To pull away. To try to protect him from the chaos of my life. He deserves...more. Safety. Security. Peace.

"Darlin'?" Perceptive as ever, even after all he's confessed, Dax turns over. "Knowing what I do, remembering every minute trapped in that shithole, losing my best friend—my brother—for six years afterwards, fuck, even not being able to see... This is who I am. I'll never forget a damn thing. But I'll share it. All of it. Any of it. With you."

Thankful he can't see the tears shimmering in my eyes, I prop myself up on an elbow and claim his mouth in a searing kiss. I need him. All of him. He's the only guide I have through the chaos, and now...after tonight...he's the only one I want.

23

Evianna

THE ENTIRE BED SHAKES, and sheets rustle. My sleep-addled brain doesn't process what's going on until a low, mournful groan comes from behind me. Then, I'm instantly awake and sitting up.

Flipping on the light, I stifle my gasp. Dax is curled into a ball, his arms around his knees, shuddering with each breath. A violent flinch accompanies his whimper, and a word that sounds almost like "please" escapes through clenched teeth.

"Dax?" I don't want to touch him. If he's trapped in some sort of nightmare, he may not know where he is when he wakes up. But I can't let him continue to hurt. "Dax, wake up."

He flinches again, hisses a breath, and tightens his arms.

Trying for my best "army whatever" voice, I bark out orders. "Dax. Wake up. Now!"

His eyes fly open, but in the next instant, he scrubs his hands over his face. Over and over again. Blinking between each attempt. "Can't...see..."

"Dax! Daxton? Daxwell?" I don't know his given name. But at this point, I'll try anything to get him back. "Officer Holloway!"

"Sergeant," he whispers as his frantic movements still.

Easing myself down, I risk wrapping my arms around him. "Sergeant?"

"Not officer. Sergeant. Evianna?"

"I'm right here, Dax. Do you know where we are?" He's shaking now, and I draw the duvet up to his shoulders. "Tell me."

"Fairmont. Boston. Fuck. I...wanted to see. For a minute...I thought maybe...I wanted it. So much. To see you." The words fade into a hoarse chocking sob, and then he tries to pull away, but I won't let him go.

Brushing his hair away from his face, I find his cheeks wet, and the idea of this strong, amazing man being scared enough to cry breaks my heart.

He twists in my arms and reaches up to touch me, his thumb tracing the line of my cheek in the dim light from the bedside lamp. "I don't know what you look like. And I've only ever wanted to see one other thing this badly since I lost my sight."

"What's that?" I smile when he slides his palm to my jaw.

"The stars the night Ry pulled me out of Hell. And now...I'd trade that for one look at your eyes. Or your smile."

"You see me, Dax. Maybe not the way you want, but you see me." Leaning closer, I press my lips to his, then brush the tears from his cheeks. "Want to tell me about the dream?"

"No." When I bristle, he rushes to continue. "I will, darlin'. Just not...tonight. Not now. Not after...earlier. I don't have anything left in me."

His heavy lids start to close, and I turn over, letting him spoon me with his arm around my waist and our fingers intertwined. "Whenever you're ready, I'll be here," I whisper, and then let myself drift off in his arms.

SOMEONE'S TALKING. Why is someone talking? It's way too early.

"Oh-eight-hundred. Oh-eight-hundred. Oh-eight-hundred."

Dax groans behind me, "Voice Assist: Cancel alarm."

"Can't we stay in bed for a while?" I ask.

He buries his face in my hair. "As long as you want, darlin'. Until Wren calls and we're still naked."

My cheeks catch fire, and I pull the duvet up to my neck. "But she's in Seattle. It's three hours earlier there."

"Wren lived in Boston until a couple of weeks ago. And is keeping Boston hours...for now." His voice cracks, and he clears his throat.

"You miss her."

"Yeah. She kept the office...human. She and Ford...they did what I could never do. Be...friendly with everyone." Dax sighs and sits up, leaning against the headboard. "I don't want you going to your office today, Evianna. It's too dangerous. After last night..."

My shoulders hike up around my ears as I slide up next to him and force confidence I don't feel into my voice. "I have to. We sign off on Alfie tomorrow. Maybe even this afternoon if the devs worked their asses off last night. If I'm not there...I *have* to be there."

Reaching for his phone, Dax taps the screen. "VoiceAssist: Call Clive on Speaker."

Clive doesn't pick up until the fourth ring, and when he does, his voice is thick with sleep. "Yeah, boss?"

"Please tell me you can work—shit. Sorry. How's your mom?" Dax rests one elbow on his bent knee and cradles his forehead. I reach up and start to gently massage the back of his neck.

"She's stable. Surgery went great, and she'll be home in two days. What do you need?"

As if Clive just gave Dax the answer to the location of the Holy Grail, he visibly relaxes. "Just a couple of hours, buddy. Escorting a priority client from the Fairmont to her office, then back again. High likelihood of surveillance, at least leaving the office, and anyone following you is definitely going to be hostile."

I'm a "priority client"? After what happened last night? Admittedly, I don't know what I'd call us right now, but...Dax is a hell of a lot more than simply my bodyguard.

Clive speaks to someone in the background while I fume, then comes back on the line. "I can do it. My brother's here, so he can take a shift with Mom for a while. What time?"

Dax arches a brow in my direction. "Evianna?"

My cheeks catch fire. We both have scratchy, raspy morning voice, and now Clive knows we're both at the Fairmont. Together. At eight o'clock in the morning. And I'm still...just a client. "Hi... uh, Clive. I can be ready to go in an hour. Then leave the office around seven."

"Okay. I'll be there. Going to stop at the hospital to check on Mom first, then I'll swing by. See ya', boss. Evianna."

The call clicks off, and I stammer, "I n-need a shower."

Snagging my wrist before I can ease out of bed, Dax holds on tight. "Are you okay, darlin'?"

"Fine." I rest my free hand on top of his for a brief moment, then pull away. I can't figure out how to put my anger, frustration, and yes...hurt...into words. I don't think he even realizes what he said—or how it made me feel, but I have to put some space between us to figure it out.

As I close myself in the bathroom, I steal one last glance at him, still in bed, and it's like someone clamped a vise down on my heart. Such a tough, strong man, muscular, scarred, and proud, and yet, the confusion written in the furrow of his brow makes him look like a lost puppy.

Swiping at my traitorous eyes, I turn on the shower, hoping the hot water will wash away these conflicting feelings before I break down completely.

Dax

Scrubbing my hands over my cheeks, I try to figure out what the hell I did. She's upset, and from her tone, it's my fault. Unsurprising, since I don't have the first fucking clue how to be...sweet. Or what I'm supposed to do when I piss someone off.

Feeling my way along the wall, I head for the bathroom and knock. "Evianna? Can I come in?"

Over the gentle patter of the shower, I think I hear her say yes. Or...at least I hope I do. "Can I...join you?"

This isn't me. Trying to be romantic. But, she makes me want to be a better man. A different man. A man who always knows what she needs.

"It's a deep tub. Stand back a minute."

The animation and tenderness is gone from her voice, and as a cloud of steam hits me, I think the shower door swings on its hinges. "I'm going to take your hand," she says. Her warm, wet fingers curl around mine, and she guides my palm to the edge of the tub.

"I'm good now. There an 'oh shit' bar on the wall?"

The weak laugh I get in response does little to calm the churning in my gut, but as soon as I'm standing next to her, she shows me exactly where it is. "Shampoo and conditioner, in order from left to right, on the little shelf just below the bar." Turning away from me, I think she raises her arms, and the tone of the water changes.

"Can I...?" Nearly knocking the little bottle of shampoo off the shelf, I flick the cap open and pour some into my hands. I need to touch her. To do something for her to fix whatever it is I fucked up.

"Dax—"

"Please, darlin'. I don't know why you're angry with me, but I need to touch you." I'm not proud of how unsure I sound, and with the shampoo dripping from my fingers, I probably look like a fucking idiot.

With a sigh, she steps closer, and her wet hair tickles my palms. Following the strands, I start to massage her scalp, and she leans against me, some of the tension melting from her shoulders. "You called me a client."

The words are so soft, I almost don't hear them over the water and my own heartbeat roaring in my ears. "What?"

"On the phone. You called me a client. I thought—" she snorts, and drops her head, "—I don't know what I thought. Never mind. It's nothing."

Oh, shit. "It's not nothing." With one arm around her waist and the other hand tangled in her hair, I press my hips to the generous globes of her ass. I need her. Want her. And my dick seems determined to make that *very* obvious. But I need her heart a hell of a lot more. More than I ever thought possible.

Gently turning her, I shield her eyes as I guide her head under the spray. "What...do you want to be?" The tender kiss I brush to her lips makes her breath stall in her chest, and she digs her fingers into my obliques. "Tell me, darlin'."

"More."

"You *are* more." *Stupid, Dax. And barely an answer.* Feeling my way around the shower walls, I find an empty space and press her back to the tiles. "I'm not a good bet, Evianna. Not someone you should want. Can't you see that?"

"No. I don't. What I *see*, Dax, is a man who's willing to do anything to keep me safe. A man who's funny—when he lets himself relax—who cares about his employees and friends, who knows just what to say when I'm feeling like my life's spiraling out of control. And a man who thinks his value is somehow tied to his sight."

The water heats my back, but against my chest, Evianna's nipples harden, and under my hands, gooseflesh rises along her arms. "You're cold," I say as I move her back under the spray, then take the soap and start massaging her shoulders. "I wish I could find the words..."

"Try," she whispers.

Sliding my hands down, cupping her breasts, I skate my thumbs over her nipples, and the tiny moan tumbling from her lips has me hard for her in a single breath. With one hand continuing to lavish attention on her breast, I trail my other to her slick folds. The scent of her arousal mixes with the steam, and fuck. I wish I could take her right here.

"Dax..." The single word holds so much need, my cock strains against her ass cheeks. Dipping my head, I score my teeth along her neck and bite down gently on the shell of her ear. Still working her nipple, I pinch her clit, and Evianna shatters. Her entire body convulses, and she throws her head back against my shoulder. "Oh God. You're...you're..."

"Shhh. Just...breathe, darlin'. I've got you." Against her ear, I whisper, "You're more, Evianna. You're...so much more."

If only I knew what...more was. Or how to figure it out.

"*Text from Clive,*" my phone says, shattering the silence that's filled the hotel room for the past half an hour.

"VoiceAssist: Play message."

"*I'm downstairs. Checked in with Ronan. No unusual activity. Safe to come out.*"

"Are you ready?" I tuck the Bluetooth into my ear and adjust my glasses. "I have all of Kyle's notes and the answering machine."

"Yes," she says quietly. "You'll...um...come get me at the end of the day?"

My eyes burn. How could I have ever put that doubt into her voice? Pulling her against me, I drop my cane and thread my fingers through her hair. She left it long today, and the silky strands let me guide her head just how I like it. When I crush my lips to hers, she parts for me, and fuck. If we had another half an hour, I'd lay her down on the bed and take my time with her. Show her just how much she means to me.

Evianna melts in my arms as I come up for air. "Darlin', I will always come for you. I promise."

"You...promise?" Her voice trembles, and she rests her forehead against mine.

"Yes, baby. I promise."

"HERE, BOSS," Clive calls as we exit the elevator.

Evianna tries to let go of my hand, but I hold tight. "Clive, this is...my..." She tenses, and shit. How can she possibly think I don't care for her? I can't say the words. I don't have them. Don't even know what they are. "Evianna. Nothing is more important than her safety. You understand?"

Maybe Evianna's right. Maybe I'm more than my blindness. Because I hear the hitch in her breath. Feel the little wobble in her knees. Her fingers tremble in mine.

"Got it, boss. Car's at the curb. You want me to stay outside her office all day?"

No. I want to stay at her side all day. Somewhere far away from here. With a bed and room service and no one else around.

"No," Evianna answers before I can respond. "No one's going to come for me at work. There are twenty other people there, including two security guards. I won't leave."

"See her all the way to the elevator, Clive. Then drop me off at Second Sight and go visit your mom. Pick me up at seven, and then we'll get Evianna from her office. We're going back to the Fairmont tonight." And maybe once we're alone again, I can fix whatever I broke this morning.

As Evianna opens the car door and guides my hand to the

frame, I don't even think about her touching me. I can sense her. Every movement. Every emotion. I don't have to see her to know her. Even though it's still the one thing I want more than anything else in the world.

The ride passes with little conversation, but when Clive pulls up to Evianna's office, I tell him to give us a minute.

"I need to get to work, Dax. I'm late already. We're so close to launching Alfie. I should have been in by seven," she says, her tone distant, though she hasn't let go of my hand the entire ride.

Sliding closer, I cup her cheek, and I can feel a muscle in her jaw tick. I've fucked this up in the worst way, and I have to fix it. "Darlin', I wish I could tell you what we are. What you mean to me. But, I don't have all the pretty words you deserve to hear."

"So you won't even try?"

Pain crushes my heart when her voice breaks. "No. Yes. Fuck." I lift our joined hands to my lips and ghost a kiss to her knuckles. "For six years, I thought everything good in me was dead. Tortured and killed and left to rot in Hell. But now..."

Clive raps on the window. "This is a three-minute loading zone, boss," he calls. "And there's a traffic cop down the block."

Holding tight for one last second, I squeeze her fingers. "Give me a little time, darlin'. Please. Don't give up on me."

Evianna opens the door and climbs out of the car. But before her heels click on the sidewalk, she leans back down so her breath whispers over my cheek. "Don't give up on yourself either, Dax. I don't need all the pretty words. Just honest ones."

24

Dax

As the car rolls to a stop, Clive clears his throat. "So, you and the client...?"

"If you value your job, don't say another word."

Except, I need him. And he knows it. After a chuckle, he turns, his voice no longer echoing off the front windshield. "I love my job. My boss is pretty cool. Most of the time. Today, he's wound tighter than a two dollar watch." The teasing tone leaves his voice. "And we both know that's when mistakes happen."

"We're getting nowhere." With a sigh, I lean forward, doing my best to meet Clive's gaze. His black sunglasses—against ghostly white skin—help me focus my stare. "I can't protect her. No one's heard from Ford and Trevor, Vasquez and Ronan are working nights, and Evianna's totally alone during the day."

"I can watch out for her. Mom's at the point in her recovery where she's ordering the nurses around and demanding we tune the television to her favorite soap operas. Give me three hours and I'll park myself outside her building."

"I can't ask you to do that."

"You're not asking." Clive gets out of the car, comes around, and opens my door. "I'll check in when I get back to her office."

I hold out my hand, and when Clive's cool fingers grasp mine, I give him a nod. "I owe you."

"Nah. Consider it my apology for Trev's packing tape adventure." He claps me on the back, and I head for the door.

"VOICEASSIST: CALL WREN." Leaning back in my chair, I take a long sip of coffee. I want to text Evianna, but after my repeated fuck-ups this morning, I'm afraid if I say the wrong thing now, we'll end up needing those separate rooms at the Fairmont.

"Hey, boss," she says. Exhaustion lends a raspiness to her tone, and she yawns over the call. "I spent the entire night on a ghost hunt. Louie Stein died seven years ago in a charter plane accident off the coast of Bimini. Honest-to-galoshes, Dax. I didn't even know Bimini was a real place. I spit out my tea."

The corners of my lips tug up in a half smile. "One of these days, you and Ry should go. It's...beautiful." Scattered memories fade, a little more every day. The beaches, the blue-green water. How long until I can't remember what *anything* looks like?

"Dax? Hey. You all right?"

Squeezing my eyes shut, I refocus. "Fine. Why?"

"Because I asked you if you found anything at Kyle's place."

"Shit. Sorry." Taking another hit of coffee, I summarize what happened the night before. "So I have an old answering machine sitting on my desk right now, and no fucking clue what to do with it."

"Like *Sneakers?*" Wren squeaks. "Holy snack cakes. You and Evianna had better come out here when this whole thing blows over. I want to meet her."

"Uh...yeah. I...sure." What the hell did I just agree to?

Wren seems surprised, because there's the distinct sound of

her choking on whatever she's drinking, followed by coughing and wheezing and a stammered apology.

The sound of typing carries over the line. "Fudgesicles," she says. For Wren, that's serious swearing. "Dax? Kyle was bailed out of jail last night. What time did you say you and Evianna were at his place?"

"Shit, Wren. We could have run right into him. Why didn't you tell me?"

"Um, excuse me if I was a little busy tracking down the guy who tried to kill Evianna. What time were you there?" Her words slow with her anger, turning deliberate and quiet.

With a sigh, I shake my head. "Sorry. I'm...not good company right now. Eight-thirty. Give or take."

"You and Ry, both," she mutters. "Hang on." More keystrokes, and shit. I wish I could see what's on her screen right now.

"Wren, you have to talk to me."

"In a minute."

Pushing to my feet, I start to pace. Five steps to the door, three steps to the far edge of the window, six steps to the other end of the office, another three steps. I make four circuits before Wren stops typing and whispering to herself.

"At seven-twenty-three, a traffic camera two blocks from Kyle's apartment caught a single image of Kyle with another man. I can't tell if it's Louie, but I'm running pattern recognition now. Whoever he is, he's holding onto Kyle's arm, and the kid looks scared out of his mind."

Dropping back into my chair, I pull out the notebooks Evianna trusted me with. "I can't do a damn thing with the answering machine on my own. But I can scan Kyle's notes and maybe...get lucky."

"Turn your glasses to transmitter mode. I'll get scans of everything you see, and we can try to figure this out together."

The last sip of coffee's half cold, but I don't care. I need something to wash down the bitter pill I'm about to swallow. "You've been up all night, Wren."

"True, but I have an endless supply of coffee, tea, and chocolate-covered espresso beans to keep me going. And do you really think *you're* going to be able to decipher all the geek-code in those pages? When I need a break, I'll take one. But for now, you're wasting time arguing with me."

I know the determination in her voice. The last time I heard it, I didn't listen, and she almost died. I'm not making that mistake again. Because this time, it's Evianna's life on the line, and if I lose her, I'm afraid I'll lose myself as well.

Evianna

The office is pure chaos. Pizza boxes litter a long table against the far wall, tiny packets of Parmesan cheese everywhere and red pepper flakes ground into the carpet. Someone ran out for a massive sheet cake an hour ago—because apparently Mountain Dew wasn't an efficient enough sugar delivery system—and now Barry, Carla, Vivek, and Priya are racing to see who can clear their bug list the fastest.

Ulysses comes in to check on me every hour or two, bringing me more tea, giving me a few moments of peace amid the cacophony. But I can't keep my door closed for long. We're so close to launching, I have to sign off on every code change, and every one of my devs has stood across from me at some point this morning.

And every spare moment I can, I bring up the diagnostics program running against my little Alfie unit and scan through the logs. "Come on..." I whisper to my computer. "Give me something."

Barry raps twice and leans a hip against the door jamb.

"Closed out that unhandled exception error bug no one's been able to track down for weeks."

Arching a brow, I hold out my hand for his tablet. "You just started working on this an hour ago. It was that simple?"

"Nope. I'm just that good." He curls his fingers and blows on his nails, then rubs them on his shirt. But in the next breath, breaks into a sheepish smile. "Seriously, though...I worked on this half the night. Didn't go home."

A quick scroll through his code, and I sign off. "Great work, Barry. Really." He brightens, and for a minute, looks like he's still in high school. Most of the time, he's an arrogant asshole. One I never would have hired. But today, he's been a star. "Um...close the door and sit down for a minute?"

He narrows his eyes at me, but snags the door with his foot, then sinks into the chair across from my desk. "What's up?"

"Tomorrow, Noah and I are going to sign off on Alfie's code. And once she's out there in the world...well...every single one of you is going to be able to write your own ticket. There isn't one person on this team who's given anything less than a hundred and ten percent the past couple of weeks, and I just wanted to thank you, personally. We haven't always gotten along. But you're an asset to this company, and at the party tomorrow, I'd like to announce your promotion to Dev Lead. If you want it."

His swallow bobs his Adam's apple, and he stares down at the tablet in his hands. "Yeah. I do." The smile's back, full force, and when he meets my gaze, determination and pride shine in his hazel eyes. "Thanks."

Pulling a terms sheet from my desk drawer, I catch sight of an alert on the diagnostics program.

Remote shutdown initiated: 18:03:45

My heart hammers against my chest, but I force a deep breath and slide the paper towards Barry. "This is the new pay and bene-fits package that comes with the position. Keep this confidential.

If you have any questions about the numbers, come see me tomorrow before close of business, okay?"

He scans the sheet, his smile widening, and then folds it and tucks it into his pocket. "Will do. Anything else?"

"Nope. Get back to work. Or...have another slice of cake. Or both."

After Barry saunters back into the bullpen, I slap a Post-in note on my door informing everyone I'm on a conference call, head back to my desk, and with shaking hands, text Wren.

Found a remote shutdown command on my Alfie unit. There's no way that should be possible.

The phone rings not more than a minute later. "What are your remote access protocols?" she asks without even saying hello.

"Any remote commands have to come from *this* office." I almost drop the phone as I sink down into the overstuffed chair by my window. "Someone *here* turned off my Alfie unit. And... tried to have me killed."

"Evianna, focus," Wren says sharply. "Are you in any danger right now?"

"I...d-don't know. I'm...we're all working. It's been tense. But... almost fun. Like it used to be. There are only a handful of bugs left, and we launch tomorrow and—"

"Stop." The single word stills my panicked rambling. "I'll message Dax right now and tell him to come get you out of there, but you need to focus."

"I...I need another hour here. I have to...I can't leave yet."

A sigh carries over the line. "Okay. So, we need to figure out where that remote shutdown command came from. Do you have any advanced monitoring software on your firewall?"

"Yes. That's how I found out Kyle made a copy of the code." I can do this. Wren's matter-of-fact, calm voice helps me focus, and I go back to my desk. "Except...I can't send those logs outside the company. So any analysis I do will have to be here."

Wren chuckles over the line. "Patience, my young Padawan. Let me show you the ways of the hacker."

"You're going to...break into my system?" My voice rises, and I curse under my breath. "Dammit. Sorry. But when we upgraded our firewall last year, we hired the best."

"I'm not going to 'break in,'" she says. "I'm going to 'break out.' Give me the specs of your firewall. Company, software version, all that jazz. And then let me work my magic for a few hours. Tomorrow, if you can install a tiny little program on one of your servers...we'll have the back door we need. Trust me, Evianna. This is what I do."

"Okay. You'll have the information within the hour."

25

Dax

AN ENTIRE DAY scanning Kyle's notebook pages has produced little in the way of leads, even with Wren translating the tech-speak. References to subroutines and shadow code are frequent, but we need Evianna to help put the pieces together.

It's a nice evening, and so a little after seven, I walk the five blocks from Second Sight to Beacon Hill Technologies. The traffic rumbles to my left, the scent of exhaust wafting through the air, but underneath, there's a sweetness I haven't smelled in a year. Lilacs.

The memories threaten, but they're muted. Faded now with time and the loss of my sight. One of the first years I lived in Boston, before I signed up for Special Forces training, I brought my mother to the arboretum at Harvard for their Lilac Festival. One of the last happy times I spent with her before I deployed and everything changed.

Her face is nothing but a blur now, though I can still some-times hear her laugh. But the flowers...the flowers are gone. My eyes burn, and I stop at the curb, wondering what else I've lost.

All the memory tricks Ryker taught me in Hell...they only work for new memories. The sights and sounds of my youth, all those images I'd filed away, to be pulled out when I was low or in pain...soon, they'll all be gone.

I'll never see lilacs again. But...maybe I don't have to. The light turns, and I sweep my cane in front of me as I double-time it to Evianna's building. She can steady me. And maybe...if she agrees to a little detour before we go back to the hotel, I can find a way to tell her what she means to me.

———————

CLIVE HAILS me when I'm about to open her building's outer door. "Dax! Hold up."

"Status report," I say quietly when he's at my side.

"All clear. I've been outside since 2:00 p.m. and haven't seen anyone suspicious. Normal businessmen and women coming and going. A twenty-something bringing in a big sheet cake, pizza delivery. You want me to get the car?"

"Yes. I'll wait for Evianna inside. I just texted her, so she should be down in five minutes. And, Clive?"

"Yeah, boss?"

"I want to take Evianna to the arboretum before we go back to the hotel. Do you have time to shadow us for an hour?"

"Yep. I'll text Ronan to let him know."

I clap him on the shoulder in thanks and head inside.

The elevator dings, and her heels click across the tile floor. Before she can ask, I hold out my arm, and when she melts against me, something in my world shifts in a way I can't explain.

"I...missed you, darlin'," I whisper in her ear. "I'm sorry... about this morning."

"Just get me out of here, please." Her voice isn't steady, and I want nothing more than to lift her into my arms and carry her to the car. But I'd trip, drop her, and fall on my face, so I settle for pressing my lips to her neck.

"Did something happen?"

Straightening, I take her elbow so she can guide me to the car, but the elevator dings again, and a booming voice calls her name. "Evianna, wait."

"My boss," Evianna whispers as she straightens her shoulders and turns. "Noah, did you need something?"

"An introduction? I didn't know you were seeing anyone."

His tone grates along my spine, raising the hair on the back of my neck. Entitled. Like he's owed an explanation. Or first right of fucking refusal. The man's cologne carries a too-sweet scent— one I think I've smelled before—and I have to force myself not to wrinkle my nose. "Dax Holloway," I say, holding out my hand.

"Noah Goset." His clammy fingers barely hold any strength, and I make sure to squeeze—hard—and his next words are slightly strained. "What do you do, Dax?"

"I run a think tank." The lie flows easily, and I incline my head towards Evianna. "We'll miss our reservation if we don't head out. You'll excuse us, Noah?"

"Don't let me keep you. I'll see you tomorrow, though—Dax? —was it? You're coming to the party, aren't you? For Alfie's release?" I must look confused, because he clucks his tongue. "Don't tell me Evianna hasn't already invited you?"

"Of course I invited him," Evianna says with a hint of indignation to her voice. "Good night, Noah. We're running late. I'll see you in the morning."

With her fingers digging into my elbow, she hurries us out of the building and right to the car Clive has idling at the curb.

I don't say anything until the door closes and Evianna flops back against the seat with a sigh.

"What party?"

"Alfie's release party. I thought I mentioned—"

Taking off my glasses, I arch a brow. "No. You weren't planning on going alone, were you?"

"God, no." She reaches for my hand, and the emotion in her voice has me linking my fingers with hers. "I just...I didn't want to think about it. About the release. About what might happen after—"

"It's all right, darlin'." Bringing her hand to my lips, I kiss her palm, then the pulse point of her wrist. Fuck. She smells like heaven, and there isn't a single reason she should want me, but dammit if I'm not going to do everything I can to keep her by my side. "I shouldn't have jumped to conclusions. Do you mind if we go one place before we head back to the hotel? There's something I want to show you."

THE RIDE to Cambridge takes less then twenty minutes with Clive behind the wheel. The man knows more shortcuts than anyone I've ever met—besides Ripper. Evianna doesn't say much as she sits too far away in the Lincoln Town Car. Clive should have opted for a coupe. Something to force us to sit close enough our thighs would touch and I could wrap my arm around her.

Her fingers start to warm in mine, and I lean over. "You're worrying me, Evianna. What happened at the office today?"

"You didn't talk to Wren?"

"I talked to Wren half the day." What the hell is going on? And why didn't Wren tell me? Making a mental note to send my favorite hacker a text later, I scoot as close as the seatbelt will allow. "Tell me."

"Someone executed a remote shutdown command that turned my Alfie unit off half an hour before you brought me home the other night. The unit was offline for fifteen minutes."

"You knew something like that had happened, though."

Her fingers tighten on mine. "Dax, I didn't put a remote shut-down subroutine in Alfie's code. But it's more than that. The only way someone could access the unit *at all*, would be from our offices. Someone at Beacon Hill—someone who's not Kyle, since he was long gone by then—is behind this whole thing."

26

Dax

THE ARBORETUM VISITOR'S Center is bustling this close to sunset, and the cacophony of voices is almost too much. "Look for signs for the Lilac Exhibit," I say as Evianna takes my arm and guides me out the door to the garden path.

"To the left. But...Dax...? Should we be out here...in the open like this?"

"Clive isn't far. You won't see him, but if anyone comes near us, he'll be here in under a minute." A breeze brings the scent of hundreds of flowers swirling around us, and I breathe deeply. "I used to come here. Before I joined the army. Before...Hell."

She presses closer to me, through another turn and down a winding path. "I never knew about this place. I've lived in Boston for three years, and outside of a couple of baseball games and one Duck Boat ride, I've never really...*done* anything. It's beautiful."

Water burbles to my right, and I stop. "Let's go down by the water. There used to be benches. Are they still there?"

"Yes. But...Dax? I...don't understand."

Taking her arm, I gesture towards the small lake that smells like it's still surrounded by lilacs. A hint of the evening sun slashes through the surrounding trees, highlighting the deep chestnut of her hair.

Our feet crunch over gravel, and when my cane finds the corner of the bench, I fold it up and tuck it in my pocket before guiding us both down onto the warm marble. "I had so many memories of this place. Before. But—" my voice cracks, and I clear my throat as Evianna links our fingers, "—they're fading. Some things you never forget. The blue of the sky. A red rose. Chinese food takeout boxes. Mickey Mouse. But this place? Every year was different. Every flower unique. I can't see them anymore. All I have is the scent. The sweetness of the lilacs. The freesia. The lilies. I need *you*, Evianna. Tell me what you see?"

She doesn't speak for so long, I start to worry. "Darlin'?"

"The lake is a deep blue. Like...a sapphire. Or...a blue jay. Tiny little ripples all over the surface. And...ducks. Three of them. A mama and two babies."

My throat tightens, and I grip the corner of the bench hard enough for the marble to bite into my fingers.

"At the edge of the lake, the lilacs... They're like a carpet. Most of them are bluish purple. But some of them are bright pink. And the closest ones are pure white." The awe in her voice makes my eyes burn.

But when she stands, hooks her arm through mine, and takes a few tentative steps towards the lake, I resist. My last memories of this place are of a steep grassy knoll, and without being able to see, I don't trust myself.

"Dax...I won't let you fall."

She's so certain. So confident, that I take a step. Then another.

"Go slow," she urges. "There's a big flagstone three feet in front of you."

When I find it, and I'm steady again, Evianna guides my hand forward until my fingers brush velvet. The sweet scent surrounds us, and I can almost see them. The flowers. So thick the color goes on for miles.

"These...are white," Evianna whispers. "The inner buds are a pale yellow. The color of...fresh-churned butter. Or...what I imagine pure sunshine looks like." She moves my hand, and the texture of the petals changes. "There's one—just one spray—that's deep purple. Like...grape juice. Each petal is identical. And...not."

Evianna bends down, and a moment later, lays a single bloom in my palm. "This one's...broken. Damaged. But it's still beautiful." Raising my hand until the petals touch my nose, she steps closer. "It fell, but...it still smells just as sweet as the rest."

A tear burns my eye, and when it hits my cheek, I crush the flower in my fist, and haul Evianna against me. How can I tell her what she's given me? A piece of myself I thought long lost. Color to brighten my world of gray. Light in all my shadows.

The words tumble around inside my head. So many words. Gratitude. Need. Joy. Sorrow. And strongest of all...*love*. I can't say it. If I do...will I wake up to find this has all been a dream? A perfect dream when I'm still trapped in Hell? In that cold, dark cave. Alone.

"Dax? Talk to me." Evianna kisses my neck, along my jaw, all the way to my lips, and she tastes like home. Sliding her fingers into my hair, she sweeps her tongue along mine, as if she knows she has to ground me. To prove we're real.

Time and time again, I try to speak. To say anything. But emotions I haven't let myself feel in six years clog my throat, and all I can manage is a hoarse, choking sound until I kiss her again.

Sinking down to the ground, I pull her into my lap, needing to feel her weight to confirm she's real. "I...you..."

Evianna traces the path of my tears with her thumbs, then

kisses them away. "Maybe...for now, it's enough that we're...us," she whispers.

Evianna

Clive hands us off to Ronan as the sun dips below the horizon. The last rays paint the arboretum in deep purple and indigo, and I wish I knew how to describe it to him.

The lilac bloom is still crushed in Dax's palm as we head for a dark gray SUV. I'm almost afraid to touch him. This strong man just broke in front of me, over...a flower. But when I turn for one last look out over the landscape, I understand. He'll never see it as I do.

"Evianna?" Dax trails a hand down my arm, and I startle, but don't turn to face him. "Come on, darlin'. Let's get back to the hotel. I'll show you what Wren and I found today, and you can check out that answering machine."

With a wink, the sun disappears, breaking the spell. Our moment, the one I could have used to tell him I'm falling for him, is over, and now...it's time to go back to reality.

I SCAN the room service menu. "What do you want?"

"They have a club sandwich or a steak?" Dax sits on the small couch in the main room, setting up his laptop, phone, and Kyle's notebooks in precise order. The vulnerability he displayed earlier is gone, replaced by determination and the hard exterior I suspect he's so used to, he doesn't even know it's there.

"Both. I'll order one of each. Medium-rare okay for the steak?"

Something clatters to the floor, and his Bluetooth earbud rolls out from under the low coffee table towards my bare toes. He stares at me, mouth slightly open, for a brief second. "It's perfect." Almost as an after thought, he says, "You're perfect," under his breath.

"I'm far from perfect, babe." The term of endearment slips out as I press the earbud into his hand. "But I like my steak medium-rare and my whiskey neat."

Wandering into the bedroom with the menu and the suite's cordless phone, I order the food, adding a bottle of red wine and a piece of flourless chocolate cake for dessert. They say it'll be forty-five minutes, and the tension in my shoulders is about to crack me in half. I can't concentrate like this.

With a quick glance at the deep tub, I smile, and I wonder... could I convince Dax to join me?

Challenge accepted.

It takes me only a couple of minutes to set the temperature and start the tub filling, and I strip off my blouse, black slacks, and camisole, tossing them in one of the drawers, before Dax's frame fills the bathroom doorway.

"We should—" I stop him by pressing my half-naked body to his, and he groans. "Evianna, fuck. Your body..." He traces my curves, his hands molding to my breasts, down to my waist, over my hips, until he cups my ass. "Perfect." Hooking his fingers into the waistband of my panties, he lowers them slowly. "And...*mine.*"

His deep, possessive timbre sends arousal flooding my core, and on his knees, Dax presses his lips to my mound, inhaling deeply. A low growl rumbles through his chest as he rises and backs me up against the counter. Feeling around behind me, he gives a quick, short nod, then wraps his arms around my thighs and lifts me, depositing my ass on the cold marble.

"Dax? What are you—?"

"Lean back and brace yourself, darlin'. I need to taste you." He sinks to his knees, guides my legs wide, and then his tongue is doing...*oh God*...things no one's ever done with such...skill.

A hint of stubble on his cheeks tickles my inner thighs, and I try not to wriggle, because holy shit, looking down at this gorgeous man on his knees, face buried in my pussy, is about the hottest thing I've ever seen.

When he sucks my clit lightly between his teeth, I whimper, my legs tightening around his head almost involuntarily. "More," I beg, and Dax reaches up and wraps his arms around my ass, easing me forward until I'm half-hanging off the counter. But I know I won't fall. He won't let me.

I've never felt more protected than I do in this moment. But then, I can't think at all as Dax slides two fingers inside me, his tongue continuing to trace rapid fire patterns around my most sensitive nub, and his grunts and appreciative moans taking me higher than I thought possible.

"I'm...oh God. Dax...I'm..."

His free arm bands around me tightly, and he scores his teeth over my clit, thrusting his fingers deep and twisting them to find my G-spot. My entire body implodes, and I can't breathe, can't see, can't hear anything but my own keening cries. He continues to drink me in until my entire body's spent, and then pushes to his feet with his arm still steadying me.

"I'll never get enough of you," he says, his voice rough, and I reach down to find his cock straining against his khakis.

Brushing my lips to his ear, I whisper, "Let me turn off the water, and then...we can take this to the bed."

"There'll be time for that...later. Get in the tub. I need to double-check the door locks, and then I'll join you."

"Dax—"

But he's already gone. Hanging my bra on the back of the door, I turn off the water and lower myself into the tub. "Oh, sweet heaven," I mutter as I rest my head against the warm porcelain and close my eyes. Between the hot water and the aftereffects of an amazing climax, I'm not sure I can move. But then I sense him, and when I force my heavy lids open, my breath stalls in my chest. He's naked, fully erect, and I lick my lips. "My God, Dax. You're..."

Dax's shoulders hunch, and he starts to turn away when I reach up and lightly touch his hip. "We need to get past this."

"Past what?" he says, his voice rough.

"Get in. There's plenty of room. I'm not having this conversation unless we're both on equal ground."

Carefully, Dax feels for the edge of the tub, and when he's across from me, the steam swirling around us, I wriggle closer, arranging myself so I'm seated between his legs, his length pressing against my ass. "Who hurt you?"

"I told you about Hell..."

"No. Who *hurt* you? After." Tipping my head back, I press a kiss to the side of his jaw. "Every time we share something...real... you shut down. Like you're sure I'm not going to understand. Or say something so horrible, you won't be able to unhear it. Someone hurt you."

"It wasn't...all her fault," he says with a heavy sigh. "I had too many demons."

"Tell me."

Dax slides his hands under my arms and scoots me forward an inch or two. I start to protest until his fingers dig into my shoulders, slowly working out the knots I've lived with for two days.

"Oh, God. Don't stop...but this doesn't get you off the hook. Tell me what happened."

"I'm...thirty-nine, Evianna. I don't think I told you that. Enlisted when I was twenty-three. Right after college. Served for ten years." He moves to my neck, and I let my head fall forward as he strokes up and down. "Right before I left for basic training, Lucy and I got married."

I stop breathing until Dax presses a kiss to my shoulder. "Trust works both ways, darlin'." As I relax again, he continues. "She was my college sweetheart. Seemed like the right thing to do. I did love her. And I think she loved me too. But, my deployment...put a lot of distance between us. And after I joined my ODA team, I couldn't tell her anything about my missions, where I was..."

Shifting slightly, Dax starts to dig his thumbs along the sides of my spine, and I lean forward, letting him work each knot, each bit of tension from my back and arms. "For most of the time we were missing, the army thought we were dead. They forced us to make a couple of videos the first month or two. But after that, when they locked us away in Hell, no one heard from us until three months before Ry broke out."

"What happened then?" I ask, trying to focus on his words even as my body wants to float away under his capable hands.

"Don't know. Someone got a signal out. A set of coordinates and the letters ODA. But that wasn't confirmation. Lucy...she did her best. Took a second job to pay for our mortgage, kept a candle burning most nights for me. But when we got out...fuck." Dax shudders, and I try to turn around, but he stops me and rests his chin against the curve of my neck. "Not yet, darlin'."

"When you got out...?"

"You spend fifteen months being treated like an animal—" his voice drops to a whisper, "—you become one. I was so angry. Scared. Had to adjust to a world where I wasn't tied up all the time, where I could eat when I needed to, not whenever they decided we'd starved enough. Shit, I couldn't even sleep in a bed for weeks unless I was doped up on painkillers. Even with all the pins in my leg and the metal brace, I managed to get myself onto the floor every fucking night."

He chuckles, a dry, mirthless laugh. "When Lucy showed up... end of my fourth day out, I think, the distance between us...she didn't know how to touch me. Hell, I didn't know how to be touched. And when I came home...six weeks later...we were strangers. She wanted to know what happened to me. I just wanted to forget it all. And back then...I thought I could."

The water's started to cool, but neither of us moves.

"We lasted three months after I came home. I don't blame her. I was an asshole most of the time. Angry. Scared. She tried...I think. I didn't until it was too late. I was too caught up in my own shit to see—" he snorts, "—or hear, I guess, how much I was hurting her. She wanted her husband back. And that man...he died in Hell."

"But..." I want to find this woman and tell her how stupid she was. Except...if she'd stayed, this amazing man wouldn't be here with me.

"Some people aren't meant for one another, darlin'. I changed. She didn't. I forgave her a long time ago. And she forgave me, too. We talk once a year or so. She remarried. Has two kids and her own yoga studio out in Framingham."

There's a knock at the outer door of the suite. "Room Service!" a female voice calls.

"I'll get it." Scrambling out of the tub, I reach for the fluffy white robe hanging on a wall hook.

"Evianna. Tell them to wait. Don't open the door without me." His command stops me in my tracks, and the reality of where we are—and why—hits me.

"O-okay," I stammer, then duck my head into the main room. "Just a minute, please."

By the time I get back to the bathroom, Dax has a towel wrapped around his waist. Water glistens all along his sculpted chest, and I wonder if he has any idea just how sexy he is—scars and all.

"There's a robe. Here." Handing it to him, I let my fingers rest on his for a breath longer than necessary. "I'm sorry about...Lucy. But...Dax?"

His eyes shimmer behind his glasses, and he presses his lips together in a thin line.

"I know who you are. And I'm here. With you. For as long as... for as long as you'll have me."

Another three raps on the door force us apart, and Dax shrugs into his robe, then takes my arm so I can lead him back into the main room. Before he opens the door, he tips my chin up so I can look into his pale blue eyes. "You're...my light, Evianna. I don't know how else to say it. You...chase some of the darkness away."

27

Evianna

I REARRANGE OUR FOOD, dividing up the sandwich and steak between us. Dax feels around the edges of his plate, and I stop with a wedge of club sandwich partway to my mouth. "Oh, shit. I'm sorry. The sandwich is at nine o'clock. Steak at three. Fries are on the plate between us. Um...two o'clock."

He swallows hard. "Thanks."

"You hate asking for help, don't you?"

Picking up the steak knife, he uses his fork to find the strip of meat, then starts cutting. "With something as simple as eating? Yeah. How many people do you know who can't manage to get food from their plate to their mouths?"

When I force the bite of sandwich down, I clear my throat. "My mom can't."

He freezes, then turns slowly to face me. Waiting.

"She has ALS. She's bedridden, can barely speak, and while she can still swallow—for now—most of her meals are through a feeding tube. When I visit her, I usually bring her a chocolate milkshake, and if I spoon feed her, she can manage a small amount of it."

"Fuck, Evianna. I'm sorry. I didn't know. She's...in Boston?"

I pour us both some wine, needing the distraction. "Yes. There's an excellent long-term care facility in Watertown. Close enough I can usually manage to see her every couple of days."

"You've been with me since Monday, darlin'. It's almost Friday. Won't she be worried?" Dax returns to slicing the steak, but his movements are more deliberate now. Calmer. And some of the anger I sensed when I described his plate has faded away.

"We email. She knows about Alfie's launch, and I promised her I'd see her this weekend." Risking a glance at Dax, I ball my hands into fists, unsure I want to hear his next response. "I can go in the evening. So Ronan can take me. Or Vasquez. If...you want..."

The knife clatters to the table, and Dax has my hands in his before I register the movement. "I can't protect you alone, Evianna. But there's no way in hell I'm letting you out of my sight —you know what I mean—until we know who's after you and stop them. And...if it's okay...I'd like to meet your mom. I...I'm with you too, darlin'. I should have said it before. I'm with you too."

Tears spring to my eyes, and I choke back a sob. "I didn't realize how much I needed..." Burying my face in the soft terry of his robe, I let myself break, knowing with him at my side, I can find a way to put myself back together.

HALF AN HOUR LATER, the dishes set outside the door, I plop the answering machine down in front of me. "All right, Kyle. Let's see just how much of a movie buff you are."

"Huh?" Dax furrows his brow, a stack of the notebook pages in his hand.

"*Sneakers* was like...*the* geeky movie of the 90s. Robert Redford, Sidney Poitier, David Strathairn, Dan Aykroyd, Ben Kingsley...oh, and River Phoenix. You never saw it?"

"No. We didn't have a lot of money when I was growing up. Movies...well...I saw *Jurassic Park* and *Independence Day*...that's about all until I was in college."

"Oh, my God. Okay, this is going to require some explanation."

"Can you put it on? The Fairmont has pay-per-view."

Now, it's my turn to stare at him, confused. "Dax...this might sound obvious, but...you're blind."

His deep laugh seems to surprise him, and he sinks against the back of the couch, takes off his glasses, and wipes his eyes. "Trust me, darlin'. I haven't forgotten. But...a lot of movies—especially older ones without all the fancy special effects—rely on enough dialogue that I can follow them pretty easily."

"Oh. I didn't..."

"Don't you dare apologize." Carding his fingers through my hair, he angles my head until he can claim my lips. "Though, I remember how much you enjoyed me stopping you."

"Enough," I say, my hands on his shoulders to force a little distance between us. "We have work to do, soldier. Tell me what you and Wren found in the notes while I hook my tablet up to the television. I have the movie on iTunes."

Dax tucks his Bluetooth into his ear, taps the rim of his glasses, and starts slowly flipping through the pages. "This one here," he says, passing it across the table as I sit back down and start the movie. "Wren says the numbers and abbreviations listed are likely subroutines and lines in the code where Kyle found anomalies."

"I recognize some of these function names. I wrote a lot of them. Or...at least the beginnings of them. When Noah hired me, he had three developers working for him. Barry, Sundar, and Raja. They'd just started Alfie's framework. Barely had an idea of where they were going or what they were doing. All Noah knew was that he wanted something that could compete with Siri. He wasn't thinking about a home unit, or car sensors, or personal security. Just the software."

On screen, Martin Brice watches as Cosmo's taken into custody, the scene fading to black, and Dax cocks his head. "So, Redford got away."

"Yep. And his buddy spent the next twenty years or so in prison. The good stuff happens in about twenty minutes." Turning over the answering machine, I find four small screws holding the housing in place. "Need my kit. What else is on those pages?"

"A lot of dates. Time stamps. Down to the second. A lot of them are crossed out. But a few of them, he circled. Then, in the corner of this page," Dax hands me a ragged-edged piece of paper that someone must have crumpled up at some point, "three words stood out to Wren."

Archo1 Remote Enabled?

My stomach clenches, dinner suddenly not sitting well. "That's the name of the computer in my office. But we don't allow remote work. We haven't since Noah agreed to turn Alfie into... what she is now. I brought in an intellectual property lawyer to advise us on how best to go about keeping Alfie a secret until we were ready to announce, and he came back with a whole twenty pages of recommendations and regulations. Including disabling all remote access to our servers."

"Most of the rest of these pages...they all look like gibberish to me. Wren says they're bits and pieces of code, so you might have more luck with them than we did."

Pouring us more wine, he cocks his head and listens. "Wait. Whistler's...*blind?*"

I laugh as I loosen the first of the four screws. "Yep. And he solves the whole damn thing. So stop selling yourself short, soldier." From my seated position on the floor, I nudge my shoulder into his knee. "Just listen to this next bit of dialogue while I get this housing off."

On screen, Robert Redford describes an office to the rest of his team, and before the blind Whistler character can make his big reveal, Dax mutters, "Son of a bitch. The guy has an answering service. He wouldn't need a machine."

"Bingo. Two points," I say. "I told you this movie was brilliant. Now, let's see what secrets this little machine has."

Setting the case aside, I frown. "It looks like your standard nineties answering machine. Except the tape's missing. And there are like sixteen more screws."

One by one, I dump the screws in my leather toolkit until I can pry the second layer of dark gray plastic off the machine's inner guts. "Jackpot."

"Uh, still blind here, darlin'. What is it?"

I press the USB stick into his palm. "Hopefully, some answers."

THE MOVIE'S LONG OVER. Dax fell asleep an hour ago, stretched out on the couch, snoring almost imperceptibly. His warmth at my back keeps me going, though the lines on the screen are starting to blur. I tuck Dax's Bluetooth in my ear, pair it with my phone, and call Wren.

"Evianna? What's up? It's really late there."

"Yeah, almost two," I say quietly as I pad into the unused, second bedroom and shut the door. "Kyle didn't delete all the copies of Alfie's code. He kept one. I found it on a thumb drive in the answering machine. It's eight months old, and the function names and line numbers he wrote down don't tell me anything. A few of them don't even exist."

"What about in the current code?" Wren asks with a yawn. I forget, she keeps Boston time, so it's late for her too.

"I won't know that until I get to the office tomorrow. I don't suppose you made any progress on that little trojan you were working on?" Now I'm yawning, and I press my hand to the thin wood door, silently promising myself—and Dax—that I'll try to turn my brain off and sleep soon.

"Almost done. I'll have it for you in an hour. Maybe less. But you're going to have to install it on the server manually. Can you do that? Without anyone noticing?"

With a sigh, I start to pace the room. "During the day? No. We have a network admin who practically lives in that room right now. But...we're having a party tomorrow night to celebrate code complete. I can do it then. As long as I'm quick, no one will miss me for five minutes."

"You're not going alone." Dax's sleep-roughened voice rumbles from behind me. "I don't trust your boss, and we don't know who else at your company is involved in this. Hell, I don't even want you going to work in the morning, but I know you have to."

In my ear, Wren chuckles. "Ry and Dax...they're a lot alike. Put him in his place, will you? But...also...be careful. And, Evianna?"

"What?" I say, glaring at Dax. I don't care that he can't see me. Maybe I'll throw in an eye roll for good measure.

"He's right. Let him protect you. Just...tell him to lose a little bit of the attitude while he does it."

Jerking the Bluetooth out of my ear as Wren hangs up, I stalk over to him. "We're...together, Dax. But that doesn't mean you can order me around."

"I'm not—fuck. Fine. I'm not above ordering you around if it keeps you alive. I almost lost you the other night, and then, I didn't feel...anywhere near what I feel for you right now. And it still almost destroyed me."

My resolve softens, and the emotion in his eyes—the same emotion written all over his face—washes over me. Neither of us have said the words. But I know right now, he feels them. As I let him wrap his arms around me, my heart swells a dozen sizes, making it hard to breathe, hard to even think.

I feel them too.

28

Dax

EVIANNA TAKES my hand and leads me across the suite to the master bedroom. "We had some unfinished business earlier," she says as she reaches for the belt of my robe.

"You needed to eat."

"I could have had an appetizer to hold me over." The robe lands on the bed, and then she's on her knees, delicate fingers wrapping around my dick and sending pure, raw need shooting through me.

"Darlin', I don't want..." And then the warmth of her mouth surrounds me, and I groan. "Fuck."

Her tongue runs along the bottom of my shaft, and I tangle my fingers in her hair. I've never been one for having a woman on her knees—not that I have a lot of experience one way or another. When she hums, my entire body electrifies, and my hips jerk against her.

Pulling back, my dick sliding from her lips with a little *pop*, I kneel next to her. "Not like this, darlin'. I want...I know I can't see you, but this...you're not a woman who should ever be on her knees."

She tastes of me when I kiss her, and shit, that makes me even harder. Yanking on the tie of her robe, I bare her breasts. They're heavy in my hands, and her nipples pebble when I roll them between my fingers. "Dax," she breathes as she tips her head back. "I need you inside me."

"Don't worry, darlin'. You'll get what you want..." Scooping her into my arms, I ease her onto the bed. "What do you like, Evianna? Tell me how you want to be touched."

Slowly, I run my hands up her thighs, and she shudders. I want to live in her scent, in this single moment when nothing matters but the two of us. One finger slides through her slick folds, and when I bring it to my lips, tasting her, I hear the hitch in her breath.

"Like that, do you?" In one fluid motion, I'm on top of her, kissing her, mingling our tastes, and her moans are the sweetest sound I've ever heard.

My dick aches trapped between us, and I'm so ready for her. I fumble for the drawer on the nightstand, desperately searching for the rest of the condoms I stowed there this morning, but Evianna beats me to them, snagging one of the foil packets, and ripping it open.

This time, I don't let her take charge. Stealing the condom from her, I take over, and when I nudge her entrance, she spreads her legs further, inviting me home.

"Go slow," she whispers. "You're...impressive, and...I want this to last."

"Yes, ma'am." Her tight channel grips me, and fuck. I want to see her eyes. Just once. Their color. To see her lids flutter. But then she rakes her nails lightly down my back, and there's only her. Only my desperate need to lose myself in her.

"More." Evianna grabs my ass, digging her fingers into the tight muscles, and I slide deeper.

"How much more?"

"All of you. Then...kiss me." Her husky tone drives me higher, and it's all I can do not to bury myself fully, slamming my hips into her like a man possessed.

But unlike last night, this is the time for slow and tender. After two gentle strokes, I pull out, slide down her body, and flick my tongue over her clit.

Evianna whimpers and clutches my arms. "Come back. Please."

"In a minute. You deserve to be worshipped, darlin'. And I plan on doing just that."

Her body does things to me I can't explain, don't ever remember feeling before. Another taste, another desperate cry, and I bury myself inside her, balls-deep. But again, I only give her enough to feel the gooseflesh under my hands as I wrap my arms around her.

Scoring my teeth over her nipple, I savor the way she arches her back, offering me her breasts like a banquet to feast on.

I want to taste her again, but she wraps her legs around my hips, and it's like I've come home after a lifetime of exile.

"You're mine, Dax Holloway," Evianna whispers against my neck. "And I want you to make me come."

I'll give her anything, and so I slant my lips over hers, thrusting harder as I slide my fingers into her hair. Angling her head, I trail kisses along her jaw, to her neck, and when her muscles start to quiver, I bite down, just enough to send her flying over the edge.

Her hoarse cries, the way she writhes under me...it's all too much, and I shout her name as I lose myself to this woman I think...I just might love.

Evianna

Dax's alarm blares a little after seven, and I roll over with a groan. He's not in bed, and from the other room, I think I hear...grunts and heavy breathing? When I peek out the door, my jaw drops open.

Shirtless, wearing only his briefs, his feet hooked under the couch, he works through a set of crunches, then rolls over for pushups.

"Like...what...you see?"

"Y-yes. Very much. How long have you been up?" I lean against the wall watching his muscles cord and flex with each precise movement.

"Not...long." After another ten pushups, he gets to his feet and stifles a wince. I rush to his side, but he holds up his hand. "I'm fine, darlin'. Just a headache. Happens sometimes. Grab my glasses for me? Left 'em by the bed."

By the time I press the glasses into his hand, he's cracked the seal on a bottle of water from the little mini-fridge and donned his robe. "Darn," I tease. "I kind of liked the briefs-only look."

Dax slides his arm around me, giving a little tug on the robe's belt. "If we had time, I'd take you back to bed. But..." His face sobers, and he squeezes his eyes shut for a moment, "Evianna, I know I'm an ass. It's part of my training. We have it drilled into us, every single fucking day, that if we aren't on top of our game, people die."

Frowning, I wrap my fingers around the robe's lapel. "But you work as a team, right? And you have to trust them."

"Implicitly."

"I'm part of your team, Dax. I don't have your training. I've never shot a gun. Never killed anyone. Never had my life threatened—until this past week. The most dangerous thing I've ever done is slap an old boss when he tried to feel me up late at night during a major network upgrade. I was twenty-three and scared out of my mind. Or so I thought. That was nothing compared to the other night." With a hard swallow, I continue. "But I know my job. Alfie's code. What she can...and can't do. I know my office. My team...well...most of them. You can't just keep me hidden and hope this goes away. You need me."

Dax brushes a thick lock of hair away from my face. "I know I need you. But I also need you to be safe. And if I can't touch you or hear you, I can't protect you. Do you understand how hard that is for me?"

"I...I think so. Just...talk to me, okay? We'll both go to the server room, but you have to do exactly what I say. I know where the security cameras are, and I can get us in and out quickly. It'd be easier if I were alone, but we'll handle it. Together."

His gentle kiss reassures me. We can make this work. Tonight's little adventure...and us.

———

TWO BLOCKS FROM MY OFFICE, Dax's phone announces, "Call from: Ford."

Dax scrambles to tap his Bluetooth, and when the call connects, his voice is strained. "Ford, where are you?"

I touch his arm, offering whatever silent support I can. "Trevor have any ideas?" he asks.

"We're here, Evianna. I can walk you to the elevator," Clive says.

I don't want to leave Dax. Not when he looks like his world is about to end. Leaning in, I whisper, "Call me when you can," and he nods, then grabs my hand as I'm about to get out of the car.

"Evianna? Be careful. I...I need you safe."

As I shut the door, Dax slams his fist against the seat in front of him. "Goddammit, Ford. What the fuck were you thinking?"

Clive cringes as we head for the building. "That's...not good.

Boss needs to hire a few more guns. Sounds like Ford could use 'em."

"Guns?" My voice isn't completely steady, but I glance over at the sandy-haired man with the easy smile next to me.

"Dax is Special Forces. Trevor is former CIA. I did a stint for the FBI, but I'm also a former Army Ranger. Ford...he's a marine. Ella was army, then a cop until she was shot in the line of duty. We're all officers. Our job is intelligence. A few years ago, Dax brought in a couple of hired guns—former enlisted guys who couldn't plan worth shit, but who could fight like nobody's business. But...they didn't work out. We didn't have enough work for them. But now...I think we might."

Clive punches the button for the elevator and waits until I'm inside the car before slapping his hand on the door to hold it open. "Remember what he said. No leaving today. I'll take him to our office, then I've got to check on my mom. I'll be back here by noon. You need *anything,* you call him."

"I promise. I'll be careful, Clive. And...thanks."

UNLIKE THE UNBRIDLED chaos of yesterday, this morning, there's an air of celebration infusing every conversation, every movement. As I drop my briefcase behind my desk, Noah knocks on my door. "We've been waiting for you."

My cheeks heat, and I fight not to stare down at my shoes. "I wanted to be in by seven, but—"

"Relax, Evianna. That wasn't a criticism. Come out to the bullpen." He extends his arm, like he's planning on escorting me personally, and my shoulders stiffen.

"I'll be right there. Just need to send one email." I don't, but at least it's an excuse Noah will believe. "Two minutes. Max."

"Any longer and I'm coming back for you," he teases.

Prick. After I lock my tablet in my file cabinet—I transferred bits and pieces of the old code from the USB drive onto the device early this morning—I smooth my hands down my skirt and steel myself for whatever public display of sexism Noah has planned.

With a quick glance at my phone and a flash of disappointment that Dax hasn't messaged me yet, I head out to the bullpen.

"There she is!" Noah says. Barry stands at his side, with Priya behind them both. "Evianna, you've been the heart and soul of this project since I hired you three years ago. You've given up nights and weekends, motivated the team, and helped us negotiate with some of our most influential partners. So, when Barry came to me half an hour ago with a bit of news, I told him we had to wait until you were in."

Great. Another subtle little dig? He couldn't just leave that part out?

"Barry?" Noah says with a flourish of his hand.

Our lead developer steps forward and hands me his tablet. "Take a look, boss."

Bugs: 0

Service Status: Up

Performance: Green

My heart crashes against my ribcage. I knew we were close. Hell, I knew we'd see this before the day was up. But it's only 9:15 a.m. Glancing around at the team, I see the exhaustion on their faces. The dark circles. The bloodshot eyes. But I see something else, too.

Pride. Relief. A sense of accomplishment no one can ever take away from them.

Scrolling through our bug list, I note the times each fix was checked in: 3:00 a.m., 4:23 a.m., 6:55 a.m. Priya fixed the last bug only half an hour ago. Five bugs wait for my sign-off, and I quickly scan each one before entering my personal digital signature code.

Months ago, when we announced our launch date, Kyle

found an old stoplight and repurposed it as our status board. It's been yellow for the past seven weeks. But as I sign off on the last code change, it flips to green, and the room explodes in cheers.

My smile is only tempered slightly by my fears. Whatever is going on with Alfie...whoever is trying to kill me...we did this. We built something wonderful. Something with the potential to help so many people.

Holding up my hand to try to quiet the team, I take a deep breath, hoping my voice won't crack. Above all, right now, I need to show strength. Not emotion. Well, not too much emotion.

"I officially declare Alfie...code complete," I say, straightening my shoulders and standing up a little taller. "She's ready to meet her public on Monday. Congratulations, everyone. I have never met a more talented, passionate, and dedicated group of people anywhere, and it's an honor to work with each and every one of you."

A tear burns the corner of my eye, and I blink hard to keep it at bay. "Alfie is going to change the world. Now let's get her packaged up with a pretty little compiler bow and get ready to celebrate tonight!"

Raising Barry's tablet in the air to a chorus of applause, "woohoos," and "fuck, yeahs," I pray whatever Wren's trojan lets me see doesn't ruin everything.

29

Evianna

BACK IN MY OFFICE, I pull up my email.

Hi Mom, I'm sorry I haven't been by this week. But we signed off on Alfie this morning! It's been a hard few days. Long hours, and some stuff I'll tell you about this weekend, in person. Would it be okay if I brought someone with me when I come on Saturday? He's...well, he's special. Love you!

It's early enough, she's probably still caught up in her morning news shows, so I tamp down my nerves over the inevitable questions she'll have about Dax. How do I explain how quickly the relationship has progressed without going into the whole "someone's out to kill me" bit?

The burner phone buzzes in my briefcase, and one bit of the tension pressing down on my shoulders eases slightly.

Ford's okay. Just...being reckless. I had to make some calls to the Turkish Embassy to vouch for them. He'll head into Turkmenistan tomorrow. Everything okay there?

I can't imagine what Ford's going through. Not knowing where his old girlfriend is, scared she's being abused...tortured.

My thoughts turn to Dax, and what he went through, and suddenly, I understand why he was *so* insistent he come with me tonight. Because he knows what it's like.

I'm about to reply when my mom emails me back.

Congratulations, sweetheart! I am so proud of you. I want to meet your special man. But are you sure you can come tomorrow? The man from your office who brought me flowers today said you might be too busy to see me for a few more days.

The man from my office? Why would anyone from my office send my mother flowers? Most of them...oh my God.

Mom, what did he look like?

I don't wait for her to answer before I lunge for my file cabinet, grab my tablet and laptop, and throw both into my briefcase. They know where my mother is, and if they can get to her...

Racing out of my office, I almost run right into Barry, but manage to side-step him just in time.

"Evianna? Where are you going? We're all ordering lobster rolls from the Chop House and Noah went out to grab some Champagne."

"Minor emergency at the house. Plumbing. I won't be long, but if I don't run home, the entire basement is going to be a total loss. Start without me!" I don't know where I pull that excuse from, but it seems to work, because he doesn't follow me or protest.

In the elevator, I call Dax. "They know where my mom is," I blurt out before he can even say hello. "I can't...I have to—"

"Evianna, stop and listen to me. You are *not* to leave your office alone. Do you understand?"

"Please," I beg as the elevator doors open and I stumble into the lobby. "I can't just do nothing."

"Not suggesting that. I can be there in under ten minutes. Where are you right now?" Despite the strain in his voice, just talking to him helps calm me, and I force myself to take a deep breath.

"Lobby."

"Wait there. Call the care facility and tell them you're coming. They're not to let anyone in to see your mother until you get there, and give them a password. I'm walking out of my office right now, and I'll text Clive, then call Wren and figure out what we can do to keep your mother safe. Do you understand?"

Swiping at the tear racing down my cheek, I stammer, "Y-yes. Hurry."

"I will, darlin'."

Five minutes later, I hang up with Watertown Longterm Care and Comfort, and find an email from Mom.

He was tall with black hair. Looked kind of like that actor...Johnny Depp? Smelled like a chimney. You should tell him to quit smoking.

Oh, shit.

The tapping of Dax's cane on the marble floors is the only thing keeping me sane, and I rush over to him, skidding to a halt a half second before I run right into him. But he senses me, or hears me, or something, because he wraps his arms around me. "Clive's three minutes away, and Wren's in my ear working on a solution for your mom right now."

"It's...Louie," I manage. "Mom described him."

Dax stiffens. "Wren? Did you catch that?" I can't hear her response, but she must have said yes, because he quickly continues, "I'll have Clive make the call as soon as he gets here. Keep working your magic. Call me back when you have something."

A horn sounds from the street. "Clive," I say, and Dax has me out the door and into the car in under a minute. It'll be okay. It has to be. Otherwise, what should be the best day of my life could turn into the worst. *I'm coming, Mom.*

I just hope we're fast enough.

TWENTY MINUTES LATER, Clive slams on the brakes, the SUV

screeches to a halt outside Watertown Longterm Care and Comfort, and I'm out of the car before Dax can even unfold his cane. "Evianna, wait," he snaps as he struggles to navigate the uneven curb.

"Shit. I'm sorry," I whisper as I take his arm and lead him inside.

He angles his head so his lips brush my ear. "You didn't do anything wrong, darlin'. I just need you to stay close."

Clive follows, his hand on his hip under his jacket. I shudder as I realize he probably has a gun.

"Can I help you?" a sweet, older woman asks as we approach the front desk.

"Y-yes. I'm Evianna Archer, and I called half an hour ago. I spoke with a Beatrice Nix. Is she here?"

"Of course. I'll get her right away."

As the woman shuffles off, Dax links our fingers and holds tight. "Once she authenticates you," he says, "let me do the talking."

"Ms. Archer? I'm Beatrice." Her gaze flicks to Dax and then Clive, and she furrows her brows. "Will you come with me, please? We can talk in my office."

I nod, but when Dax steps forward with me, Beatrice holds up her hand. "Only family members are allowed in the back, gentlemen. I'm sorry."

A low growl rumbles in Dax's throat, and I drop his hand, grab Beatrice's arm, and whisper, "Nutella. Please. They're with me..."

The password settles her, and she angles her head towards the hall. "Fine. This way."

Dax turns to Clive. "Stay here. No one comes in or out unless you vet them. Wren sent you the picture?"

"Affirmative." He takes position by the front door, his hand resting on something black and decidedly gun-like at his hip.

Beatrice's office is small, decorated with pictures of babies, teenagers, and adults. All who bear a striking resemblance to her. "Ms. Archer, this is a safe facility. Can you tell me why you think your mother is in danger?"

Dax shuts the door behind us. "Ms. Nix, I'm Dax Holloway with Second Sight Security Services." Digging into his pocket, he withdraws a small leather wallet and passes it to the woman.

"A private investigator? But...you're blind."

"I'm quite aware of that, Ms. Nix. I'm also aware you're sixty-two-years-old, have three children, four grandchildren, and a dog named Chester. Now can we table the discussion of my blindness and talk about the safety of Ms. Archer's mother?"

Anger and frustration radiate off Dax's stiff frame, and if he squeezes my hand any harder, I'm worried he'll break one of my fingers. But his little speech does the trick, as Beatrice takes a step back and stares down at her desk.

"My apologies, Mr. Holloway. But Mrs. Archer isn't in any danger."

"She had a visitor this morning," I say. "He brought her flowers, claimed to be from my company. We didn't send anyone."

Beatrice sits, taps a few keys on her computer, and nods. "Yes. the gentleman had identification. Benjamin Denik. He stayed for ten minutes, and your mother was quite happy with the flowers."

"There's no one working for Beacon Hill Technologies named Benjamin Denik," I protest. "He lied to you."

Dax gives my hand a gentle tug, and I stop, turning towards him. "We have to—"

"Ms. Nix, the man you admitted this morning is a professional hitman. He tried to kill Evianna several nights ago. She's been under Second Sight's protection ever since. Mrs. Archer isn't safe here, and unless she's moved, immediately, neither are any of your other patients or your staff."

Dax's phone buzzes, and he taps his Bluetooth. "Excuse me for a moment," he says. "Wren? Tell me you have a solution."

He listens for a minute while Beatrice stares, her cheeks at least three shades paler than they were when we walked in here. When he hangs up the call, he nods. "Two unmarked, specially outfitted transport vans will be here in twenty minutes. They will pull up to your loading dock, side-by-side. We need to have Mrs. Archer ready to go by the time they show up. There will be no paperwork, no record of this transfer. Evianna will continue to pay your bill for the next ten days, or until we can guarantee Mrs. Archer's safety and return her to your care. Do you understand?"

Holy shit. I think I just met Sergeant Holloway, Green Beret.

Beatrice nods, then, when I arch a brow at her, adds, "Of course, Mr. Holloway."

"How DID you do all of that so quickly?" I ask as I lead Dax towards my mother's room.

"A lot of people owe me favors." He offers me a half-smile. "And you can accomplish just about anything with enough money."

"Oh God. Tell me what I need to send you, I'll—"

"Nothing, darlin'. It's done."

I don't know whether to yell at him or hug him. "You're not paying for all of this. No."

Dax stops, curls his arm around my back, and pushes me against the wall. "You're mine, Evianna. And I protect what's mine. No matter the cost."

His words send a little thrill through me, but I still won't let him pay for this whole damn thing. "We'll talk about this...later," I say, then kiss him, the feel of his lips and the taste of him— coffee and a hint of toothpaste—settling me and warming me down to my core. "Mom's room is right here."

I knock twice, and then step through the door. "Hi, Mom."

She smiles, her eyes lighting up, though one side of her mouth ends up higher than the other. *"What are you doing here?"*

The mechanical voice doesn't sound anything like her, but I can still hear her. It's in the way her eyes move, her brows, her lips.

"Mom," I approach the bed, "there's something we have to talk about. And it's scary and complicated, but you have to trust me."

"Are you in trouble? Who is that?"

Dax steps forward, but he doesn't take my hand. "Mrs. Archer, my name is Dax Holloway. I'm a private investigator. Please don't say anything else until I give you the okay." He pulls a small black plastic box from his pocket, flips the switch, and waits until the thing beeps twice. "All right. If there are any bugs in this room, they're jammed now."

"Bugs?" The word escapes on a squeak. "You really think—?"

"No clue, darlin'. But he was in this room. If I were trying to get a bead on you, I'd be listening."

"Evianna, what is going on? Tell me."

If Mom were still mobile, she'd probably be shaking me right now. With a sigh, I ease a hip onto the edge of her bed. "Dax? Can you...um...come closer?"

His cane slides across the linoleum until it hits the bed, and I take his hand. "Mom, this is the man I told you about. Dax is... protecting me." Glancing up at him, I see the conflict in his eyes behind his glasses. The fear. "And we're involved. Dating."

"You're in danger. Why?"

As quickly as I can, I give her the highlights, leaving out the part where the man who brought her a large spray of red, white, and yellow daisies threatened to kill me. "Dax arranged to have you moved to another facility for a few days. Just until his people can find the guy."

Mom fixes Dax with a hard stare. *"Young man, give me one reason why I should trust you."*

Dax wraps his arm around my shoulders. "I'm Special Forces, ma'am. Retired. Injured in the line of duty, awarded the Medal of

Honor, a Purple Heart, and a Silver Star. The United States Special Forces fight for those who can't fight for themselves. We don't lie, cheat, or steal, and we absolutely never leave one of our own behind. Evianna is...mine. I would die before I let anyone hurt her."

I don't breathe. I'm not sure I can. To hear my soldier, the man I'm falling for, say he'd die for me...the absolute certainty in his voice, the strength of his arm around me... I wish I could tell him how I feel. But now isn't the time.

Mom moves the little joystick on under her hand, all while the silence in the room turns into a physical weight.

"What are you waiting for, then? Let's go."

30

Dax

EVIANNA'S VOICE carries an undertone of fear as she tells her mother about signing off on Alfie's code this morning and the upcoming party. I stay close but out of the way as the nurse and three EMTs Wren hired unhook Olivia Archer from the tubes, wires, and sensors that help her stay alive and load her into an unmarked ambulance.

We climb into the back with her, and once we're belted in, I reach for Evianna's hand, offering her what little reassurance I can. "The second ambulance is a decoy, darlin'. It'll go off first, lights and sirens, then we'll follow silently. After ten minutes, our lights will come on. And we'll weave through the city for at least half an hour to make sure we're not being followed."

"You have done this before," Olivia says.

"For almost ten years, this was my job, ma'am."

Evianna's knee bounces against mine until her mother's computerized voice breaks the silence.

"You love my daughter. Call me Olivia."

"M-Mom!"

Pressing my lips to Evianna's temple, I whisper in her ear, "It's all right, darlin'." Turning my focus to her mother, I clear my throat. "Olivia, are you comfortable enough?"

"You don't worry about me. You keep my daughter safe."

BY THE TIME we return to the Fairmont, it's after four, and we're both on edge. Evianna's been on and off her phone for the past two hours, keeping in touch with Beacon Hill, approving the final version of Alfie's code, and making excuses—all related to a massive water leak in her basement.

Ella dropped off a garment bag and small duffel with the concierge a few hours ago, and when we're back in our room, Evianna lays the bags on the bed. "What is all of this—?"

"Precautions." Patting the bed, I find a clear spot, sit, and pull the duffel bag closer. Everything's coded for me, little Braille dots embossed on the tag for each canvas pouch. "Comms," I say as I open a black plastic case the size of my palm.

"They're so small."

"Wear your hair down tonight. It should cover the earbud. We'll be on with Wren the whole time. She'll monitor things from the camera in my glasses, and will be able to walk you through anything you need to get her spyware installed."

"And the rest of this stuff?"

I don't want her to see the rest of my kit, but I also can't lie to her. I won't. "I don't carry a gun, Evianna. With enough light and the right contrast, I might be able to hit someone center mass, but it's too dangerous. That doesn't mean I can't defend myself. Let's see what Ella brought us to wear."

As Evianna unzips the garment bag, I pull out my modified tactical vest. Running my fingers over the thin canvas, memories assault me. Ryker barking orders. Ripper shouting for air support, Gose tying a tourniquet around Hab's leg. But then the images shift. The first time I put on that Green Beret and patch. The day I walked into the barracks to find my assignment: ODA 5150. Ry's easy smile and strong handshake when he welcomed me to the team.

"Dax? You're...somewhere else, aren't you?" Her soft voice pulls me from the past, and I reach out, finding her cool fingers and giving them a squeeze.

"Right here with you, darlin'. Is there a dress shirt in there for me?" I ask.

"Yes. A black one."

"Makes the vest less visible." With a light brush of my lips to her knuckles, I take the shirt from her, strip off my long-sleeved Henley, and shrug into the pressed shirt. The vest is next, and as I secure the buttons, I stand up a little straighter. I'm still capable. Still a soldier. But also, still...blind.

"Wow." Evianna slides a hand down my arm, and I realize I can sense her coming. Feel her warmth, pick up on the subtle scent of freesia from her perfume. "You clean up nicely."

I wish I could return the compliment. "What are you wearing?"

"Black pants, black heels, and a gold tank. And Ella brought me a black beaded purse." She fiddles with something on the bed for a moment, then gasps. "With two USB drives."

"Wren's program. One for each of us...as backup." Holding out my hand, I accept the little plastic and metal data drive, and tuck it into an inner zippered pocket of the vest.

I'd give anything to avoid the next few minutes, to be able to keep the potential for danger from this woman I think I love, but she's right. We're a team, and she has to know what we could be up against.

"Sit down, darlin'. I need to explain a few things."

As she moves, the light hits her gold tank, and I can see a hint of the shimmer. For the thousandth time, the longing ache blooms in my chest. To be able to see her. Just once. To have her image in my head, know what she looks like when we kiss. When I have her naked against me.

Reaching into the duffel bag, I pull out a zippered, leather folio, set it on the nightstand, and open it. "You need to know what I'm carrying, and where, so if anything happens, you're not defenseless. Understand?"

"Okay. Do you really think—?"

"I didn't think you were in danger at your house the other night. Or that they'd come after your mother—though I should have anticipated that one." With a small shake of my head, I feel for the folding blade. "See the metal crescent here on the handle? Press it to extend the blade. It'll snap, so be careful. Press it again to collapse the knife. Right side pocket."

"Got it," she whispers as I tuck the knife away.

"Spare comm units in the left side pocket." Holding up the tiny, plastic case, I wait for her confirmation, then stow that as well.

"This is important, darlin'." I take off my belt, roll it up and tuck it back in the duffel, and then grab the one from the folio's inner pocket. Twisting the buckle, I wait for her reaction.

"Oh, my God. Who comes up with this stuff?" she asks as she reaches out to touch the tiny set of lock picks.

"Trevor, mostly. Ten years with the CIA. The man's...scary." After I've secured my belt, I add a metal window punch, a credit card tool with a tiny screwdriver, GPS chip, and glass cutter, and a second Bluetooth earbud to the vest.

All the while, Evianna fidgets with the duvet, and when I'm satisfied everything's in its place, I sink down next to her and take her hands. "Evianna, when we get to the party, you have to be my eyes. See what I can't. Watch everyone. If you see anything suspicious, tell me immediately. Someone at this party tonight wants you dead. But they also want something from you first. So don't go anywhere without me. Not even the bathroom. Understand?"

"Yes." Her voice cracks, and she rests her head on my shoulder. The soft silk of her hair brushes my cheek. "I'm...this was supposed to be the day of my dreams," she whispers. "The day to celebrate everything I've worked so hard for the past few years. And now..."

"I know, darlin'. But I'm with you. And we're going to find out who's after you and stop them. I promise."

31

Dax

CLIVE OPENS the door of the Town Car at the curb. "I'll park the car around back and wait. There's a service entrance I can get through in under a minute if you get into trouble, and I'm on comms."

I hold out my hand to help Evianna up, then tuck her against my right side. "As soon as we get into the building, darlin', we'll do a comm check. The mic is on all the time. So don't fiddle with your ear, don't touch it to make sure it's still there. Got it?"

"Uh huh."

She's been so quiet since we left the hotel, I'm worried. But we have to go through with this—and it has to be tonight. "You'll be fine. I'll be by your side the whole time."

Clive clears his throat. "Just got a text from the two hired muscle outside your mom's room. Everything's been quiet, and your mom's watching *Law & Order*."

With a shudder, some of the tension leaves Evianna's body. "Oh, thank God. And they'll stay there?"

"She'll have round-the-clock protection until this is over," I say. "These guys are ex-Israeli military. Meanest fuckers on the planet—unless you're under their protection."

With a chuckle, Clive agrees. "Eitan already texted Yosef to bring your mother a chocolate milkshake when he comes on duty."

Evianna's delicate snort settles me, as does the relief I hear in her voice. "Mom always has been persuasive."

"Ready, darlin'? The sooner we get this over with," I lower my voice and brush my lips to her ear, "the sooner we can get back to the hotel."

"Hey!" Wren's voice says in my ear. "Your comms are hot, boss."

"Shit. Sorry, Wren." Unfolding my cane, I feel out a semi-circle in front of me. Clear. "We're going in now."

WHEN WE STEP off the elevator, one floor above Evianna's offices, the heavy bass beat of the music sets my nerves on edge. "Wren, can you hear us over this shit?" I murmur as I angle my head towards Evianna's.

"Loud and clear, boss."

"Evianna!" a booming voice calls from a few feet away. "We were getting worried!" Her boss, Noah, claps me on the shoulder, and I jerk back. "Dax, was it? It's Noah. Evianna's boss."

His voice is unnaturally loud, even with the volume of the music in the room, and I grit my teeth. "I'm aware, *Noah*. Next time you want to say hello, do it with your voice, not your hand. And I can hear you just fine."

"Boss," Wren says in my ear, "calm down. You're supposed to be playing nice."

Evianna angles her body between me and Noah. "Plumbers are notoriously late, Noah. I had to wait almost two hours for the guy to show up. My basement's a mess."

"Well, you're here now. Have some champagne. You too, Dax."

"In a few minutes," Evianna says. "Ulysses and Cyndi did a great job. You'd never know this place was empty three days ago."

"Absolutely not." The words come a little slower, a little softer, almost like he's distracted. "I should mingle," he says and brushes past me.

The scent of his cologne wafts over me, and I stiffen. I know where I've smelled it before. Outside Kyle's apartment. But...for all I know, one of his neighbors might use the same one. "I don't like that guy," I grumble as Evianna wraps her arm around my waist.

"He's a jerk, but I think he's harmless. He hired me. Paid for all my moving expenses from San Francisco to Boston...hell, he bought extra insurance coverage when Mom was diagnosed so I could get her into a better facility." Evianna guides me across the room, towards bright lights that make my eyes hurt.

"What's in front of us, darlin'?" Turning towards her, I adjust my glasses, hoping to stave off my headache until the end of the party. I'm no use to anyone if I can't concentrate.

"The bar. Well...one of them."

"And a disco ball? Or strobe lights?"

Evianna picks up on the strain in my voice and locks her arm through mine. "Let's go to the other one. Across the room. Barry's over there. We've butted heads off and on this whole project. He's one of three employees Noah hired before me. Well, the only one left."

"Who were the others?" I keep my eyes mostly closed as she leads me across the large space.

"Sundar and Raja. I don't remember their last names anymore. Sundar took a job at Google not long after I came on board, and Raja moved back to India after a family emergency."

We have to stop four times before we reach the bar, and Evianna introduces me to some of the developers who worked on

Alfie's code. Most are already tipsy, but friendly, and I shake hands, try to make jokes, and listen to Wren and Evianna's running commentary about the layout of the room.

High-top tables are spread around the edges of the space, but there's a dance floor in the center, and a long table off to the left with a very large sheet cake surrounded by gift bags.

The *pop* of the Champagne bottle makes Evianna flinch, and I give her hand a squeeze. "Relax, darlin'. We should get some food, see if we can find a free table in the back. Let people get used to us standing in one spot. Then, we'll leave our glasses and plates, maybe even your purse. Like we're coming right back."

She presses a glass into my hand, and when we find a table, I nuzzle her neck. "Noah rubs me the wrong way. And Priya is nervous about something. Lauren idolizes you, and Barry is drunk off his ass."

"I hired Priya. She's the sweetest woman you'd ever want to meet," Evianna replies. "And I'm pretty sure Barry was drunk at 10:00 a.m."

"Is anyone watching us right now? Be my eyes, darlin'. Check the whole room. Slowly. Try not to be obvious."

"Noah's chatting with Cyndi, his assistant. Barry and Walt are at the bar with the bright lights getting more beer. Priya and Alice are laughing over something." She goes around the entire room, and I commit every detail to memory. In my ear, Wren asks the occasional question—last names, descriptions, how long they've been working at Beacon Hill.

For two hours, we try to slip away, but every time, one of Evianna's coworkers comes up and engages her in conversation. I stick to our agreed upon story—I own a think tank a few blocks away, and we met at a single's mixer three weeks ago.

Nursing my glass of Champagne, I wish I had something stronger. Having to wait this long sets my nerves on edge, and if we don't get out of here soon, we're going to lose our chance.

"Incoming," Wren says. She's watching the entire party

through the small camera in my glasses, and two seconds later, Noah comes up to us.

"Evianna, we shouldn't keep the troops waiting any longer," he says. "You don't mind, do you Dax? If I take your lovely date away from you for a few minutes? We only have the room until midnight, and we can't cut the cake until after Evianna gives her speech."

"Go, darlin'. I'll be right here, watching you." I grab her around the waist and haul her against me, slanting my lips over hers in a searing kiss. Just before I pull away, I score my teeth along the shell of her ear and whisper, "If I leave right now, he won't notice I'm gone. I can be back before you're done with your speech."

Her fingers tighten on my arms, and I can feel her panic. "I don't like it either. But you're in a room full of people. With Wren in your ear."

She's pulled away from me, and I want to punch her boss in the face. Or maybe the balls. But as her warmth disappears from my side, she calls out, "I won't be long, baby. If you can...get me another drink while I'm up there?"

"Break a leg," I reply. As I turn, I murmur, "Good job, darlin'. Gives me an excuse to walk away. And you'll hear me the whole time."

"Wren? I need you." My cane sweeps across the floor until I reach the elevator, and I feel around for the call button.

"Right here, boss. Are you sure this is a good idea?"

"No. It's a terrible idea. But it's been hours. I want to get Evianna the fuck out of here." Finding the button for the fifth floor, I jab it with more force than necessary, then wince. "You're going to have to guide me. I have no idea what I'm doing here."

"I have her passwords. I can get you through this." Wren's

voice holds an odd note, nerves, I think. Or maybe I'm projecting. The idea of leaving Evianna in a room with someone who wants to kill her makes my skin crawl, but I can hear her congratulating her team—though Wren's turned down her volume a bit to avoid distractions.

The elevator doors slide open with a *ding*, and I take two steps forward, then turn around in a slow circle, giving Wren a 360-degree view of the room.

"Okay. You're good to go. No one here. Head to your right, approximately thirty feet, and there's a door with an electronic keypad lock."

When my cane finds the door, Wren blows out a breath over comms. "Okay. Enter seven-six-two-five-nine-one."

The door beeps, and after a metallic *thunk*, I'm in.

"The server you want is all the way in the back. Be careful. It's kind of a maze in there. Stick to the far left wall, and watch the cane."

Evianna announces Barry's promotion as I reach the back corner of the room, and in my ear, cheers and applause break out all around her. Noah's voice cuts through the din, and his condescending tone bleeds through comms.

"I really don't like that guy," Wren says. "But he's a flippin' boyscout. Not even a parking ticket."

"Wren, focus. Where am I going next?"

"Three o'clock. Take five steps in that direction, then you'll find a tall, metal server rack. The keyboard is on a tray approximately belt-high."

She walks me through entering the password and navigating to the right directory, though the process is painfully slow, and by the time she tells me to take the USB drive out of my pocket, I'm ready to beat my head against the wall.

"The slot for the drive is on the front of the server. Seven o'clock. No...lower," she says when I try, and fail, to find it.

"That's not seven o'clock. That's six-thirty."

"Snack cakes, Dax. I'm doing the best I can. Ry's been at the warehouse training all damn day, I have both you and Evianna in my ear, and I'm walking a blind man through how to break into a secure server."

"I'm sorry. I'm just...on edge. I need to get back to Evianna." Finding the slot, I plug in the drive and breathe a sigh of relief.

"She's fine. Now type exactly what I say."

In less than five minutes, the trojan is running, and I grab the little USB drive, tuck it back into my pocket, and head for the door. "Wren, tell Clive we'll be on our way out in three minutes. And turn up Evianna's comms again."

"Got it, boss," Wren says as I close the door to the server room behind me.

But a second later, the comms go silent. "Wren?"

Pain explodes along the back of my head, and I fall to my knees. Another blow catches me in the ear, and my entire world fades into nothing.

32

Evianna

I CAN'T MAKE my way out of the crowd surrounding us, and the music's so loud, Dax and Wren have only been a low murmur in my ear for the past fifteen minutes.

Noah presses a glass of Champagne into my hand, then raises his own glass, and half a dozen developers, including a very drunk Barry, do the same.

"To Beacon Hill and Alfie. May this be the first of many celebrations we have together," Noah says, and I force down a single sip of the drink while scanning the room for Dax.

"Excuse me for just a minute," I say, finally fighting my way out of the circle of people. "I need to grab a bottle of water."

Noah tries to stop me, but I'm just quick enough, and hurry towards the bar. "Dax? Wren? What's going on?"

I can't hear anything, and my heart threatens to beat right out of my chest. "Wren?" Snagging my purse from the table, I pull out my cell phone, but then a heavy arm drapes around my shoulders.

"Noah, shit. Don't *do* that," I protest, but he tightens his grip, and then I feel a pinch along my side. "Get your fucking hands off me."

But when I turn to him, his face blurs slightly, and his voice is muffled, like he's on a bad cell connection. "Come with me, Evianna. Time to get some air," he says.

Air? I don't need air. I need Dax. But my lips don't want to move, and he leads me towards the stairs.

What...did you...do...? My head lolls to the side, and I think I can see Barry staring after us. "N...oah," I manage. "I..."

"Be quiet. You've had too much to drink, and you need to sit down. It's nice and cool in the stairwell. You'll feel better in just a couple of minutes."

No...I won't...

I try to unlock my phone, but my fingers don't want to type in the code, and then Noah snatches it out of my hand. As the gray metal door to the stairs clicks open and we spill out onto the landing, I stumble, losing one of my shoes. It makes a loud, clanging sound as it bounces all the way to the next landing, and I watch it fall, almost in slow motion. I can't keep my eyes open. It won't hurt to sleep a while. Alfie's done. Released to the world. But Dax... Where's Dax?

Have...to...find...him...

I'm moving. Floating. And then...I'm not.

Dax

I can't feel my fingers. My shoulders burn. Where am I? Oh fuck. It's dark...only a dull reddish glow from somewhere above me. Jerking my hands, I start to hyperventilate. No. Not this. Anything but this. My wrists are bound behind me, zip ties, I think. My ankles too.

A low moan escapes my throat, one I almost don't recognize,

except my cheek scrapes against the cold cement floor as my entire body starts to shake, and the sound changes pitch.

I can't... this... no. Fuck, no. Struggling against the restraints, I rub my wrists raw, and the scent of blood burns my nose. My blood.

I'm cold. Back in Hell. Alone. "Ry..." I croak, my throat tight. "Help...me."

As I try to sit up, my head spins, and then I'm down again, my temple smacking against concrete.

Evianna.

I'm not back in Hell. I'm...somewhere else. "Wren?" Pressing my ear to the ground, I curse under my breath. They took my comms unit. Of course they did. And my glasses. Fuck. My vest too.

I'm alone, blind, with none of my tools. And Evianna could be anywhere.

Pain consumes the whole right side of my face, the migraine turning my limited vision white, then I'm floating. Away. Somewhere I can't feel anything at all.

THE THROBBING in my wrists registers first. Then my shoulders. The server room. I planted the trojan. But then...someone came. Hit me. Tied me up here. But where is here?

"Evianna," I groan. The room is almost completely silent, just a low hum that seems to come from everywhere.

Focus, Holloway.

Inhaling, I try to find some hint as to where I am. It's...stale down here. And musty. Like I'm underground. And then...there's a hint of something else. Something...familiar.

Freesia.

Evianna. She's here. Somewhere. I have to find her. But moving even a few inches takes everything I have. How long has it been? My mouth is bone dry, and between my shoulders and my head, the pain is almost too much.

"Keep moving, brother."

Ryker. I'm back in Hell. Trying to stay awake when it's cold enough I can't feel my hands and feet. We'll die of hypothermia if we fall asleep.

"Move your ass, Dax. Now."

Freesia. A whiff of Evianna's perfume brings me back, and I roll onto my stomach. I can do this. Find her. One inch at a time.

Evianna

My lids are heavy. Trying to force them open takes everything I have. And when I do...I don't understand what I see.

Dark gray. Nothing but dark gray.

A dull scraping sounds behind me, and I whimper before I realize that might not be such a good idea.

"Evianna?"

Dax.

I shove up on an elbow, but the entire room spins around me, and I cover my mouth with my hand as my stomach pitches.

"Darlin'? I can't see you. How far away are you?"

His voice is strained, and I fight against the urge to vomit as I turn over. "Dax!" Crawling over to him, I cup his cheeks, finding sticky, dried blood at his temple. "Shit. What did they do to you?"

"They didn't tie you up." With a groan, he struggles to rise, and I wrap my arms around him and pull him against me. "Fuck, Evianna. I thought I'd lost you." He nuzzles my neck, and the gesture makes my eyes burn.

"You'll never lose me," I whisper. "I...lo—"

"No, darlin'. Not here. Not like this," he begs. A single, hoarse sob stalls in his throat, and when I pull away, his pale blue eyes shimmer with tears.

"Yes. Here. Now." I press my lips to his, fingers tangling in his shaggy hair. He kisses me back with such fervor, I feel it down to my toes. "I love you, Dax. I don't know how we get out of this. But you have to know. I love you."

With a guttural roar, his entire body strains, the muscles of his arms cording, and a sharp *snap* echoes in the dim room as he breaks free from the zip tie. Then...his arms are around me, holding me tight.

"I love you," he whispers, over and over like a mantra. "I love you. I love you."

33

Evianna

WHEN DAX LETS ME GO, the coppery scent of blood clings to me, and I scan his body. "Oh shit. Your wrists."

"I've had worse," he mutters, and bends his knees to feel for the zip tie around his ankles. "I need something for leverage if I want to snap these. Look around, darlin'. Tell me what you see. Where are we?"

"I don't know." My eyes don't want to focus for more than a minute at a time, and I grab onto his arm as the room spins for a few seconds. "Noah...he did something to me. I'm...dizzy."

"Evianna, take a slow, deep breath in. Focus on a point on the wall. Just one point. Release the breath for a count of six. One, two..."

By the time Dax reaches six, my heart has stopped hammering against my chest and we're no longer on a tilt-a-whirl. "I'm okay. How'd you do that?"

He traces patterns on the back of my neck, and the slow, rhythmic motion calms me even more. "Training. Now what do you see?"

"It's not a big room. Maybe...fifteen by fifteen. Low ceiling. There's a stack of pallets in the back corner. The wooden ones. With slats. Flattened cardboard boxes behind them. Empty. It's some kind of storeroom, I think."

"Any of those pallets broken? Can you get me a piece of wood?"

"Maybe." I crawl across the room, not trusting myself to stand yet. But all of the pallets are intact. I kick at them, thinking maybe I can break one of the planks, but then realize I'm only wearing one shoe.

Shoe.

"Dax, will the heel of my shoe work?"

"Maybe?" He rubs his temples, wincing. "Worth a try."

By the time I reach his side again, I feel like I've run a marathon. "There's nothing else in here. No water. No food. They can't keep us here forever...can they?"

Dax caresses my thigh, skimming his hand down my calf until he finds my black pump and eases it off my foot. When he speaks, he keeps his voice low. "They tied me up, but not you. Which tells me they don't want to put any marks on you. So they're planning on using you for something—going somewhere, making a public statement. But me...they're probably keeping me alive as leverage."

"Leverage?"

I flinch as he wedges the heel between his ankles and yanks, hard. The zip tie snaps, and he stretches his legs out with a groan. "Leverage, darlin'. To get you to do whatever they need you to do."

"How do we get out of here?" I say, my voice cracking on the last word.

"Get me to the door?" He tries to climb to his feet and ends up on his hands and knees.

"Together," I say, wrapping my arm around his waist. After three tries, we're upright, and I lead him, my legs trembling, to the rusty door. "There's no handle. It's...folded over on itself or something." Taking his hand, I rest his fingers against the mangled metal.

"Fuck. Look up. Vents. Cameras. Anything we can use. Anything at all."

I take my time, scanning the entire room, floor to ceiling, one wall after another. "There's an air vent. Opposite side of the room from the pallets—almost in the corner. But...that's it."

A loud *thud* sounds from outside the door, and I yelp. "Dax? What do we do?"

"Across the room, darlin'. Stand in the corner. Look scared. Try to distract them."

I stumble, almost crash to the ground, but I make it to the pallets as the door opens. Broad shoulders, a solid gut, and the ugly version of Johnny Depp's face fill the narrow opening, and I don't have to act scared. I'm terrified.

"Don't...please," I beg, trying to wedge myself behind the pallets.

Dax shoves the door at Louie, but the hitman is ready, and takes a quick step into the room. Dropping his shoulder, he rams into Dax's stomach, sending him slamming back against the wall with a grunt.

"Dax!"

"Stay...back," he orders, and brings his joined hands down hard on the back of the big man's neck. Louie sends Dax flying over his shoulder, and he lands on his back, the air leaving his lungs in a loud *whoosh*.

"He has a gun!" I cry, except I'm wrong. It's not a pistol, but a Taser, and the twin prongs fly, embedding themselves in Dax's chest.

The man I love twitches and spasms uncontrollably, then lies still as the door opens again, and Noah strolls in.

"Unless you want me to have Louie start cutting off body parts, Evianna, I suggest you come with me. Right now."

Louis drops to one knee, grabs Dax's hand, and presses a knife against the joint of his thumb.

"Stop!" I take one step forward, my hands raised. "Don't hurt him. I'll...do whatever you want. Just...let me make sure he's okay. Please."

Noah nods once, and I fall to my knees next to Dax. "Please, open your eyes, baby," I whisper. "I...I love you."

"Enough," Noah says, and Louis grabs my arm and drags me out of the room. Right before the door slams shut, I think I see Dax's eyes open.

The hallway's just as dark as the room we were in, and between the fear and the after-effects of whatever Noah gave me, I can't focus on any details. Not with how fast Louie's walking. We take a corner, then another, and Noah steps aside.

I scream, and as I pull against Louie's hold, he releases me, but just as quickly, wraps his arms around me from behind and lifts me off the ground, carrying me into another small, window-less room, and depositing me on a metal chair.

"Hold her down. Gently," Noah says, and reaches for a roll of duct tape on the table in front of me.

It's like the world's worst bear hug, tainted by the disgusting scent of stale cigarette smoke and body odor. Noah wraps the tape around my torso and my left arm, leaving only my right free, then starts on my thighs, binding them to the seat of the chair.

"I do apologize, Evianna. But none of this works if the police find marks on you."

"None of what, asshole? You drugged me and brought me... where? That's kidnapping, assault, probably a half-dozen other crimes."

Taking a seat across from me, Noah opens a folder and with-draws a piece of Beacon Hill Technologies letterhead. "You couldn't simply let things go. Instead, you had to start investigating me. I shut the server down, you know. The one your boyfriend tried to hack."

Shit.

I try to wriggle in my chair to test the tape, but Louie slams a hand down on my shoulder. "Keep moving, bitch, and I'll go have some fun with the blind guy."

"What do you want, Noah?" I stare him down, but I don't know what I hope to accomplish. I'm duct taped to a chair, for fuck's sake. And Dax...he's trapped and alone.

Digging into his jacket pockets, he sets a pen, then a container of prescription sleeping pills on the table. Louie hands him a bottle of water, and Noah cracks the seal. "I want you to take responsibility for Alfie's security breach. And after you've done so, you'll take ten of those little pills, and fall asleep. By the time they discover your body, I'll have all the information I need for many, many years."

"Suicide?" My voice breaks, and I shrink back—as much as the hard metal chair will let me. "Noah, please. We've worked so hard..."

"Don't make me hurt your boyfriend, Evianna. Write the note, and I promise you this: His death will be quick and painless. A single bullet to the head, and we'll dump his body in the Charles River. I'll make sure your mother is taken care of too...for the rest of her natural life."

Tears spill onto my cheeks. "Mom," I whisper. "No."

"I'm not a monster, Evianna. She won't want for anything." Noah leans forward, and the earnestness in his hazel eyes makes me want to vomit. He's actually serious. "I lost my father to Alzheimer's. Did you know that?"

"N-no." I can barely force the word out, my tears dripping down my chin and onto my tank. I don't want to die. Not like this. And Dax...I've killed him too. "P-please, Noah. D-don't d-do this."

"I'll do this with or without your cooperation, Evianna. I could simply pour those pills down your throat and type your suicide note from your work computer. But handwriting is so much more...irrefutable."

"Wh-why? We...we built...something great, Noah. Something...th-that w-will change the w-world." My tears lend a shimmer to the room, and I can't stop shaking.

"Because I'll never have to work another day in my entire life. The amount of information I'll be able to get from Alfie in her first few days...it'll set me up for life." He sits back and crosses his arms over his chest. "I need an answer, Evianna. Right now."

Louie steps up to the table and opens the bottle of pills. The look in his dark eyes...he'll do it. Force me to swallow the pills and that'll be the end of everything. Of me. Of Dax. Of...us.

But...by now, Clive knows we're gone. Wren probably has half of the Boston Police Department looking for us. I just have to stall. And maybe...someone will find us.

"L-let me...talk to my mom. Just one more time. I...I won't say anything about you. I'll...make it sound like...like I'm about to kill myself. I just want to tell her I love her. P-please." I stop fighting my tears and let myself sob, praying he has some small shred of compassion left.

But Noah just glances up at Louie, and the asshole pours a dozen pills into his hand. I grab the pen, bite off the cap, and spit it on the floor.

I'm sorry. I wanted to create a product that would change the world. But I lost my way.

Lifting my gaze, I try one more time. "Please, Noah. I won't fight you. I just...I need to tell her I love her. If...you'd had the chance...with your dad...wouldn't you have taken it?"

Noah's gaze softens, and he almost seems...wistful. "Yes, I suppose I would have." He rolls his eyes. "Fine. Louie, get her phone. She can record the message there." He rises, pulls his handkerchief from his pocket, and wipes away my tears. "I'm sorry, Evianna. I tried to set Kyle up to take the fall, to spare you. But he refused to cooperate. And then Louie got a little overzealous convincing him, and...well...Kyle was useless once his neck was broken. I'll give you a few minutes to think about your final words to your mother and make whatever peace you need with your maker."

His footsteps echo on the concrete, and when the door slams behind me, I scream until my voice is hoarse, hoping somehow, someone will hear me.

34

Dax

MY LIMBS ARE LEADEN, but my heart races, and I struggle to catch my breath. What the fuck happened?

Evianna. I can't hear her. Rolling onto my side, I feel wires drag over my arms. Taser. That fucking prick Tasered me and took Evianna.

Yanking the twin prongs out of my chest, I force myself to breathe deeply. Evianna described the room. I'm close to the door —or was, when that fucker dropped me.

Slowly, I feel my way along the walls. The door's locked again —big surprise—and I keep going. On my knees, not trusting myself to stand yet, I let my hands and memory guide me until I come to the stack of pallets.

"There's an air vent. Opposite side of the room from the pallets."

Based on where we were standing, the vent is to my left. But the pallets are only two feet high, and while I'm tall, I doubt these are eight-foot ceilings.

Sinking down onto my ass, I drop my head into my hands.

Noah has her. And whatever he needs her for...he can't keep her alive for long. Not without putting marks on her. And he sure as hell won't bring her back to me. Not unless he needs to hurt me to get her to cooperate.

She's going to die. All because I was too broken, too slow, too...stupid to protect her. I should have *known* they would come for her at the party. Should have sent Clive in as her date instead. Fuck. I should never have left her in the first place.

The cold from the concrete floor seeps through my dress pants. So much like Hell—with fewer rocks. Less shit, too. Just as much pain. Only this time, it's my heart that's shattering—not my bones.

"Get the fuck up, soldier."

"Ry?" I can hear him so clearly, it's like he's right next to me. But when I raise my head, I know I'm still alone. Fucker's so big, I'd see his shadow no matter how little light there is from the overhead bulbs.

Before the insurgents captured the last of us...we were bleeding, out of ammo, and had been trapped on the side of a mountain for more than twenty-four hours. No water left. Sun beating down on us during the day, winds whipping through the canyon at night.

But Ry...he kept us alive. Kept us going. Trying to climb. To escape.

"Get the fuck up, soldier. Now. You think you deserve to wear that Special Forces patch? That green beret? You do not give up until you've exhausted every possibility. Until you've spilled your final drop of blood. Until your heart beats for the last fucking time. Now move."

"Yes, sir. Moving, sir."

The memory curves my lips, and I almost laugh. That was the first, last, and only day I ever called Ry "sir." And he gave me shit for it until they finally caught us.

Pushing to my feet, I feel for the top pallet in the stack. If I stand it on its end, it's almost four feet tall. Maybe...if I'm the luckiest son of a bitch on the planet, I can make it into that fucking vent.

My muscles still twitch involuntarily every few minutes, and I stumble more than once as I drag the pallet across the room. It doesn't feel stable, so I add a second, leaning in the same direction, then push the remaining four pallets against the first two, praying I don't end up on my ass—or breaking my neck.

Not to mention...I don't even know exactly where the vent is. I have to hurry. That asshole knew I was behind the door, so there's probably a camera in this room somewhere.

Wedging my dress shoes in the spaces between the slats, I climb until I can touch the ceiling. There. The edge of the vent. Stripping off my tie, I wrap it around my fist, then punch the vent cover. It bounces, and I grab it and toss it to the floor.

Climbing to the very top of the pallets, I fit my head and shoulders through the vent. The muscle of my mangled thigh protests as I tense, but I ignore the pain and jump up, then wriggle forward.

But...now what? I don't know where I am. Or where Evianna is. I may be out of that room, but for all I know, the next few vents I encounter could lead to escape—or the big thug with the Taser.

"Think," Ry says in my head. *"You saw the shadow as they dragged Evianna away. Which direction?"*

"Left of the door," I whisper.

"And which way are you facing?"

"Right."

"So back the fuck up, Sergeant."

My head pounds, and my entire body aches, so I don't take time to examine why a man who's all the way across the country is inside my head. But...maybe he's always been there. I wriggle backwards until I find a cross-vent.

"Which way, Ry?"

"Think. Remember what I taught you."
Look. Listen. Count.

The first directive won't do me any good. Up here, everything's dark, only the occasional dull glow from a vent. But... when I still my breathing, I think... Oh fuck. I can hear Evianna screaming. Words. Unintelligible. But definitely words. Angry words. Turning my head, I try to isolate where the sound is coming from.

Contorting my body, I choose the left path, and the sound starts to get a little louder.

At another junction, I pause. Footsteps.

"Count them. And listen."

They're not rushed. And then I hear Noah's voice. "Once she's signed the note and taken the pills, get her out of here. Take her up to Maine. She has a favorite hotel up there. It's in the file. Barry will handle the reservation system. She won't be found for three days. By then, we'll have everything we need."

"How long you going to let her stew?" the hitman asks.

"Another few minutes should do it. Go get her things." The two part, their footsteps heading in opposite directions. Which one is which? I can't tell. I should know this. But Ry...Ry was always better at this than I was.

"Focus. Breathe. Assess the risks, and then act."

I try, but Evianna's stopped screaming. Fuck. Another few minutes. I have time. I just need to find her. Squeezing my eyes shut, I concentrate, ignoring the ice pick digging into my skull, the fire in my shoulders, the cramps wracking my muscles.

"This one's...broken. Damaged. But it's still beautiful." I can feel the petals of the fallen flower brush my nose, hear her whispering to me as the last rays of the setting sun warm my cheeks. *"It fell, but...it still smells just as sweet as the rest."*

I love her. And if I don't find her in the next few minutes, it'll be too late.

Evianna, darlin'...give me a sign. Something. Help me.

Freesia. I can smell her. So faint, it's barely there. I pray this isn't my mind playing tricks on me. Straight ahead.

Ryker's face—what it looked like the last time I saw him— swims behind my eyelids. *"You're a soldier, Dax. A survivor. And the strongest man I know. You can do this."*

I can do this. I don't need my sight. Training, determination, and love will get me back to her. I just hope a little luck can save us both.

Evianna

After screaming obscenities for several minutes, I haven't managed to do anything other than exhaust myself. Clearly we're somewhere Noah doesn't think anyone will hear me. Struggling against the tape only exhausts me, and I try to contort my free arm to find an end, but Louie was too smart for that.

I have the pen. Oh God. All those old *Law & Order* episodes I used to watch with my mother come back to me. Post-mortem bruising. If I can't get out of here...I can at least do *something* so Noah won't get away with this. Gripping the pen so hard my knuckles turn white, I press down on my thigh over the tape. *N. O. A.* Halfway through the *H*, the pen punches through the thick, gray tape with an audible rip.

Holy shit.

If I can cut through all the tape, I'll have a chance to get out of here. Flipping the pen around to use the sharp tip instead, I start hacking through the tape. Sweat dots my brow, and my heartbeat roars in my ears. I have to hurry. Noah won't leave me alone for long.

The last of the tape around my legs tears, and I go to work on the loops around my torso. This...is harder. Contorting so I can keep the rips under my free arm...so I can hide them from Noah if he comes back before I finish...and still having enough strength to punch through four layers... But...I'm close. So close.

The lock *snaps*, and I'm out of time. Shaking, still bound to the damn chair by an inch or so of tape, my shoulders slump, and I drop the pen on the table.

"I hope you've thought about what you want to say, Evianna," Noah taunts as he rounds the table and drops a bag on the floor. He places my phone between us. "Unlock code, please?"

"Eight, two, nine, one, one, three," I say, my voice stalling on the last word.

"There's no service down here, but I'll attach your message to the email I send her as soon as you're gone." Noah taps the screen a few times to launch the voice recorder. "Say anything I don't like, and I'll make your boyfriend suffer. He's famous, you know. Dax Holloway? One of the only two Special Forces members to survive fifteen months in the worst of the Taliban interrogation camps? I can make him relive those days. Let Louie go to work on him, keep him tied up, starve him...for days. Weeks even."

"Please," I beg. "D-don't hurt him. He was just trying to protect m-me." A fresh round of tears spills onto my cheeks, and an icy ball of fear sits on my chest, making each breath harder than the last.

With one touch of the screen, he activates the recorder.

"Mom? I'm...I'm sorry. I...didn't...don't...want to leave you, but I can't...I don't have a choice. I did something. Bad."

Noah gestures for me to get on with it, and I glare at him through my tears. "I love you, Mom. So much. I...don't know how to say goodbye, but I...I love you."

Tucking my phone back into the bag on the floor, Noah smiles. "So touching. But now...please finish the note so we can get on with this. I need to be seen by my doorman in an hour."

"Please, Noah. I won't tell...anyone. I'll just disappear. You don't have to kill me."

"This will be the largest data breach in the world, Evianna. Big names. Business men and women, government officials, billionaires, foreign and domestic alike. Alfie records *everything*. Credit card numbers. Bank access codes. Over a few days, it'll track patterns, passwords... I'll have enough information stored to blackmail the rich and powerful for years. There's nowhere you could hide." Sadness wells in his hazel eyes. "I really didn't want it to be you. But...it makes so much more sense than pinning the whole thing on Kyle. Now write."

He unscrews the top on the prescription bottle and pours a dozen pills out on the table. I can't tear my gaze away, and my hand shakes as I pick up the pen.

What I did was wrong. I know that now. I can't keep pretending it wasn't.

I look up, pleading with Noah one last time, but he arches a brow and gestures for me to continue.

The crash as the door slams open makes us both jump, and I feel the last bit of the tape under my arm give way. Louie rushes in and whispers something to Noah. Something that makes him very angry.

"Go. Now. I don't care what you have to do, but make it hurt," he growls.

Oh God. Dax.

As soon as Louie shuts the door, I shift my grip on the pen and lunge for Noah. The tip of the pen drives through his cheek —shit, I was aiming for his eye—and he roars in pain as blood spurts over my fingers. He rears back, and I lose my grip on the pen.

"You *bitch!*" Noah yells, though the words are a little muffled as he's clutching his cheek and trying to pull the pen free. Ripping at the tape, I manage to tear it off my left arm and chest, but then Noah springs for me, and I fall—still in the chair—my head slamming against the ground.

Stars fill my field of vision, and Noah presses his entire forearm against my throat. I can't breathe, and I buck my body, trying to get him off of me. My right knee is all I can really move, and I slam it into his balls. With a yelp, he curls in on himself, but he's still half on top of me.

Something crashes to my left, followed by a low grunt. I can just make out his black shirt and pants. "Dax! He's...on...me!" In my panic, I can't figure out the clock time. "Go...a little right!"

"Get the fuck away from her," he growls and springs for me. Noah turns just in time and tackles him, and both men land on the floor a foot away.

Fighting to free myself from the last of the tape, I stagger to my feet, grab the chair, and swing it—hard—catching Noah in the back.

Dax lands a sharp punch to Noah's jaw, and shoves him to the side. "Is he unconscious?" he rasps. "Quickly, darlin'. I need to know."

"Y-yes." Dropping the chair, I'm in Dax's arms in three steps. "You came."

"I promised." He kisses me hard, then pulls back to skim a hand over my hair. "Are you okay?"

"I think so. But...we have to get out of here."

"Any idea where *here* is?"

"No. Just that we're underground. Far enough there's no cell signal. But—oh!" Extricating myself from Dax's embrace, I reach for the black bag next to the table. "Vest, glasses, phones, your cane...they're all here. No comms, but everything else."

"Give me the vest and the glasses." As he zips up the vest, he offers me a wry smile. "You know...I was coming in here to rescue you. But, you were doing a pretty good job all on your own."

"Never been much of a damsel in distress." I cup his cheek,

brushing away a smear of blood. "Now let's get the hell out of here."

"Stay right next to me," Dax says, touching his forehead to mine. "Tell me everything you see, as quietly as possible, and if I tell you to run—at any time—you run. Don't look back. Just go."

I won't argue with him. Not now. We don't have time. But I'm not leaving his side. No matter what.

Wiping away the last of my tears, I stand up as straight as I can and lead him to the door. "I'm ready."

35

Dax

With Evianna's warmth at my side, a part of me settles, even though we're far from safe. Grasping the folding knife in my hand, I nod, and she cracks the door. I hate having her exposed. I want her behind me. But I need her eyes.

"Empty," she whispers.

"Take us the opposite direction from the room we woke up in."

Her fingers tighten on the back of my vest, and she guides me to the right. Pressing ourselves against the wall, we creep forward. "Pipes along the ceiling," she says.

"Follow them."

Her bare feet make little noise, and I learned how to mask my footsteps years ago, so the sound of someone rushing towards us is deafening in the silence of the hallway. Evianna hears it too, and urges me forward at a run. "Left turn. Fifty feet," she hisses.

The shot is deafening, and her scream sends my heart into my throat. Grabbing her, I shove her in front of me, pushing us faster, until she yells, "Turn!"

A second shot grazes my side as we skid around the corner, and I grunt at the impact. It doesn't hurt yet, but it will. "Too far," she says, and the hopelessness in her tone stops me in my tracks. "Stairs. But we'll never make it."

"Stay behind me. Don't run until I engage, and ignore the next thing I say." Raising my voice, I shout, "Go! You can make it. I'm right behind you."

I feel her tense at my back, and then she's fumbling with the bag slung over her shoulder. *What the hell is she doing?*

The burly hitman's footsteps are so loud, he sounds like a baboon, and he's not slowing down. "Back up five feet. Now," I tell her.

She does, the sound of my cane unfolding barely audible over the stampede headed right for me. Crouching down, I brace myself for the hit, and when the asshole barrels around the corner, I ram my shoulder into his gut, jerk the knife upwards, and catch him under the arm.

Roaring, he grabs my right wrist, yanking it behind me hard enough my shoulder strains to stay in the socket. The pain sends me to my knees, and he rolls away, then...I hear him cock the hammer.

"You're dead, blind man. Where is the girl?"

What? Evianna was right behind me.

The gun jams against my temple. This is it. I'm going to die. But if Evianna got out...got anywhere. Maybe...I can die if I know she'll live. She's all that matters.

"Fuck you, asshole." Dropping my head, I wait for the inevitable. Unable to see, I don't have a chance at disarming him.

"Did I teach you nothing, soldier? Listen. You see with more than just your eyes, brother."

Ryker. Again. I'm losing it. Fear, the blows to the head. Another one sends me sprawling, and then Louie grabs the collar of my shirt and shoves me against the wall, the barrel pressed to the back of my neck. "Where's the girl?"

I can hear him breathing. Feel where the warmth of his body ends. He's behind me, but off to one side. My left side. My good, dominant side. I can do this.

A feral, high-pitched scream, the likes of which I've never heard before, pierces the still, dank air, and Louie takes a step. Just one. But it's enough. Spinning, I grab for the gun, finding his wrists and forcing them upward, then to the side, using his joints as the weak point.

The gun clatters to the floor, and then there's the sound of metal hitting something solid. Again and again. Louie falls, and metal hits the floor. "Come on!" Evianna cries and grabs my hand. "Your cane's dead. Sorry about that. I'll buy you a new one."

We sprint for the stairs, and she warns me about them just in time. Bursting through a door, I smell fresher air, but we're still not safe. "Keep climbing," she says, pulling me after her. Another door, another set of stairs, then another, and another, and then... we're outside, the sounds of traffic not far away.

"People. Find people. Somewhere we'll be seen. Then call Clive." My words escape strained and hoarse, and the graze on my side starts to burn like someone just lit a match and is holding it to my skin.

With my arm around her shoulders, we keep going, and then Evianna slows, pushes against something, a door that makes a heavy *whoosh* sound. The sounds of conversation swirl around us, and she leads me another few steps, then takes my hand. "There's a bench, right here. We're out of the way, but in plain sight."

"Where...?"

"The Kilted Scotsman. It's a pub, and there's a sports match on the big screen. Cricket or something."

"Can I help you?" a big, booming voice says. "Uh, lady, you need shoes if you want to stay."

"Please..." Evianna's rummaging in the bag, then presses my wallet into my hand. "He's hurt, and someone's after us. Can we just...stay here for a few minutes? I'm calling someone...right now. Don't make us go back out there—"

"Whoa," the man says as I hold up my PI license. "That shit real?"

"Yes, this *shit* is real." I push to my feet, wincing, as I hear Evianna say Clive's name. "And we're staying. Right here. Until my team can get to us. You have a problem with that, I should warn you, I'm fucking Special Forces and I've had a really bad night."

"Prove it."

"Excuse me?" I'm not in the mood for this shit, but I rip open the cuff on my left sleeve and yank the shirt halfway up my forearm. "*De Oppresso Liber,* motherfucker."

"Hooah, man. We cool. Rangers, 75th Regiment. Come into the back room. Ain't no one getting to you there. They'd have to go through me."

"Where'd you train, soldier?" I can't see the guy—for all I know he could be lying to me, but something in his voice tells me he's not.

"Fort Benning, Georgia, sir. Now you gonna trust me or not?"

"Clive is twenty minutes away," Evianna says, her voice barely audible over the music and the crowds and her own fear. "We're... across town from Beacon Hill..."

I hold out my hand to the Ranger. "Could use a little help, 75th. I'm blind. But lead the way."

"Demetrius Washington," the man says as he pumps my hand. "But you can call me Tank. You were seriously gonna try to take me? Blind?"

"Still might." Pulling Evianna against me, I arch a brow in Tank's direction. "Give me your arm. At the elbow. Get us out of sight."

Tank walks us down a short hallway, opens a door, and steps inside. "There's a couch along the left wall. What you need? Water? Towels? Couple fingers of scotch?"

"All of the above. You got a first aid kit?"

"Top desk drawer. I'll be right back."

When we're alone, I turn to Evianna. "Darlin', I'm pretty sure it's just a scratch, but I need you to get the first aid kit and see if I'm still bleeding."

"O-okay." She hisses out a breath after the first step, but as I sink down onto the couch, I hear the drawer opening, and then she's at my side and pulling up my shirt. "Shit."

"How bad is it?"

"About...a quarter inch deep. It's...not bleeding...much." She's barely holding it together, and as she swipes an antiseptic pad over the wound, I grit my teeth and try to steady her hand.

We stay like that, the alcohol burning, but her fingers under mine, for several seconds until I feel like I can speak. "Had a lot worse, darlin'. Every damn day for fifteen months. This is nothing. Just clean it up and slap a bandage on it and I'll be good as new tomorrow."

"Yeah, right," she scoffs, but her voice is stronger now, and she moves quickly. Two more cold, stinging pads, then a square of gauze, a couple of pieces of tape, and I start to relax.

Tank returns a few minutes later. "Got water, scotch, clean bar towels, and a plate of fries. You two look like you're about to pass out. You said you got people coming?"

"Yes," I say as Evianna wraps my fingers around the glass of water. "Three guys. They'll identify themselves. Clive, Ronan, and Vasquez. Anyone else comes asking, don't say a damn thing about us."

"Roger that. I gotta get back out there. You good?"

"We good, darlin'?" Wrapping my arm around her shoulders, I stifle my wince as the bullet wound protests. But all of my pain fades away in an instant when Evianna answers.

"We're good."

36

Dax

THE COMMOTION from the hall warns us Clive's on his way a few seconds before Tank opens the door. "These your people, Special Forces?"

"Yes," Evianna answers as she burrows closer to me. We finished the fries—and the scotch—and she cried the whole time, even though she tried her best to hide it. But when her tears started soaking into my shirt, she gave up, apologizing three times for "losing it" when I was the one who got shot. We're going to have a serious talk about her incessant need to apologize later.

"Boss. Thank fuck. What happened?" Clive asks as Tank shuts the door. The wall of men in front of us is a black-clad blur, and I take off my glasses and rub my eyes. I need to sleep for a week, and so does Evianna.

"Short version: Evianna's boss is responsible for this whole damn thing."

She shudders, then sits up. "Longer version: Barry Nolan's involved too. Kyle's dead—I don't know where his body is—and Noah was planning on killing me and making it look like a

282 | PATRICIA D. EDDY

suicide. Complete with a note and a goodbye message to my *Mom*." She stifles a sob, and I try to comfort her, but she straightens her shoulders and swipes at her cheeks. "Louie *shot* Dax when we were trying to escape, but it's stopped bleeding now. Mostly. I checked the map on my phone a few minutes ago. He had us four floors underground in the building at 42 Harvest Street. When we escaped, we knocked them both out. But that was more than half an hour ago now."

I turn to her, wishing, yet again, that I could see her face. "I love you, Evianna. You're...perfect. Perfect and strong and...mine."

The silence in the room against the low bass beat from the pub confuses me, until I realize what I just said, and I sigh, rolling my eyes at my men. "Yes. I love her. Can we get back to the part where one of you calls the police and the others go see if either of those two shitstains are still where we left them?"

"On it, boss," Vasquez says, and he and Ronan double-time it out of the room. Clive crouches down in front of us. "You two have any liability here?"

"Not unless we actually killed one of them," I reply. "But call in Decker. We wait much longer, we won't be able to explain the delay."

"Who's Decker?" Evianna asks.

"Our Boston PD contact. He works homicide, but he's been on the job for a hundred years," Clive explains. "He's got seniority everywhere. We start with him, we get a fair shake."

"Make the call. Then wait outside the door." I pull Evianna back against my side. "I need a few minutes with her before Decker gets here."

When we're alone, I find her lips, infusing as much calm and reassurance as I can into our kiss. She melts against me, and fuck. If I could just pull her into my lap and never let go, I would.

"Darlin', I need to tell you what's going to happen next. We're going to be taken down to the local precinct, separated, and questioned. You tell them everything that happened. *Everything.* Even the break-in at my apartment. But you hold one thing back. Just one."

"What?" The tremble is back in her voice, and she clings to me like she doesn't ever want to let go.

"Your mother's location. Decker's a good guy. Solid. Fucking incorruptible. But you know how easy it is to hack into a computer system. Do *not,* under any circumstances, mention the name of the facility. And tell them why."

My phone buzzes, then the calm, British voice says, *"Call from: Wren."*

She doesn't even wait for me to say her name before she starts talking so rapidly, I can barely understand her. I'm not even sure if she's speaking English.

"Wait," Evianna says. "You got a complete copy of Alfie's code? And you isolated every single one of the differences between the earlier code and what we signed off on? Seriously? In...what...? Six hours?"

"Five and a half," Wren huffs. "What else was I supposed to do when I was worried out of my mind about the two of you? Well, besides run facial recognition on every traffic camera feed in the whole flippin' city. So...you want the report or what?"

"Hell, yes! Noah said he shut the server down. I thought... we'd lost any chance of proving he was involved."

"Puh-leeze. As if I'd write code that didn't immediately propagate itself to every machine on the network. That's amateur hour."

Evianna touches my cheek. "Dax, I'm sorry. I know what I said earlier, but I'm in love with Wren now."

"You'll have to go through Ry," I say with a weak smile.

"What did I miss?" Wren asks. "Wait...never mind. I figured it out. I expect both of you to come out to visit us in Seattle by the end of the year. Now back to the evidence. Evianna, every single code change was logged from your workstation."

"Shit. So they could still blame this all on her?" Anger prickles along my spine. "Wren—"

"Let me finish, boss. I got more than just the code change logs. I got a record of every single badge swipe in and out of Beacon Hill's offices. And I can prove Evianna badged out for the day hours before any of these changes were made. *And*," she continues, "that one Barry Nolan badged out less than half an hour *after* each one of these changes."

"That's it," Evianna says. "Wren, will you marry me?"

"Send us everything." I grab the phone and double-tap the power button to hang up the call. Turning to Evianna, I take her hands. "I love you. And after that prick Tased me, I thought I'd lost you. I don't ever want to be without—"

A brisk knock cuts me off, followed by Decker's gritty voice, roughened by age. "Holloway, what the fuck have you gotten caught up in this time?"

37

Evianna

A LITTLE PAST 4:00 a.m., someone wakes me with a gentle hand to my shoulder. "Ms. Archer?"

I blink up at him, not understanding where I am or who this kindly, older man is. "Dax?" I croak, suddenly terrified our escape was all a dream, and the lumpy couch I'm stretched out on isn't real. Maybe I'm dying. Maybe—

"He's right across the hall. They're just wrapping things up with him. Louie Stein was shot dead by two uniforms an hour ago, and Noah Goset was killed when he tried to run across a busy street and got pancaked by a bus. We're still searching for Barry Nolan, but he won't be able to hide for long."

Sitting up, I bite down on my bottom lip to keep it from wobbling. I've cried enough in the past twelve hours. My eyes burn, and they're swollen to twice their normal size. "You're...sure?"

"I'm sure."

Now I remember him. Detective Decker. Not more than two minutes after Dax and I arrived at the police station, they separated us. Questioned us for hours, made us repeat our stories half a dozen times. When Decker was satisfied, he led me to this empty office and told me he'd come get me when they were done with Dax.

"Thank you," I whisper.

"Come on. I'll take you to Dax." He holds out his hand, and I let him help me to my feet.

As soon as the door across from me opens, I see him. He looks so tired. But still proud. Still strong. "Dax?"

He's up and out of the chair in a heartbeat, feeling his way around the table until he reaches me. Nothing, in my entire life, has ever felt so right than being in his arms.

"Let's get out of here, darlin'. I need you...alone."

RONAN AND VASQUEZ take us back to the Fairmont and promise us that they'll be at either end of the hall until Clive and Ella relieve them in the morning.

I lock the door, and then lead Dax into the bathroom. "Come on, soldier. Let's get you cleaned up."

Steam surrounds us, and I strip off Dax's torn and stained shirt, kissing each bruise. Skimming my fingers over the cuts on his wrists, the gashes on his head, I say, "You should have gone to the hospital."

"Would have kept me away from you," he replies, his voice rough and strained. Pulling off my bloody tank, he reaches around me to unhook my bra. "Nothing...will ever keep me away from you, darlin'. Not again."

I undo his belt, then let his pants fall to the floor so I can strip off his briefs. His cock stands at attention, the tip already glistening, and despite the exhaustion, the pain, and the tears, my core heats, and arousal floods me.

"Get in. Let me get this stuff off the floor and I'll join you."

Dax threads his fingers through my hair and brushes a gentle kiss to my lips. "I don't know what angel smiled on me the day I met you, darlin'. Or why. But you are...perfect. You're my everything. My only. And I love you."

I can't respond. I almost lost him, and every time I close my eyes, I see the blood seeping from his side. See him spasming on the ground after Louie tasered him.

"Evianna?"

"I'll...be right there. I promise." Sweeping the clothes under the sink where he won't trip over them, I follow him into the shower, wrap my arms around him from behind, and lay my cheek against his shoulder blade. "I love you, Dax. I...didn't want to tell you in the middle of that room. I wanted..." Swallowing my sob, I tighten my hold on him to stop him from turning. I don't want to see his face right now. I have to get this out while I can.

"I wanted to take you somewhere special...to me. Show you with...words. Let you...know me. More...of me."

Dax wraps his fingers around my wrists and carefully loosens my grip. His cock nestles against my stomach, hard and hot, and he eases me under the water. Running his hands through my hair, he groans softly. "You smell like freesia. And you're so soft. And so...strong. You're brilliant. During times of extreme stress, you respond one of three ways. You joke. You narrow your focus to *only* what needs to be done. Or you turn your attention to others. Take care of them. Like me. Like now. I know you, Evianna. I *know* you."

We take our time. Washing away the blood, the stale lingering odor from that dingy room. The last vestiges of the drug still lingering along the edges of my mind.

And when we fall into bed, we're both asleep in seconds.

Dax

Her soft breaths tickle my cheek. Our legs tangle under the blankets, and our hands are joined between us. A shaft of sunlight cuts in through the drapes, and I can make out the rich chestnut of her hair. But for the first time since we first met, I don't long to know what she looks like.

Because I know. She's beautiful. Strong. Capable. Brave. And she loves me. Blind, scarred, with nightmares, anger issues, and a complete inability to ask for help when I need it. For her, I'll be better. Go back to my shrink. Work on rebuilding my friendship with Ry.

With a gasp, Evianna sits up, and I'm up right next to her. "What's wrong, darlin'? We're safe. You're safe."

"Alfie!" In a heartbeat, she's out of bed and fumbling for something on the desk. "It's...Saturday, right? I mean...shit. It's after noon."

"Evianna? Talk to me." I slide to the edge of the bed, the wound in my side throbbing.

"Alfie's code goes live on Monday. It's an automatic push to every Alfie unit around the world. And it's *broken*. I have to fix it." She fiddles with something in her hand, and then says, "Ulysses? Yes. I'm fine. No, I *didn't* leave without saying goodbye. Well, okay. I did. But it wasn't my choice. No more questions. Just listen. I need you to call in every single developer except for Barry. Do not, under any circumstances, call Cindi. You won't be able to reach Noah. Don't even try. Get everyone into the office ASAP. I'll be there in under an hour. Order enough food to keep everyone going for at least twelve hours." She pauses for a brief moment. "Yes. I'm serious. Have you ever known me to joke about something like this? Do it. Now."

Her phone clatters to the desk, and then she's at my side. "I have to fix Alfie. Noah and Barry...they don't get to take this success away from the rest of my team. Do you think Wren would be willing to help?"

"I think Wren would kick your ass if you tried to do this without her. But, darlin', you know I'm not leaving your side today, right?" I arch a brow as I link our fingers.

"Dax, I'm going to be glued to my computer the entire day. In an office full of people."

My voice drops to a whisper. "You were in a room full of people last night, and I almost lost you. I have my own work I can do. But don't ask me to let you do this alone."

Her embrace is so sudden, so fierce, I fall back against the pillows with her on top of me. "I'm sorry," she says. "I didn't think—"

With a searing kiss, I quiet her apology. Maybe I don't care if she ever stops with these unnecessary "I'm sorrys." Not if I get to do this every time. Between us, my dick hardens, and when her hips grind against me, I roll her over and cage her with my arms.

"We'll go. Along with Clive and Ella. Conference Wren in. But first, there's something I need."

"What?" Evianna breathes.

"You."

Sliding my fingers into her hair, I angle her head and trail kisses along the curve of her neck. She shudders under me, and damn if that doesn't make me even harder. This woman is mine, but more than that...I'm hers, and I'll give her anything. Everything.

She grabs my ass and pulls me closer, and her sweet arousal perfumes the room. "Dax," she whispers as I kiss my way down to her breast, cupping the heavy globe in my hand and pinching her nipple. "Oh God. Harder!"

I oblige, rolling one taut nub between my fingers while I use my tongue and teeth on the other. Her hips writhe, her back arches, and she grits out, "I'm...on birth control."

As her words sink in, I stop, my breath catching in my throat. "I'm...clean. You're...the first, the only...in more than six years."

"I want you inside me. Just you. Right now." Evianna pushes herself up on an elbow and cups my cheek. "As talented as that tongue is, soldier, I need to feel you. I *need* you to take me. Right now. Please."

I don't have to see her face to hear the emotion in her words. To know...in my heart...the exact look in eyes I've never seen, and never will.

I love her, and as I bury myself in a single thrust, she wraps her arms around me. "Don't let go, Dax. Don't ever let go."

EPILOGUE

Evianna

ALFIE'S LAUNCH IS EXHAUSTING. For almost thirty hours straight, we work to pull out all the insecure code. Wren was a godsend, and we spent so much time together—virtually—untangling Barry and Noah's messes, I feel like we've forged a real friendship —something my life has been sorely lacking the past couple of years.

Explaining what happened to the team...that nearly destroyed me. But with Dax at my side, I survived. Even if I did have to close myself in my office and sob in his arms for ten minutes afterwards.

During those thirty hours, Dax never left my side, until finally, at 3:00 a.m. on launch day, I declared victory, and he took me back to his apartment, where his housekeeper had pulled off a minor miracle and restored the whole place to its former spartan order.

Not wanting to be involved in any of the press surrounding the launch, he hired private security for me, and for the past two days, Tank—the now-former bouncer from the Kilted Scotsman

—has been standing just outside my office for eight hours a day, arms crossed, staring daggers at anyone who dares look sideways at me.

But amazingly...everything else...is working out. Noah's death forced our PR company—well, *my* PR company now, I suppose, to do some serious dancing.

The official story? He was out celebrating after the party, drunk, and walked right into the path of an oncoming car. Dax made some calls, and details of his other injuries—as well as his negligible blood alcohol level—are buried forever.

The day after the first units come online, I walk out of my office at 5:00 p.m. on the dot, join Tank in the elevator, and don't bother to hide my smile.

Dax waits for me in the lobby, dressed in a pair of black jeans and a blue Henley, with a new cane in his hand. I can tell the exact moment he hears my footsteps, because he smiles, and though the man never truly relaxes, some of the tension leaves his shoulders.

"I think I read all the news reports today, darlin'. And the interview on WBZ? I'm so fucking proud of you."

Stepping into his arms, I feel safe. Protected. Whole. For so long, I thought Alfie's success would be the thing to give true meaning to my life. But I was wrong. I ignored almost everything else these past three years. I worked, visited my mother, and slept.

Now...I realize how much I've missed.

"Let's get out of here," I say against his ear. "I want you all to myself tonight."

Dax offers me his arm, and Tank follows us to the waiting car. "You need me any longer, Dax?" the big man asks.

"Not tonight."

I offer Tank a smile. "See you tomorrow?"

"Yes, ma'am."

"Evianna. And...I ordered you that kick ass chair I told you about. If you're going to be protecting me eight to ten hours a day, you're going to be comfortable."

Tank doesn't even try to stifle his grin as he high-fives me. One of these days, Dax will relent and agree that I no longer need round-the-clock protection, but for now, I let him be as overprotective as he wants.

After the car pulls away from the curb, Dax turns to me. "Do you trust me?"

"With my life. You know that." He's...nervous. Why is he nervous? "Why are you nervous?"

"I want to take you home. Your home."

My heart lands in my throat. I haven't stepped foot in my house since the attack, and I'm not ready. "Dax...can't we go back to your place instead?"

He takes my hand, holding it between both of his. "If you don't want to stay, we won't stay. But...it's like being thrown off a horse, darlin'. You have to get back on sometime."

After a long minute, I take a shuddering breath. "Okay. Let's go."

The ride passes in silence as I stare out the window, remembering the fear, the helplessness I felt as Noah's hitman held me down. But then the memories shift. The first time Dax put his arms around me. How he took care of me. By the time Dax gets out of the car and offers me his hand, I'm steadier. I can do this.

It still takes me three tries to get my key into the lock, but once I do, I gasp. The house smells...clean. Like freesia and lilies. Two steps down the hall, I understand what he's done.

"You took care of everything," I breathe as he shuts the door behind us.

"This is your home. I didn't want you to come back here and have to see it...broken. And...Ry has a contact at the best home and business security company in the United States—maybe the world. There's a top-of-the-line system protecting every door and window. I want you to feel safe here."

I turn slowly, terrified to ask the next question. "Is this your way of saying...you want me to start staying here again?" I leave out the two words I can't bear to say. *Without you.* We've spent every night together since the attack, and though I know our relationship went from zero to a lifetime—at least in my heart—faster than it should have, I can't imagine my life without him.

"I'm fucking this all up," he says as he shakes his head. "Can we go upstairs? There's one more thing I need to show you."

With my hand around his elbow, I guide him up the stairs. My bedroom looks almost exactly like I expect, with one difference. Little Xs of tape on the floor under the bedposts. At the corners of the dresser. My gaze trails around the room, until it lands on my bed.

"Oh, my God."

My eyes brim with tears as I gently cradle the jewelry box to my chest. "How...?"

"This is a big city. Didn't take long to find the best wood-worker in Boston." Dax runs a finger over the lid, all the way to the dented corner, which still bears evidence of the fall, but is now smooth and polished—almost like it was dented from the start. "It'll never be...what it was. Never perfect again. But, it's whole. And it'll last."

"You're wrong about one thing," I whisper. "It *is* perfect." Easing his hand off the box, I lift the lid and stop breathing.

Dax sinks to one knee as I stare at the intricately designed platinum ring with an emerald-cut diamond cradled among the whorls.

"I know it's soon," he says, his voice rough as he stares up at me. "But...you're it for me, darlin'. I think I knew that very first night we spent together. Something about you quieted my demons. With you, I'm...not the man I was, but the man I think I'm supposed to be."

He clears his throat and holds out his hand. When I lay my shaking fingers against his palm, he swallows hard. "Evianna, I love your strength. I love your heart. I love your mind. But most of all, I love *you*. All of you. Will you...marry me?"

A single tear races down my cheek and lands on our joined hands. Dax sucks in a sharp breath. His words tumble out in a rush, almost colliding with one another. "I...we can wait as long as you want. A year, two, we don't even have to legally—"

"Yes." Sinking down next to him, I set the jewelry box on the bed and then wrap my arms around him. With my lips only a breath away from his, I say it again. "Yes."

Dax

Kissing Evianna goodbye the next morning as Tank holds the elevator door, I think I catch a flash of light from her engagement ring, and smile.

The late May morning is warm and sunny, and I slide my briefcase strap over my shoulder and extend my cane. The short walk centers me, and gives me the courage to do the one thing I've avoided ever since we escaped that basement and certain death.

As I drop into my desk chair, I tuck my Bluetooth into my ear. "VoiceAssist: Call Ryker."

"Dax," he says after the second ring. "About time, asshole. I had to find out you were okay from Wren."

I still haven't gotten used to hearing his voice again after all the years and the pain between us, and I put this one off for too long. "I didn't know what to say to you, Ry."

"The fuck?"

"This...is going to sound crazy. Hell, I lived through it and don't believe it happened."

"Explain. Now."

I stifle a laugh. Ry has always been a man of few words.

"When Noah and his goon had us, they took Evianna. Tasered me, and left me in a locked room. I didn't have my glasses, my cane, or any weapons. No lock I could pick. I...I almost gave up, Ry."

"Dax...brother..."

"You wanted an explanation, you shut up and let me finish." There's no harsh edge to my voice, but my words have the desired effect. Ry grumbles something under his breath and quiets. "You were the best damn commander in the whole fucking army, Ry. You taught me how to survive. You kept me going in Hell. Protected me." My voice stalls until I force the words out, "You came back for me."

"You're family, Dax. That's what family does."

"I know. But...Ry...you did more than that. You saved me in that basement. I was lying on the floor, barely able to move. And...I heard your voice. You told me to get up. To move. To think."

"Dax, how hard did they hit you?" He sounds genuinely concerned now, his voice strained.

"There's nothing wrong with my head, fucker. I know it wasn't *actually* your voice. I'm trying to thank you. To tell you..." I clear my throat, trying to find the words through the weight of the emotions pressing down on my chest. "You saved me. You saved Evianna. And she's...she's everything to me. You don't have to worry about me anymore, brother."

Ryker doesn't speak for almost a minute. When he does, there's a thickness, an awkwardness to his tone that tells me he's as close to tears as I am. "I'll always worry, Dax. That's what brothers do."

"I love you, man. And...your whole New Year's wedding plans? Any chance you'd want to make it a double?"

"Fuckin' A, brother! You've got yourself a deal."

HELLO,

Thank you for reading *Second Sight*. When I started writing this book, I wasn't sure I could do Dax justice.

After all, he's blind. And—at least when I wear my contacts— I can see. To write Dax's story, I talked to a number of people with limited amounts of sight.

Whenever I write, I try to put myself in the characters' shoes. But Dax...his shoes were very hard to put on.

In some ways...Dax and Ryker are two halves of one whole. Brothers in every way that counts, each of them almost...can't exist without the other. In some ways, this is as much *their* book as it was Dax's and Evianna's.

Bringing them back together was so rewarding. And yes, that wedding will be in a future book.

In On His Six, I told you that I write characters I call "beautifully broken."

Dax is definitely broken. He's blind, angry, and alone. But with Evianna, he finds a way to feel...whole.

Dax still has a bit of a journey to go on. But now that he's reconciled with Ryker and has Evianna at his side, he'll take that journey. And he won't be alone.

I want the Away From Keyboard series to continue on for many, many books.

Ford's story, *BY LETHAL FORCE*, is available for *PRE-ORDER NOW* and will be released on June 11, 2019.

After that, there's a surprise story coming. But Trevor, Clive, Graham, and Ella will all get their own books soon.

I hope you'll come along for the ride. See the Also by section for a list of the other books I have available or visit my website: http://patriciadeddy.com. I love talking to readers, so email me at patricia@patriciadeddy.com.

If you'd like, sign up for my newsletter or come find me on Facebook. You can also join my Facebook group, **Patricia's Unstoppable Forces**, where we talk about books, life, and everything in between.

Love, Patricia

P.S. Don't forget to *PRE-ORDER BY LETHAL FORCE* today!

THE END

ABOUT THE AUTHOR

I've always made up stories. Sometimes I even acted them out. I probably shouldn't admit that my childhood best friend and I used to run around the backyard pretending to fly in our Invisible Jet and rescue Steve Trevor. Oops.

Now that I'm too old to spin around in circles with felt magic bracelets on my wrists, I put "pen to paper" instead. Figuratively, at least. Fingers to keyboard is more accurate.

Outside of my writing, I'm a professional editor, a software geek, a singer (in the shower only), and a runner. I love red wine, scotch (neat, please), and cider. Seattle is my home, and I share an old house with my husband and cats.

I'm on my fourth—fifth?—rewatching of the modern *Doctor Who*, and I think one particular quote from that show sums up my entire life.

"We're all stories, in the end. Make it a good one, eh?" — *The Eleventh Doctor, Doctor Who*

I hope your story is brilliant.

You can reach me all over the web...
patriciadeddy.com
patricia@patriciadeddy.com

facebook.com/patriciadeddyauthor

twitter.com/patriciadeddy

instagram.com/patriciadeddy

bookbub.com/profile/patricia-d-eddy

ALSO BY PATRICIA D. EDDY

Elemental Shifter

Hot werewolves and strong, powerful elementals. What's not to love?

A Shift in the Water

A Shift in the Air

By the Fates

Check out the By the Fates series if you love dark and steamy tales of witches, devils, and an epic battle between good and evil.

By the Fates, Freed

Destined: A By the Fates Story

By the Fates, Fought

By the Fates, Fulfilled

In Blood

If you love hot Italian vampires and and a human who can hold her own against beings far stronger, then the In Blood series is for you.

Secrets in Blood

Revelations in Blood

Contemporary and Erotic Romances

I don't just write paranormal. Whatever your flavor of romance, I've got you covered.

Holidays and Heroes

Beauty isn't only skin deep and not all scars heal. Come swoon over sexy vets and the men and women who love them.

Mistletoe and Mochas

Love and Libations

Away From Keyboard

Dive into a steamy mix of geekery and military might with the men and women of Emerald City Security and North-West Protective Services.

Breaking His Code

In Her Sights

On His Six

Second Sight

By Lethal Force

Restrained

Do you like to be tied up? Or read about characters who do? Enjoy a fresh BDSM series that will leave you begging for more.